ADVENTURE TO
DESTINY

Volume One
in the
UNITY OBJECTIVE SERIES

SANDRA GOLDEN

Published by:
Southern Yellow Pine (SYP) Publishing
4351 Natural Bridge Rd.
Tallahassee, FL 32305

www.syppublishing.com

This is a work of fiction. Names, characters, places, and events that occur either are the products of the author's imagination or are used fictitiously. Any resemblance to actual persons, places, or events is purely coincidental.

The contents and opinions expressed in this book do not necessarily reflect the views and opinions of Southern Yellow Pine Publishing, nor does the mention of brands or trade names constitute endorsement.

ISBN-13: 978-1-59616-107-8

ISBN-13: ePub 978-1-59616-108-5

Library of Congress Control Number: 2020934115

Printed in the United States of America
First Edition
February 2020

DEDICATION

I dedicate this book to my son, James Robert Golden. Your smile lit up every room you entered. Your energy electrified all those you met. Your talents amazed us, and your need for adventure always got you into trouble. You will forever be in our hearts.

Love you forever and a day

THE UNITY OBJECTIVE

ADVENTURE TO DESTINY

Book 1

CHAPTER ONE
PAST, PRESENT AND FUTURE

The late afternoon sun was just beginning to fade, and the calm waters off the coast of Washington made for easy passage for the ferryboat. No one ever expected anything to go wrong on that routine trip back to Hope Island. The private ferryboat, which carried the residents of Hope Island to the coast of Washington State and back, was carrying ten passengers and three crew members back to the island. The boat was approximately halfway between the island and Washington when a sudden pop from below deck shut down the boat's progress. The ferryboat quickly filled with smoke. Within seconds, an explosion was triggered that turned the small boat into a fire ball, blowing it out of the water and turning it into billions of minuscule pieces. It happened so fast that the life jackets didn't have time to be secured properly onto the ferry's passengers. Every soul was lost. This tragic incident happened in early May, and the people of Hope Island still mourned the loss. But none more than their Guardian, William Unity.

William Unity, the sixty-four-year old leader of the people on Hope Island and the CEO of Unity Corporation, was supposed to be on the ferryboat that afternoon. Instead, he had used the company helicopter to return to the island early. He had an unexpected emergency conference call he needed to attend in the privacy of his home office. William had observed the explosion from the safety of his balcony outside his office. It shocked and horrified him and sent him into deep mourning. He also felt guilty because he couldn't keep his people safe. His family and the people around him kept telling him that there was nothing he could have done. That it was an accident. He didn't believe it. But he couldn't prove it either. There was nothing left of the ferry. The biggest piece they'd recovered was the on-board refrigerator, and it didn't give them any clues as to what had happened. The forensics experts told him that the engine was stripped apart so badly that it was unrecognizable and useless in the investigation.

It wasn't just the loss of the souls on the ferryboat that bothered William. It was everything happening to his people all around the globe. In Florida, two of their most brilliant scientists had been kidnapped and tortured for information. The F.B.I. had rescued them after two days. Unfortunately, the four men who'd held the scientist's captive where all killed during the rescue. This lost the corporation the opportunity to question them about who was pulling their strings. Other attempted kidnappings, attempted hacks into their computers, and attempted break-ins at their private holdings were happening all over the globe. It was a battle every day, but so far, the Guardians around the world had not allowed their secrets to be discovered. They knew that those who wanted to expose them were powerful and held influential positions; they just didn't know who they were.

William felt his people and the secrets they kept were in danger. It was his job as a Guardian to keep them safe, and his job was getting harder as the days passed. William Unity thought about all this as he stood on his balcony on a sunny day in late June, watching the sea gulls dive in and out of the waves. A shiny glint of light caught the corner of his eye, and he turned his body slightly to get a better look at it. It was a move that saved his life, because it moved him out of the way of the bullet that whizzed past his face. The bullet came so close to William that it burned the tip of his ear. It came to rest in the concrete wall behind him. Immediately, his wife, Jennifer, was at his side, screaming in fright and crying hysterically.

It was at that very moment that William decided to become proactive instead of reactive. It was time to fish out those who were behind these attacks and stop them at all costs. The agents they had planted in strategic places needed to come through for them. It wasn't yet time to reveal themselves or their secrets. Soon all would be known, and all would be safe. But first in just a few weeks, a new generation would come into power, and they would take over this huge responsibility. More importantly, "The Ones," would soon be discovered and begin their destiny to save them all.

* * *

Twenty-four hours after the attempt on William's life, security on Hope Island was practically doubled. Every Guardian on Earth took huge measures to protect themselves and their ten secret and concealed cities. More agents were deployed, and everything was done to smoke out the evil that could destroy what they were working to achieve. The evil that sought to destroy them didn't know that Unity Corporation was the very thing that was going to save them from a horrible fate. William wished he could make them understand, but he didn't know how to do that without exposing themselves.

It was a few days before William's retirement and when his Guardian duties would be turned over to his son, David. He would then become an Elder in their community. Tomorrow, his family and the board of directors would arrive on Hope Island, and the next few days would be busy with meetings, brain storming ideas to deal with the threat, and wrapping up his duties as Guardian and CEO before William and his sister's Fourth of July birthday. It was the day of their retirement and their sixty-fifth birthday.

It was late in the day when William's wife, Jennifer, came bursting into his office with a tray of chocolate chip cookies and tea.

"William, I am tired of you shutting yourself in your office. You can't carry the problems of Unity on your shoulders. Even though they are strong and sexy shoulders," she teased. "You have to turn it all over to the new Guardians, and trust in yourself that you have done the best that you could."

"I'm trying but—"

"No buts," Jennifer demanded. "You need to let go! I also don't think that you've fully processed the fact that someone tried to kill you the other day. You need to let people in, and stop pretending it didn't bother you, when I know that it did."

"And how am I supposed to do that my darling wife?"

Jennifer thought about that as she placed the tray down on a small table. "It's easy! And it is as simple as trusting that the next generation of Guardians are wise. Since we raised our next Guardian, I know that the job is being passed down into good strong hands."

"It's always good to have extra warriors," William protested. "And yes, I know our David will make a wonderful Guardian. That's not the problem."

"It's not your problem now," Jennifer smiled. "Our ancestors had it all written out for us. I think we should get out the Story Chamber and let them remind us of the grand plan. Then you will see that you must move on."

"I think that is a great idea." William looked at his beautiful wife. It was hard to believe that she was a grandmother. She was just as beautiful as the day they had met. "You had this planned out, didn't you? And you even brought refreshments."

Jennifer rolled her eyes at him. "Just get out that machine."

William went to the carefully hidden closet and pulled out the Story Chamber. As the tall machine settled on the floor in front of them, William smiled. The Story Chamber was a sacred relic of their people, and the stories it held within it always gave him comfort, as well as insight on sometimes impossible situations. It stood over six feet tall, was made of a clear substance, and was shaped like a big test tube, although closed on the top and bottom.

Before he brought the machine to life with just a touch, he looked over at his wife. "What, no popcorn?"

"Not tonight."

William touched the Story Chamber, and it whirled to life, playing out a story like a movie. The Story Chamber is sensitive to the operator's feelings and thoughts and plays back the thing that is at the forefront of the operator's mind. Unfortunately, what was on William's mind was the tragic ferry accident, and the pictures of it began playing before them.

"William, stop it! Stop it please!" Jennifer begged as she covered her eyes. "I can't watch that!"

William touched the machine, and the Story Chamber stopped. "I'm so sorry dear."

"Shut your eyes and think about what is important, why we are here, and your heart's desire."

William shut his eyes and it only took him a brief moment to know what he needed to see. He reached out and touched the Story Chamber and sat down next to Jennifer. The tall clear machine came to life again with a tornado of color. The picture began to clear up, and the story began. No sound was necessary, the pictures said it all.

The story began with the image of a large planet in a distant galaxy. The planet which their ancestors came from eight generations ago. The planet becomes larger and larger until they saw the beauty of the landscape, the happy faces of the people, and the beautiful life that was enjoyed by all. A sadness came in the form of a dark and aggressive disease that turned the planet black and took the lives of all that lived on the planet. A darkness they called Black Cell Disease, or simply BCD. Black Cell Disease turned living healthy cells—in plants, animals, and all living creatures—black by robbing them of oxygen, thus turning the cells black. Eventually this destroyed tissue, then whole organs. It was a long and painful death for those who hosted BCD. It spread slowly, but eventually it destroyed everything, including the air they breathed, and the water and food they needed for survival. Finally, the evil entity took all that was left. This was the reason they had to leave.

In fast forward, they watched as ten massive ships were built over the next two generations. The ships were loaded with the people who had survived BCD and with everything they needed to make the trip to their new home on Earth. William and Jennifer watched the ships arrive at their new homes and disappear into the landscape. The story moved forward showing them pictures of their people's accomplishments and failures. The Story Chamber showed them their family through the generations. It ended the story by reminding them of what was important, and why they must fight. It showed them the beautiful planet they now called home. It focused in on the millions upon millions of people they called neighbors, friends, and family. The story ended with a picture of their family, focusing on their grandchildren. It then focused closer, leaving only two faces smiling at them. Those faces belonged to their granddaughter, Helaina Unity, and their grandnephew, J.R. Black.

The picture in the Story Chamber faded out and swirled around like a tornado before it was sucked back into its memory bank. William looked at Jennifer and saw she was fighting back tears of pride and love. She playfully hit him when she discovered him looking at her.

"That, William, is what is important. Our past, our present, and our future."

"As always, my dear, you're right."

Jennifer's words echoed in William's mind, "Our past, our present, and our future."

At that very moment, William realized something important. Something he needed to share with his family when they came to the island. He would have to find the time to talk with them privately after all the business was concluded and before the official retirement ceremony. William knew that the next few days would be busy and emotionally charged for everyone involved. And he was right.

Hope Island's population was just over twenty-five-thousand people. It was a private island owned by Unity Corporation, one of the largest conglomerates in the world. Everyone who lived on the island was employed by Unity and under their protection. During the next few days, the island's population nearly doubled as leaders of Unity came not only to conduct important business, but to Celebrate Independence Day. A celebration that also marked a new era for Unity.

William Unity, and his sister, Hanna Unity Black, were celebrating the holiday, and they were celebrating their sixty-fifth birthday. This date also marked their retirement as CEOs of Unity Corporation and the end of their duties as Guardians. These duties would now pass down to the next generation. David Unity, Williams's son, and Charles Black, Hanna's son, would become the new Guardians and CEOs.

***

It was one day before the big celebration and the family estate was busy with preparations; chefs were busy in the estate kitchen, preparing gourmet delights. Workers decorated the compound, putting up lights, and setting up the tables and chairs for tonight's banquet. The band was doing a sound check and going over the list of music to be played. That evening only family and the board of directors would be present for a more intimate celebration. The board of directors of Unity Corporation consisted of all the Guardians. Tomorrow the town's residents would celebrate the occasion, which would be broadcasted around the world so their people could take part. First, there would be a big parade in the morning followed by a picnic in the park. The day would end with a concert followed by the largest fireworks display the island had ever seen.

On the second-floor balcony, the elder members of the family were relaxing. Present were William, Hanna, David, Charlie, and their spouses. All business had concluded yesterday, and now the family was taking time to catch up on family news and to enjoy their island paradise and all the festivities. The younger members of the family were under the watchful eyes of two of the island's security personal and their nannies as they played lawn games or swam in the cool water of the Olympic-sized pool down in the courtyard.

Helaina Unity lay stretched out on a deck chair with her young curvy body dressed in a one-piece designer swimsuit that showed off her long tan legs. Helaina had thick, curly dark hair which she kept in a ponytail. She had the darkest brown, almost black eyes, anyone had ever seen. If you looked closely, you could see that gold streaks appeared to radiate from her iris when she got angry. Helaina's cousin, J.R. Black, short for James Robert, was at her side. J.R. was the same height as his cousin, five foot ten, but there the similarities ended. J.R.'s hair was the color of wheat, and his eyes were bluer than the ocean. It was when he was concentrating on a problem that the gold streaks appeared in his eyes. The gold streaks in J.R. and Helaina's eyes were an inherited, Unity family trait. Both looked and acted like typical fifteen-year olds. But typical they weren't.

"Helaina, did you bring that rat with you?"

The animal that J.R. referred to was a sugar glider that Helaina's parents had given her for her recent birthday.

"She isn't a rat, she's a sugar glider, and she has a name; it's Peanut."

"Sorry! You don't have to get so touchy."

"What are you working on over there? Is that a new iPod?"

"Yes, it's an iPod. I'm modifying it."

"Why?"

"You sure ask a lot of questions."

"I know, I like asking questions; that's how you learn, and besides it drives you crazy when I do."

This would be a typical conversation between two teenage cousins except for one thing, not one word could be heard by the people around them. This conversation was being conducted using their minds, a talent they discovered when they were at the tender age of eight. They could hear what the other was thinking. Their talent didn't extend to other people that they knew of, and this frustrated them to no end. The cousins would like nothing better than to hear what other people were thinking. They never told anyone, keeping this talent a secret from everyone, and they believed that they were the only ones with this special talent.

Up on the balcony, William Unity watched the two teens with fascination and amusement. William Unity was Helaina's grandfather and J.R.'s great uncle, but to the all the kids he was just, Granddad. William was a large teddy bear of a man; he stood six foot four inches tall and was very muscular with a slightly rounded belly thanks to his wife's cooking. William was a commanding figure and a highly respected CEO and Guardian. He was a leader who was watchful of what was happening, but most of all he cared and loved his people. The two teens didn't know that William was able to listen in on their private conversations. For a reason unknown to him, he had recently acquired this particular ability. This came in handy especially when J.R. and

Helaina decided to get into mischief or to do something they shouldn't. They could never figure out how William always showed up in time to prevent disasters from happening.

David Unity, Williams's son, and his successor, approached his father carrying a plateful of cookies. David was a much younger version of his father, the same dark brown hair, without the gray, the same eyes, and the same medium skin tone. Like his father, he was a great businessman, but William thought David took more after his mother in personality. He was one who sometimes preferred solitude and didn't like sharing his ideas until he had worked them out fully on his own.

"I see you found the cookies your mother made for the picnic tomorrow."

"She can't hide them from me; besides she makes the best chocolate chip pecan cookies in the world, and I just can't resist them," David told his father.

"You do know she makes several batches so that the rest of us can enjoy them also? She just lets you think that you found her secret stash so you'll leave the rest alone."

"I know. It's a little game we play. Besides, if I did'nt go searching for these little delights, I think she would be hurt."

"I think you are right about that." They were both laughing as Charles Black, Charlie to friends and family, joined them. Charlie Black was the same age as his cousin and partner, David, thirty-six, but he was the total opposite of his cousin in looks, having golden blond hair and blue eyes. Charlie was known as the family prankster; he was always looking for ways to make things, even work, fun. He believed his cousin took life to seriously and often dragged David into one of his schemes. It was the differences which William and his sister Hanna believed would complement each other, making them strong partners as Guardians for their people.

"Uncle, have you and Mom discussed who will precede us as Guardians?"

"Hanna and I made the decision a while back; I guess it is time to reveal our choice."

It was a tradition in their culture that the new Guardians give their retiring counterparts the privileged of choosing those that would follow them when it was their time to retire.

This time the choice was simple. Knowing what was to come, Hanna Black came and stood beside her brother. As much as her brother was outgoing, a big kid at heart, and everyone he met was a friend, Hanna was quiet and reserved. She kept mostly to herself and her family, trusting no one, and questioning everything. Just like her niece, Helaina.

"Hanna and I have thought about this for some time. The next generation of Guardians was an easy choice, the only choice really, and it should not be a surprise to anyone in this room." Everyone's head was nodding in agreement.

"J.R. and Helaina will make excellent Guardians. Usually at the age of eighteen, the next generation of Guardians begins to learn about their heritage and what we are about. But not this time; this time something is different about our future Guardians."

"Dad, you do realize they just turned fifteen, on June sixteenth."

"Yes, I know, but J.R. and Helaina are different from previous generations. Charlie, David, when did the two of you make your connection, knowing what the other thought, how they felt, and start your private communications?"

Charlie and David looked at each other. Then they answered in unison, "We were seventeen."

"It happened to Hanna and I when we were nineteen." William paused, knowing what he was about to say was unheard of. "J.R. and Helaina were able to mind speak together when they were just eight years old."

Joanna, David's wife spoke up, "Dad, how is that possible? And why didn't you tell us?"

"I don't know how. And I didn't tell you because I didn't want you treating them differently. I have two of our best scientists working on that question. I believe that J.R. and Helaina are proof that we are evolving, getting stronger, wiser, and more sensitive to our environment."

William walked over to the desk, pulled open a drawer and retrieved a little pink notebook. Immediately Joanna, David's wife, recognized it.

"Joanna, do you know what this is?"

"Yes, it's my daughter's little book that she writes her thoughts in."

"It's much more than that, I'm afraid. Yesterday morning I was walking in the gardens before breakfast. I found Helaina sitting by the water fountain writing. I asked her what she was writing. She told me they were her, "Dream Stories." And that she had to write them down because she didn't want to forget, because she, "Felt them in her heart." Curious, I asked if I could borrow one of the notebooks so I could read her stories. Helaina was hesitant but let me take this one notebook. She had two others with her."

William took the pink notebook and handed it to his wife, Jennifer. "Jenny my love, you are our fastest reader, read a few of Helaina's Dream Stories, then you tell us what they are."

Within seconds Jennifer Unity was turning page after page, reading them at a remarkable pace. When she was finished, she closed her eyes and laid the little book on her lap. Letting the words she just read sink in, she looked visibly shaken, and her son and daughter-in-law immediately went to stand by her side.

"Mom, what is it?"

"I don't understand; there is no way that she knows. This has never been written down before, and it's only in video files. These are things only the elders and Guardians should know."

William spoke softly, "She knows them as dreams."

David asked, "Are you two going to tell us?"

Jennifer looked around the room and took a deep breath. "Helaina is writing down the, "Truths," as if she were present and witnessing them firsthand. She believes they are dreams, but, it's the truth about us, our heritage, and what we are doing to help them evolve. She even wrote about ten ships that traveled to a new home. Also, she wrote about powerful people with special abilities. And somehow she dreamed about how a watcher was sent to Earth."

11

The room became silent; the Guardians began to think, trying to reason out the problem.

David spoke, "I will talk to my daughter; she needs to know that she must not share her, *Dream Stories*, with anyone."

"Yes son, she needs to know that what she writes can impair what we are trying to accomplish. Don't discourage her or frighten her; handle the matter with gentle hands. Remember she is a sensitive child, but an incredibly intelligent one. It might be best if she lets you keep her, 'Dream Stories,' in a safe place." William continued to make his case to the family.

"There are other signs which tell us that Helaina and J.R. need to start their education. Hanna, what was that gadget that your grandson gave you as a present?" Hanna was William's older sister by just three minutes. Out of the two, she was the creative thinker.

"J.R. presented me with this beautiful watch for Christmas. He told me that it could tell me how much energy a person had. What he really produced was a meter which told exactly how much of our DNA was in a person. When held up to William and I, and Charlie, you see that the needle points to 100%. We know that Katie's father was a half breed, and her mother a full blood, which makes her three quarters, watch the needle when I get close to her."

The family looked closely as the little gold watch correctly foretold Katie's, Charlie's wife, heritage.

Hanna spoke quietly but confidently, "There has never been an instrument created to correctly identify how much of our makeup or genes are in a person. That is until now! Since I have had this little device, I have tested it countless times, and it has always been correct. I have had our best technical engineers analyze it, and none of them can figure out how J.R. produced it."

The room became silent, everyone's mind calculating the possibility of how such a device could be constructed by a fifteen-year-old. It was the mothers of the two children who spoke up. Joanna Unity, Helaina's mom and David's wife, spoke first. Helaina had her mother's beautiful hair and her long legs but there the resemblance ended. Helaina was definitely her father's daughter when it came to appearances, but her personality came from her mother. Both mother and daughter were nurturers. Both were the happiest when they were taking care of a child or an animal; both were very cautious, detailed orientated, and meticulous organizers.

"William is right! If the children are exhibiting such knowledge now, can you just imagine how much more their young minds will take in? Such knowledge brings much responsibility and power. They need to learn now how to accept that responsibility for the good."

It was then Katie Black's turn to join in the discussion. Like her son, J.R., she never wanted to be left out of anything. Katie and Charlie were both the adventurers in the family, and their children took after them. "I agree, even though they are very young. I think it would be best for Unity that William begin their education. Helaina and J.R. would benefit from his knowledge, and they enjoy spending time with him and Jennifer. Besides, he knows how to make things fun for the kids, being a sixty-five-year-old teenager himself."

The family laughed, Katie always seemed to know how to remove the tension from a tense situation, because she always saw the good in everything. She then continued, "Joanna and I think that it would be best for them to spend the summer months here on Hope Island with William and Jennifer, then in the fall return to a more traditional schooling. What do the rest of you think?"

***

As the family discussed their future, J.R. and Helaina played a carefree game of Marco Polo with their siblings and other cousins, enjoying the hot summer day as only the young could. An odd feeling came over Helaina; she got out of the pool and walked to the edge of the garden. With the hot sun making the water droplets on her skin look like shimmering diamonds, she stared out towards the beach. Suddenly she shriveled, goose bumps appearing on her young body. J.R. had followed his cousin, sensing that something was not right.

"Is something wrong?" J.R. wanted to know.

13

"Yes! I have a feeling someone is watching us. And I am not talking about nannies, parents, or staff. I don't think this is good, I feel like..."

"Like someone is threatening us," J.R. finished Helaina's thought.

"That's exactly it! J.R. can you feel it? Can you feel that we are changing?"

"They call that puberty."

"No! That's not it. I don't want to be different. I want to be like everyone else. I'm really scared!"

"You sure jump from one subject to another! Of course, we are different; we can talk to each other within our heads silly. That just makes us special. Mom once told me that everyone's unique in some way. Because if everyone in the world was the same, the world would be a boring place to live in." J.R. was trying hard to comfort his cousin the best he could; he wanted to protect her from the unknown eyes that were upon them. "And yes, I feel like I am changing, but change is good, right?

"I guess so. But who is watching us?"

"Don't worry about that right now. Just remember that Hope Island is one of the safest places on the planet, and with the Secret Service here this week, we couldn't be safer. Now come on let's go play spy games before my dad and yours take over the video game, playing one of their endless tournaments."

CHAPTER TWO

J.R.'S VERSION OF THE BIG BANG

Everyone was dressed in their best evening wear. After eating the best steaks and sea food money could buy and listening to all the boring speeches, the younger children were tired. As the tables were cleared away for dancing, they were taken to their rooms to rest up for the all the excitement that would come tomorrow. This left the adults, family members above the age of ten, and honored guests to enjoy the music and to dance the night away. It was a perfect summer evening. No cloud dared to appear in the sky, the heat from the day had cooled to a comfortable eighty degrees, and every star looked like someone had personally placed it on the black velvety background of the night sky.

Helaina danced with her father, dressed in a pink chiffon dress made especially for her by her talented mother. Her hair was falling down her shoulders with stylish pink feathers clipped on. Her mother also made the matching accessory. The accessory, which Helaina protectively wore close to her side, looked like a small rectangle bag, about four inches wide, and six inches long, and was hanging on a long decorative chain. One would think that the bag held the things that young girls used like lipstick and a comb. But inside the bag, curled up in a tight ball and secured with a little collar and leash that attached to the inside, was Helaina's favorite companion. A sugar glider her father had given her for her fifteenth birthday. The little animal was only a few weeks old and was dark gray with a dark brown stripe running down her small body. When she curled up into a tight ball, she looked like she was the size of a large peanut. That was the name Helaina had given the little marsupial, Peanut.

While she danced with her father, Helaina spotted her cousin J.R. sneaking off down the garden path on the way to the beach. When the dance was finished, she followed him, kicking off her shoes as she reached the sandy beach. She then ran after her cousin. As she ran, she could hear Peanut noisily protesting the fact that she was being roughly bounced around. Peanut wasn't shy about expressing her discomfort to her human when she wasn't happy. Helaina took one hand and held the bag close so that Peanut could have a smoother ride and continued following J.R. She caught up to him just as he reached the barge holding the fireworks for the celebration the next night.

J.R., dressed in dinner jacket and slacks, with his discarded tie carelessly tucked into his back pocket, didn't need to turn around to know that Helaina was following him; he just knew she was near. When he reached his destination, he turned around and waited for her to catch up with him.

"Go back and dance with that handsome prince I saw you drooling over at dinner."

"He's a terrible dancer. He stepped on my new shoes and scuffed them all up. What are you doing here?"

"I'm working on a surprise for our dads."

"That's the barge with the fireworks; Granddad said that everyone was restricted from being near that because it was dangerous. Only the explosive expert and his crew are allowed here. We will be in trouble if they catch us."

Helaina looked around to see if any of the security personal had followed them, but none had. Security was tight, but right at that moment, every security personal was protecting all the VIPs. None of them were interested in, or concerned about, two mischievous teenagers.

"Stop being a mother hen. Besides I'm not going to touch the fireworks. I just want to get into the computer that controls them to upload a program."

"And what does this program do?"

"It's a program that will make the fireworks dance to a song."

"Cool! And what song would that be?"

"*A Country Boy Can Survive*, by Hank Williams Jr.*"

"That's our dad's favorite song! They sing it at campfires when we go camping, when they go fishing, and I swear my dad sings that song every day in the shower. That's why I think it would be nice to have the fireworks perform with that song. After all, they are the new CEOs, and they should have their favorite song performed for them."

"That's a wonderful idea. Come on; I'm going to help."

It took J.R. and Helaina just five minutes to find the computer that controlled the fireworks and install the special program designed for their fathers. They were back at the estate and eating chocolate cake before anyone knew they were gone, so they thought. Both sets of grandparents sat at a table near the edge of the patio enjoying cocktails and watching the younger generation dance. They saw the two mischievous grandkids sneak back into the party. They looked at each other, and they all started laughing, all thinking the same thing. "*What are they up to now?*"

"I think maybe we're all in for a little surprise tomorrow," William remarked.

***

As the festivities took place outside, one lone person was on another mission. Hired by the Unity Corporation to pilot their guests to and from the island in the corporate helicopter, he had developed a trusting relationship with his employers. For two years he watched, he listened, and he waited. Taking a walk yesterday, Jack Webber stumbled upon a conversation between granddaughter and grandfather. He had listened and watched William's interest intensify after reading a few pages in the little pink book Helaina was writing in. His instincts told him he might have stumbled onto something his other employers might be interested in. As everyone enjoyed the celebration, he sneaked into the house. He was dressed like one of the security guards so no one would question why he was there. If anyone asked, he would say he was making sure the younger children were secure in their rooms. Jake took the house elevator to the second-floor study. When he opened the door, there was the diary, right on the desk. Just like he knew it would be. He walked over, put the little pink book in his jacket pocket, and went back to the party.

Security checks had been made on the mainland before anyone was permitted to come to the island. Since the attempt on William's life, law enforcement on the island had been doubled. The normally small sheriff's office, which had eight trained police officers to take care of the residents of the island, now had sixteen members. The family felt safe on the island, protected from the outside. However, this was no ordinary, rich family, and it was Jack's mission to uncover the secrets they were protecting from outsiders and pass it along to his boss.

***

Despite the late night, everyone was up early the next morning. Everyone would participate in some way in the parade that would travel down the main street of the little town on Hope Island. The children had decorated small floats, their bicycles and wagons, and wore patriotic costumes that their mothers had sewn especially for the occasion. Helaina made Peanut a special bag to ride in. It was a red velvet bag she decorated with white and blue stars made from glitter. She put a tiny little bandanna around Peanuts tiny neck, but not without a lot of fussing from Peanut, who wouldn't cooperate with her.

The parade was great fun. The whole population was out this special morning to celebrate the holiday and to celebrate the retirement of their outgoing CEOs. The community was showing their support and showing them how much they would be missed.

First the island's high school band performed, "The Star-Spangled Banner." They were followed by William and Hanna, along with their spouses, riding in a 1940 Ford convertible painted red, white, and blue for the occasion. Following them in a blue 1915 Studebaker SD touring car were David and Jennifer Unity and their children, Helaina, and her little sister Cassie. Next came Charles and Katie Black, with their children J.R., Paul, and Tina; they traveled in a fire engine red 1947 Chevrolet convertible. The rest of the family followed them, all in antique cars that were owned and maintained by William Unity himself. It was his favorite pastime, restoring what was old and not working into useful and beautiful machines. The parade also had clowns, stilt walkers, and people who made balloon animals. Floats showed off the prize-winning, oversized vegetables that some of the residents grew. There were street venders handing out free cold drinks and hot dogs. The different clubs on the island had floats that had been judged and awarded prizes for their efforts by the parade's organizers. It was a typical Independence Day parade like any small town would put on for their residents. The outside of the stores and businesses along the route were decorated for the celebration. The participants, as well as those who watched from the sidewalk, enjoyed this time of celebration. Unknown to them, among the crowd were two FBI agents who were watching closely, looking for anything that was not what it was supposed to be. They were there at the invitation of William Unity and Hanna Black.

Following the parade, the ocean front park was opened. There were carnival rides, a petting zoo, and lots of games that awarded the winners big stuffed animals. Barbecue teams set up their grills and began cooking various meats, fish, and poultry. The first official duty of the new CEOs was to judge the team's best efforts and award them cash prizes. What a tasty way to begin their new positions.

During the day, no one was granted passage to the island, and patrol boats kept watch like they did on normal days. Hope Island was a happy secure place, and no one had any worries, at least not today. Soon the day turned to night, the stars brilliantly shown down upon the beautiful island, and a soothing breeze cooled everyone's sun burned skin. David and Charlie handed out the last of the trophies and big checks to the winners of the barbecue cooking contest. Colorful ribbons were given out to those who won the watermelon seed spitting contest, the pie eating contest, the cake decorating contest, and the best decorated bike, and the cutest animal costume. Unfortunately for Helaina, Peanut refused to wear her costume and preferred to remain sleeping throughout the whole day. J.R. teased Helaina, telling her that Peanut should have gotten a prize for sleeping through all the noise. It seemed that everyone on the island had their hands filled with prizes and good food. It was now time to sit back and relax on the beach and enjoy the concert and the elaborate fireworks display.

Young children raced up and down the beach playing with friends, while the teenagers preferred to congregate near the stage where they danced along to the rock and roll music. After a few short speeches, thanking those who had worked so hard for a successful and pleasant day, it was now time for the big finale of the day. The fireworks show was about to begin.

J.R. and Helaina were more excited than most of the children or teenagers gathered on the dock to get a waterfront view of the dancing lights. For half an hour, rocket after rocket was fired into the sky, exploding into colorful lights. Music played over the speakers, the brilliant colored lights danced in unison to the variety of music that accompanied them, like a well-choreographed Broadway show. Since it was now dark, Peanut awoke and sat on Helaina's shoulder. She watched the display with interest and didn't seem to be disturbed by all the noise. Suddenly the sky above became quiet, the lights on the beach were dimmed, and the music came to a temporary halt. Excitement and anticipation for what was to come built up in the crowd on the beach. But not more than in the two teens who were sitting together on the dock, with their bare legs swinging over the platform, their feet cooling in the ocean waters.

J.R. whispered to his cousin, "It's time."

"I know. Be quiet."

But J.R. was too excited to be quiet. "Now you are going to see what a real genius I really am."

"You idiot, we are both geniuses, remember that test we took?"

"Taking a test doesn't show your true potential."

"I know, now shut up, it's time."

Suddenly the music began, within a few notes Charlie and David knew what song was playing. Helaina and J.R. looked over and saw their fathers smiling and singing along to the music. They looked at each other and smiled, taking joy in knowing that they made their parents day a little more special. The fireworks joined the music and they were spectacular! The crowd began to sing along as they watched. Then without any warning the music sped up, the rockets shot from the barge faster and faster, causing the mechanism to begin smoking. That's when the two little schemers stood up and moved towards the back of the crowd where they couldn't be seen. Helaina took Peanut off her shoulder, placed her in her bag, and zipped it up, which made the little animal chatter in anger.

The rockets stopped shooting into the air, which was really not a good sign of things to come. Everyone stood up to watch what was about to happen; the beach became silent. The smoke got worse, yet the music still played. No one was singing now. It was a good thing that the barge was a good distance from the beach. It was also good that the technician who controlled it all worked in a little tower and not on the barge itself. If anyone was close to that barge, they would have been in grave danger. The technician in the control tower tried to override the program and stop the rockets, but it was too late. The rockets got jammed in their silos, causing them to overheat, which caused the remaining rockets to be ignited, which caused the whole barge to blow up in one big spectacular ball of colorful fire that even the residents living on the coast from Spokane to Alaska could see.

The patrol boats quickly responded to the situation and put out the fire within minutes. Then the crowd broke out in applause. William and Hanna, wanting to defuse the unexpected ending took the stage, along with David and Charlie.

Taking the microphone Charlie began speaking, "What an explosive way to begin our new positions at Unity Corporation." Everyone laughed and broke out in thunderous applause. Charlie waited until the applause died down before he continued.

"We want to thank everyone for coming and celebrating the beginning of a new era with us. Let's give a big round of applause to everyone who made this day one to remember."

Everyone on the beach applauded and cheered, showing their new CEOs and their predecessors how much they were appreciated. Hanna and William hugged their sons, and standing shoulder to shoulder, hand in hand, raised their arms together. A new generation had come into office, and there was a promise of great things to come for them and the world. It was a proud and heartwarming moment of celebration.

The family left the stage all smiles. At the bottom of the stairs they met with people wishing them well. It wasn't until they had safely returned to the house that they felt they could let loose with the laughter they fought to control. They knew who was responsible for the unexpected display. They weren't angry, and they weren't concerned. They knew J.R. and Helaina just wanted to show their love for their parents. They had to admit it was a brilliant idea that had ended in an unexpected way, and when they thought about it, it was hilarious; they just had to laugh about it. Just not in front of the people. After all, they had to keep the illusion that they were the ones in control, right?

As for J.R. and Helaina, after the barge blew up, they headed to the house with the other family members, not saying a word, wondering if anyone knew what they had done. They quickly retired to their rooms where they lay in the dark all night, wondering if they would be in trouble the next morning. What better punishment could there be? And their elders agreed.

CHAPTER THREE

J.R. AND HELAINA LEARN THEIR FATE

The next morning everyone was busy preparing to go home and back to work at the various companies that the Unity Corporation owned. At breakfast, everyone discussed the previous day's activities. The teenagers were surprised that not one single person accused them of last night's mishap.

Some of their cousins and siblings talked about the exploding barge, and how cool it was when all the remaining rockets exploded and what a beautiful display it made right there on the water. The younger kids talked about how cool it would have been to be on a patrol boat to help put out that fire. Before J.R. and Helaina could go back upstairs to pack their bags for the trip home, they were told to go to Grandfather's den because their fathers wanted to talk to them. Slowly they made their way to the second floor, not saying a word, using mind speak to communicate.

"This was all your idea!" Helaina accused her cousin.

"You wanted to help."

"What kind of punishment do you think we will get?"

"Maybe we will have to go clean up the beach. Grandma made me do that once when I blew up the trash dumpster," J.R. smiled slightly at the memory.

"Maybe we will have to rebuild that barge. If that is the case, maybe we can stay here for a few more weeks. I sure hate working with hammers and nails. I always end up smashing my fingers!"

"That would be cool. Staying a few more weeks, not smashing your fingers," laughed J.R.

As the two teens climbed the stairs, Peanut woke up and climbed out of her travel bag, and with her harness and leash securely on, climbed to sit on Helaina's shoulder. J.R. reached out a finger and rubbed the small animal's soft fur. They now stood at Granddad's door, but before they could knock, the door opened to let them in. They walked in with their heads down, looking as remorseful as possible.

Helaina's dad spoke first, "You two look like you are headed to the electric chair. Cheer up; we have wonderful news for the two of you."

Helaina and J.R. looked up in confusion. Using their Mind Speak and in unison they said, "They don't know! Great, maybe we are going to get away with it!"

William came up behind them, putting his hands on their shoulders and making both teens a jump. Their hearts beat rapidly and Peanut raced into her carrying bag. William smiled, knowing what they were saying to each other but not letting on to their secret.

"Sit down kids; your parents have come to a decision about the rest of your summer."

"Maybe they do know." They were still using Mind Speak, as they called it.

"Why are they torturing us like this?" asked Helaina.

"Why don't they punish us and get it over with?"

"Maybe they—"

Their conversation, not heard by anyone but their Granddad, was interrupted by Charlie. "Kids it has been decided that you will spend the remainder of your summer with your grandparents. They have much to teach you and would love spending a little more time with you."

Helaina jumped up excitedly, causing little Peanut to curl into a ball and start shaking from fear. "That's wonderful, really! That's great." Not wanting to hurt her Dad she added, "I will miss you and the camping trip we had planned."

This was a dream come true for her. She loved being on the island with her Grandparents. The more time they spent on Hope Island, the better.

"Don't you worry about that; you will have a few adventures with your grandparents. I assure you; you will have lots of fun."

J.R. spoke, "Do we have to rebuild that barge that blew up last night?"

"Now son, why would we make you do that?" Charlie asked his son.

"No reason, I was just wondering." Then he thought for a minute and asked, "Can I work on some of the antique cars?"

"I have something a lot more interesting to show you. Now go and tell your brother and sisters good-bye. They are going to be envious of you getting to stay here with us. Then go help your mothers pack the luggage into the cars," William Unity instructed his grand-daughter and grand-nephew.

In unison they said, "This is going to be great!" J.R. and Helaina looked at the men in the room. "Why do we keep speaking together like that?" they asked.

David and Charlie smiled, and together, in unison, they said, "One day you will know the answer, but not now."

The kids looked at their fathers with quizzical expressions.

Just as they were about to leave Williams's office, David stopped them. "About the fireworks last night, I think that it was extremely lucky no one got hurt."

"We do too!"

"I think in the future only those with the skills and knowledge to execute events should program the controls. This will help prevent dangerous mishaps from happening and prevent injuries to innocent bystanders. What do you two think?" David asked the two teens.

J.R. and Helaina looked at each other and turned back around to face their fathers and grandfather. "We think that you are probably right," J.R. answered for both of them.

"We're glad you think that," Charles Black told his son. Now both David and Charlie smiled at them, and Charlie continued, "Boy! We were very surprised to hear our favorite song. And it was sure cool to see the fireworks performing it. It was a nice thing to do, and it was our favorite part of the day. Something we will remember the rest of our lives."

"Even the barge blowing up was cool!" said David. "But dangerous! And we are sure that something like that won't happen again, right?"

"Right!" everyone agreed. Then J.R. and Helaina left the elders, going to do as they were instructed.

The rest of the morning and a good part of the afternoon was spent saying good-bye to brothers and sisters, moms and dads, and aunts and uncles. Small planes filled with family, friends, and board members took off to the mainland. From there, they got on flights that took them all over the country and all over the world, back to their homes and back to their jobs at the various companies owned by Unity Corporation. The residents of Hope Island were now hard at work cleaning up and putting things back in order, getting ready to welcome in a new week.

At the helicopter receiving room at Washington's International Airport, helicopter pilot Jack Webber stood waiting. Two men dressed in dark suits approached him, without exchanging pleasantries, without any expression at all. The taller of the two simply said, "The package please!"

Jack pulled out the small pink notebook that he had wrapped carefully in brown paper from the inside pocket of his black leather flight jacket. Then he handed it to the men. Without a word, they took the package and walked away. Jack suddenly felt regret, he worked for two companies, both secretive, both looking out for their own interest. It was a good thing Jack knew who the good guys were and who were the bad guys, and he always made sure he was on the good side of both. Just for insurance, he had removed some of the pages from the girl's pink Dream Stories journal. He didn't know why he had done that; he just knew deep down inside that he should.

After all the good-byes were said and everyone was gone, J.R. and Helaina went down to the beach, dressed in their scuba gear and dragging a small inflatable raft. William and Jennifer Unity watched from the second story balcony. The kids swam out to where the barge had been, collecting the wood and debris from the water and placing it in the raft. When the raft was full, they pulled it back to shore, emptied it into a trash dumpster and went back to collect more.

Jennifer turned to her husband of nearly forty-five years. "They're good kids."

"Yes, my dear, they are. They have good hearts."

For the next hour they watched as Helaina and J.R. cleaned up. They then went out and joined them.

CHAPTER FOUR
THE ADVENTURE BEGINS

Breakfast the next morning was served on the patio near the swimming pool. Since there were only Jennifer, William, J.R., and Helaina, there was no need to mess up the big dining room. After the four finished breakfast, William announced he had arranged a special trip. The kids were excited to hear they were going to take the new yacht and travel down the coast towards California.

The Unity's yacht was one of two identical ships; the second had been given to Hanna Black. It was a 44 Steel built in Italy. She was a beautiful ship, 144 feet from stem to stern. She had a top speed of seventeen knots and cruised comfortably at fourteen knots. She was outfitted with a large recreation room, a lap pool, a basketball hoop, a theatre to watch television or the latest movie, a large restaurant style kitchen, and sleeping quarters for eight. Below deck was a tender garage which held a small submersible and a small cabin cruiser to take passengers to shore. The yacht was equipped with the latest computer and navigational technology. The *Unity One* was given to William as a retirement gift; The *Unity Two* was given to Hanna Black and was delivered to her at her seaside home in Florida. This would be *Unity One*'s first trip.

J.R. and Helaina were excited about being the first to travel on the *Unity One*. They went to pack their bags. Helaina made sure she packed plenty of special food for Peanut and brought along Peanut's rather large cage. Of course, she couldn't forget to bring along at least three books to read and one of her little pink notebooks. J.R. made sure he had his laptop computer and the newest gadget he was working on. However, he did forget to pack socks, but who needed socks when you were on a luxury yacht in the heat of summer? Helaina on the other hand packed enough clothes for a month, with matching accessories for Peanut of course.

Captain Elijah Alexander had received orders from his employer to prepare the *Unity One* for a one-week voyage. Elijah Alexander had retired from the Royal British Navy and moved to Hope Island with his wife ten years earlier to be closer to their daughter and her family. When William needed someone to captain his yacht, Elijah was the perfect choice, having plenty of experience piloting small and large sea vessels. Elijah welcomed the opportunity and enjoyed this part-time position. He loved the chance to get back out on the water.

Elijah's friend and second mate, Mason Johnston, was down below checking the engines and making sure everything was in working order. Mason had worked for William for over thirty years, starting when he was twenty-two and just out of mechanic school. They had bonded over their love of antique vehicles. Everyone considered him family and a trusted friend. The third member of the crew was Sophia, Jennifer Unity's assistant in all things home related and her dear and trusted friend. Sophia had already boarded the *Unity One*, stored her things away, and was busy putting away the food in the big walk in freezer. Elijah, Mason, and Sophia were the only crew needed on the *Unity One*.

The family arrived at one in the afternoon, and at one thirty the *Unity One* pulled away from her dock to begin the maiden voyage. They journied south down the coast towards California. Elijah and Mason had taken this trip many times on William's old yacht the *Jenny*, named for Jennifer Unity. Elijah and Mason were happy the family had purchased this new vessel. The *Jenny* was an old relic that constantly needed repair, and parts for her engines were getting scarce. For years they had pleaded with William to retire her, but his love for antiques and everything old kept him from doing so. Even now the *Jenny* was traveling to a dry dock to be refurbished. William just couldn't let her go.

Once they were on their way, William brought J.R. and Helaina up to the pilothouse. J.R. was interested in all the gadgets. Helaina, with Peanut riding on top of her head, was more interested in using the binoculars to find sea lions and dolphins; she believed the pilothouse was the perfect look out spot. Elijah had to stop J.R. from touching the controls and noticed the interesting watch he was wearing.

"J.R., that's sure a cool watch."

"Thanks, I made one for my grandma for Christmas."

"You made two watches?"

"Sure did," J.R. said proudly and extended his left arm so Elijah could get a better look.

"What does this gage here measure?"

"It measures people's energy; it says here you are fifty percent."

"Fifty percent of what?"

"Fifty percent of our energy. Look when I point it at Granddad it says he is 100%, so is Helaina…, and me."

Elijah looked over at William, instinctively knowing what his eyes were asking; William nodded yes to his silent question.

J.R. opened a drawer and discovered some random parts and an old radio from the *Jenny*, plus fuses and wires. "Elijah, do you need these things?"

"Not right now, but you never know when you will need some spare parts."

"Can I have them? Do you have more?"

"No, you can't. Besides what do you want with those?"

"To put them together to make things. Do you have a welding torch?"

That's when William interrupted, knowing that if he didn't this could go on for hours.

"J.R., we don't need you setting our new yacht on fire with a welding torch. Elijah might need those parts for repairs if anything breaks down. Why don't you and Helaina go and try out the pool. I bet Sophia and your grandmother have a snack waiting for you."

"Okay, come on Helaina. By the way, your rat just went pee on your hair."

"No, she didn't, and she is a sugar glider for the thousandth time."

As the two teens went out the door, Elijah relaxed.

"Thank you, my friend, for rescuing me. Boy can he be persistent?"

William laughed, "You don't know the half of it."

"Does that watch of his really do what I think it does? And he made it himself?"

"Yes, it does, and yes he did. That boy is always making things. Our best people haven't figured out how he did that. He's talented. Better keep the control room locked or he will take everything apart just to see how it works."

Elijah laughed, "Yes sir, I will do that."

"I'm serious; that boy took my Model T apart last summer and when he helped me put it back together, he had the thing going ninety miles an hour. The fastest one on record never went above fifty," William told him with a chuckle.

William remembered how J.R. put modifications in the engine that Ford himself never thought of, and how he was so proud of the boy's accomplishment that he had bragged about it to all his friends.

"I will remember that!" Elijah laughed.

***

William joined his family near the pool. At dinner that evening, Helaina must have asked a thousand questions. But it was her last question that shook up her grandparents.

"Grandma, where did our family come from?"

After a few seconds of trying to think of a plausible answer, Jennifer decided to take the offensive.

"Why do you want to know?"

"Well Elijah is from England, Sophia is from Spain, and I have a friend whose family came from Germany. So, where does our family come from?"

"Well Granddad was born on Hope Island, and I was born in California."

"Okay, thanks."

"You are very welcome."

Later that night as William and Jennifer lay in bed reading, William took a break to compliment his wife, "You did a great job tonight answering Helaina's question."

"Thank you, my love."

"I'm sure glad she didn't want more information."

"She's young; usually kids just want simple answers."

"You are very wise."

"Well isn't that the reason you love me? You know the questions will become harder and very soon; J.R. and Helaina are special."

"That, my dear, is what I am worried about," William told her.

All through the night, as the family slept, the luxury yacht moved effortlessly through the Pacific water towards their destination. Elijah, taking William's words seriously, brought one of the vessels comfortable lounge chairs to the control room. He slept with one eye open and an ear to the door. He woke up every two hours to make sure they remained on course. The *Unity One* was completely capable of piloting herself, but Elijah had a hard time trusting all the modern equipment.

William was up at five a.m. the next morning. He was an early riser and was always the first one at the corporate offices. First, he went to the galley and made coffee. Taking two hot steamy mugs, along with some donuts, he made his way up to the pilothouse. Elijah was already at work checking the instruments and making notes in the logbook.

"Good morning, William. Did you sleep well?"

"Like a baby in her mother's arms."

William put the tray down and handed Elijah a cup of coffee.

"Thanks, I was just thinking about going below deck and fixing some. Those donuts look good."

"Is everything running properly?"

"Right as rain, and right on course. Later I will radio the *Oceanic One* and give them our ETA. We should be there around four tomorrow morning," Elijah told William, taking a sip of the steaming cup of coffee.

Elijah looked out the viewing window and saw that Helaina was sitting at a little poolside table writing. "William looks like you aren't the only one who likes to get up early. Looks like Helaina beat you this morning."

"I think I will go fix her some hot chocolate and join her. You need anything?"

"No sir, I am just fine. I'll talk to you later."

William went back downstairs and fixed another tray with donuts, hot chocolate, and another cup of coffee for himself and went out to join Helaina.

"Good morning, sweetie, you're up early."

"I couldn't sleep, I'm too excited. Besides I had another Dream Story and wanted to write it down."

"Did your dad talk to you about your Dream Story diaries?"

"He said that they are special because I wrote them, and that I should let him keep them safe so the wrong people can't read them. Who are the wrong people?" she asked all in one breath.

"People who wouldn't understand what you were writing about. They would get really angry about some of the concepts you talk about in those stories."

"I don't want that. Besides, I don't think anyone would get upset about my dreams. Maybe one day I can publish them in a book. Can I have the diary I gave you the other day? I wasn't finished with that one."

"Your dad didn't give it back to you?"

"No." Helaina reached for the steaming cup of hot chocolate on the tray. "Thanks for the chocolate."

Helaina took the cup off the tray and took a few sips, then a few bites of a donut.

"It's nine o'clock in Maryland; let's call your dad. I have a question to ask him."

"Can I talk to him? I want to make sure they give Iggy, my iguana, her calcium."

"Sure you can. Let me get him on the phone first. Should be easy, he likes getting up early like we do."

The phone rang three times before David Unity picked up. "Dad, how's the trip going? Is my girl driving you crazy with all her questions?"

"We are having a wonderful time; its smooth sailing here. I was wondering, did you take Helaina's pink diary off my desk and take it home with you?"

"No! But I talked to her about keeping them safe for her. When I went to the den to retrieve it before I left, I couldn't find it. I thought you put it in the library safe or gave it back to her."

William walked to the railing so Helaina couldn't hear what he was about to say next. "We have a problem. I don't have it and neither does Helaina. We must find that book. Call the house and have them search it, and call me. She wrote dates and names in those books that were right on the money. They can't get in the wrong hands."

"I agree. Is Helaina with you now? I know she doesn't sleep late, even on a holiday. Can I speak with her?"

"You're right about that; she's right here."

William walked over and handed Helaina the phone.

"Princess, your dad wants to talk to you."

Helaina put down her pen and took the phone from her granddad. "Hi, Dad, the *Unity One* is great, and last night I beat J.R. at Dragon Wars. He got frustrated because I beat him six times in a row. How's everyone?" Without taking a breath, Helaina continued with her questions. "Can you remind Cassie to give Iggy her calcium? Did you get my cell phone fixed? Peanut loves the—"

"Goodness girl! Can you take a breath so I can answer your questions," her father laughed. "First, great job in beating J.R. Tonight play your grandma; she beat me twice while we were on the island. Everyone's fine, and Cassie is taking good care of Iggy, and your phone couldn't be fixed. Your mom will get you a new one. Next time, try not to drop it in the pool, okay."

"Okay, Dad."

"Now can I ask you some questions?"

"Sure, but I usually have more than you do."

"That you do, baby. Now, can you tell me how many of those little pink books you have?

"Well mom ordered them from your secretary. They are the usual notebooks that the employees are given to keeps notes in. You know, the ones with the company logo on front. I wanted some pink ones to write in, and mom had your secretary order me some. She even got the printers to put Dream Diary on the front and my name in gold. Isn't that cool."

"Yes, that is, and it was nice of Sandy to do that for you. I will ask your mom how many she ordered. Can you tell me how many you already used to write your stories in?"

"I didn't count them. They are on my bookshelf in my bedroom closet, all but four of them. Those are the ones I brought with me. Did I do something wrong?"

"No, Princess, you didn't. We just want to keep them safe like I told you. I am going to take the ones you have at home and put them in a safe place. Is that okay with you?"

"Sure. But who do I have to keep them safe from? And why are you so worried? They are just dreams that I have. No one would be interested in those. And they are in a safe place already."

All Helaina's questions exhausted David's mind at that early hour. Yet, he needed to tell his daughter something. "I believe that we should discuss this next time we are together. In the meantime, I will take your books and put them in our home safe."

"I can get on a computer and set up a video chat. Granddad's phone is old, and we can't FaceTime on it." Helaina got up from the table and began walking into the galley to retrieve her tablet. Her father's next words stopped her.

"Not right now. I have a meeting in a few minutes. You have a great adventure with your grandparents and let me worry about all that. Now give the phone back to your grandfather. Love you."

"Love you too!" Helaina said a bit to sharply, frustrated that her father wouldn't answer her questions.

Walking over to William, she pushed the phone into his hand and stood there to hear what William would say to her father. William started talking about the Yacht, knowing it would take only a few seconds for Helaina to get bored with the subject. He was right, because a minute later, she picked up her drink and book, stomping her way back to the gallery, and they were able to finish their conversation.

At breakfast, it was decided that they would stop for a few hours so that the kids could go scuba diving with William and Elijah. It had been about six months since the kids were certified as divers, and they needed the practice. Elijah anchored the *Unity One* as Mason prepared for the dive. Mason would stay on board the luxury yacht with Jennifer and Sophia. They planned to make cookies and work on needlework projects. But first they planned to take the smaller cabin cruiser for a little ride to shore. They wanted to have some fun and do a little shopping. Mason would monitor everyone by radio and keep a watch out for any dangers with the underwater radar system.

After opening the bay doors Jennifer and Sophia were off. They headed straight for the docks of a nearby town. The two men and the two teenagers, dressed in wet suits, checked their equipment and dropped into the crystal, clear waters, diving down about twenty yards before leveling off.

J.R. and Helaina swam in front as the two men followed behind them. J.R. was the first to see the old shipwreck and pointed it out to everyone.

"Let's go explore the wreckage; we might find gold."

They headed down slowly, letting their bodies adjust to the pressure. Finally, they were on the deck of the old ship and having a great time exploring. J.R. picked little things up off the deck that interested him and placed them in his dive bag. The two men explored the wreckage, taking notes as to where it was found and noting any identifying words or symbols that might identify the origins of the vessel. Later they planned to send a salvage crew to retrieve her. Helaina slipped away from the group and swam through a passageway, chasing after a school of fish. As Helaina slipped out of sight, Mason called down to Elijah to tell them about a few sharks that appeared on the radar screen back on the *Unity One*.

Mason's main responsibility was to keep the family and crew safe from harm while at sea, so he quickly informed William of the danger. J.R. was within sight and heard them through his earpiece. Helaina didn't; the thick metal of the ship blocked out any communication from the others. Before they could go after Helaina, the sharks were upon them, circling just above their heads. The three of them took cover in the wheelhouse. Thankfully it was fully enclosed, and the windows were too small for the sharks to enter so it provided a safe haven. Elijah took out his underwater flare gun. Before shooting the flare gun, he informed Mason he was going to try to distract the animals and send them off in a new direction. He fired, and the flare flew through the water. But the sharks weren't interested in following it. The sharks seemed more interested in what had caused the noise and stayed where they were, staring at the three men. The three of them must have looked like yummy sea lions in their dark wet suits. And sharks are known to snack on sea lions.

"J.R., keep trying to contact your cousin on the radio. She went into that passageway, and I am afraid that she was distracted by something and isn't paying attention to what's happening. Tell her to stay where she is until the sharks move on. I'm positive that they can't fit through that passage, and she will be safe where she's at."

"Roger that."

J.R. tried to contact Helaina, first by radio, then by Mind Speak, but the rusty metal of the dead ship prevented her from hearing him. Meanwhile, the men checked their gauges; they were good. They figured they had about forty-five more minutes before the air tanks were empty. When that was done, they radioed Elijah to inform him of the situation. They decided not to fire their last flare until it was absolutely necessary. J.R. was worried about Helaina. When something caught her attention, she would forget everything else to go investigate.

Helaina was having a great time collecting some treasures of her own when suddenly, she heard a voice on her radio, but it was unclear. She tried to call the three men but got nothing. She decided that it would be best to go find them. She emerged from the passageway, and she tried to adjust the radio station. When this didn't work, she swam to the deck of the wreckage.

Finally, she heard J.R. in her head. "Helaina go back into the passageway."

But it was too late, one of the sharks was now blocking the entrance, and she couldn't go back in. Elijah and William motioned for her not to move and not to panic. Finally, she was able to get her radio to work. She also saw that two sharks had trapped the men in the wheelhouse and another was headed in her direction.

"Granddad, they aren't going to hurt you."

"Helaina, darling, please don't move."

"But it's alright; they are just curious. Watch!"

Helaina then did something that almost gave William and Elijah a heart attack. She held out her arms, extending them away from her body with palms up. She stayed as still as possible. She didn't appear to be afraid; in fact, she looked relaxed and had a smile on her face.

"Girl, what are you doing?"

"Be quiet please; you are going to scare them."

"Hell! Girl, they are scaring us!" William yelled at his granddaughter.

"Just give me a minute; watch me, and be very quiet and still."

Elijah and William were pulling their knives from their sheaths and were about to go rescue Helaina. Before they could swim to her, they froze at the sight before them. The two sharks approached Helaina. One shark was on her left and the other on her right. They nuzzled her open palms and she laughed. Then she wiggled her fingers and began rubbing their soft skin as she looked straight ahead, not making eye contact with the sea creatures. Slowly, she brought her arms together in front of her, and the sharks followed the movement. They were now directly in front of her, not attacking, not moving, just watching her. She rotated her hands slowly, palms down, and fingers extended. She stroked between their eyes, and they seemed to enjoy it. Helaina smiled at them, making eye contact with each of them. Then they turned around and swam away, taking their friends with them. Helaina swam to her grandfather once they were gone. All three of her companions were astonished at what they had just witnessed.

"I told you they didn't want to hurt you."

William, the first to regain his voice, was the first to speak. "What did you just do?"

"I showed them that we were harmless. I showed them that they were scaring you and that they should go."

"You spoke to them? You can't do that!" J.R. said

"Yes. No. I mean that I can't actually talk to them. I picture in my mind what I needed them to know and send them those pictures. And they send me pictures."

"You weren't scared?"

"Of course not. I would have known if they wanted to hurt me."

"And how would you know that?"

"I don't know. I just do."

Elijah informed Mason they were fine, and the group of explorers headed back to the *Unity One*. As they swam, William asked himself, *what other abilities do these children have? Are there others of their generation capable of doing amazing things?* All he knew was that he would have to watch them carefully in the future. He also knew he had to speak to their parents about this new development.

***

The group of divers returned to the *Unity One* and discovered the cabin cruiser had also returned. Helaina got out of the cool water and quickly removed her wet suit and returned it to the storage locker. Then she ran off to find her grandmother to show her the treasures she'd found. Mason joined the divers to help assist them with their equipment and to refill the air tanks When J.R. finished putting up his equipment, he asked Mason to show him his workshop and the inside of the little submersible. William cautioned him not to take things apart and went to the pilothouse with Elijah to prepare to get the yacht moving again. He also needed to get on the computer for a video conference with David and Charlie to discuss what he had witnessed. He wasn't surprised that Helaina could communicate with creatures; that trait was common in their kind. He was surprised that one so young could do it and do it with such threatening creatures.

That evening at the dinner table, everyone talked of their adventures. Jennifer and Sophia shopped while in town and bought something for everyone. Helaina got a new dress and a swimsuit. They found J.R. a ham radio kit to put together, hopefully distracting him enough that he wouldn't take apart any of the new equipment on board the *Unity One*. William got a new hat and the newest Dan Brown novel which he wanted to read. They even brought Mason and Elijah something.

Jennifer and Sophia had discovered a bakery and brought back some delicious breads and pastries. Sophia Fernandez worked for William and Jennifer as their household manager. She was skilled at making pastries. That day the two women enjoyed a stop at a little tearoom for a snack. They then bought some homemade chocolates, a cake, and two apple pies for everyone to enjoy on the trip. Of course, this got them out of baking the cookies they had promised Elijah and Mason. They enjoyed one of the pies as they watched J.R. work on his ham radio kit. Sophia and Jennifer had been friends since the day Sophia arrived at Jennifer's home as a young exchange student. When Sophia returned to her home in Spain, after her year of studying English, the two women continued their friendship through long letters. Years later, when Sophia lost her family in a tragic land slide, Jennifer encouraged her friend to come to Hope Island. Sophia never regretted that move.

Before going to their staterooms, J.R. and Helaina showed off the trinkets that they had found on the sunken ship. Helaina found an old pocket watch, some beads, four silver teacups with their saucers, and a china teapot. The watch, she gave to her cousin, the tea set she gave to her grandparents, and she kept the pretty beads for herself. J.R. dumped his bag on the table. His treasures consisted of a few antique tools, some very odd looking, and a few old knives—the kind men kept with them when they hunted. He gave one to William, another to Mason, and kept two for himself. He also had some leather bags that looked like they had been created to hold gold coins, unfortunately they were empty. Everyone was exhausted from their adventures that day, so they retired early. Everyone except for Mason, because it was his turn to keep watch on deck that night and make sure that they stayed on course. To pass the time, he played video games on the computer, and later he raided the kitchen for a few of those pastries. He was thankful that Miss Jennifer and Sophia brought them back, because he had a tremendous sweet tooth. Mason really liked Sophia and wanted to ask her out, but that would have to wait until they returned to Hope Island.

CHAPTER FIVE
THE SEA LAB

Around three in the morning, the *Unity One* reached her destination. Mason stopped the engines, put down anchor, and took a nap while he waited for everyone to wake up. The first thing J.R. and Helaina noticed when they awoke was that they had stopped moving. Excited to know where Grandfather brought them, they dressed quickly and went on deck. They discovered they were anchored in the middle of the Pacific; there was no island, no port, and no nothing. There was nothing around them but blue water. They were confused.

"Where do you think we are?" Helaina asked her cousin.

"In the middle of the ocean."

"That I know, nimrod."

"Don't call me names."

"Sorry, do you think we are going diving again?"

"Don't know," J.R. curtly remarked back.

"Okay. Why are you mad at me?" Helaina demanded, crossing her arms and giving him a look of frustration.

"I'm not mad!"

"Yes, you are!"

"Alright, I am mad! Because I am wondering just what else you can do. What other superpowers do you have?" J.R. yelled back at his cousin.

"I don't have superpowers! You idiot! I just communicate with creatures. You have seen me do it thousands of times, so what's the problem?

"I saw you talk to animals the normal way people do. But I have never seen you communicate with anything like the way you did with those sharks! That is completely different."

Just then William and Jennifer joined them on the railing. Jennifer sensed that something was wrong because suddenly, the kids became quiet. Even going so far as to give each other dirty looks and turning their backs to each other.

"What going on here?" Jennifer asked as she glanced back and forth between the two kids.

"Nothing!" they said rather harshly.

"Why did we stop here? There's nothing here," J.R. asked William.

"There is something very important here; something that Unity has been working on. We want to show you some of the things we are doing so you understand what Unity Corporation and our family are working for."

Jennifer handed the kids each a backpack that she had retrieved from a storage locker, and told them to go pack some clothes, because they would be gone from the *Unity One* for two days. But before they ran off to pack, the kids had a few more questions.

"Grandma, can I bring Peanut with us?"

"Not this time, Sophia will take good care of her. I promise."

"Are you coming with us?"

"I wouldn't miss this for the world. Besides, it will be nice to visit with an old friend," said Jennifer. Before J.R and Helaina could ask "What friend" she asked a question of her own. "Do you know why your parents let us have you for the rest of the summer?"

"Because they want us to begin learning about what Unity does, and because they know we love spending time with you because you spoil us."

Jennifer and William laughed at J.R.'s insight.

"Are we taking the submersible?" J.R. wanted to know.

"Yes, we are."

"Who gets to drive it? Mason or Elijah?"

"Neither. They are staying aboard the yacht. Your grandma will be piloting the submersible."

Now for any other person having your grandmother pilot a submersible would be quite unusual, but for J.R. and Helaina being unusual was a normal fact of life. Take Helaina's Grandma Jennifer for instance. Not only was she William Unity's wife, and mother to David, Rebecca, and Connie, she was also a professor of English Literature and a life-long student. She quit teaching when her children came along, but when she was not busy with the family, she learned how to pilot a small air-craft, a submersible, and even a hot air balloon. She also learned to speak several languages and master several culinary cuisines to the delight of her family and friends. But what amazed everyone was that she learned all this on her own, without taking a single class and still passing every one of the certifying tests with high scores. The Unity family was unusual to say the least. Right now, Jennifer Unity was playing the role of grandmother, a role she enjoyed the most.

"Go and pack your bag. Helaina don't try to sneak Peanut in your bags. The pressure under the ocean would be too much for a little animal, and it could kill her."

"Yes Grandma; let's have pancakes and bacon for breakfast."

"Sure, meet me in the kitchen in ten minutes, and you can help me make the pancakes. Now hurry along dear."

William and Jennifer had already packed their backpacks, and as the kids went hurrying down the stairs, they headed to the pilothouse. William had asked Elijah to make a call to their son, David, who was now waiting to talk to them.

"David, did anyone find that diary? I'm a bit worried."

"Good morning to you too, Dad," David said with an audible yawn.

"Good morning!" both his mother and father said together.

"About the diary!" William said in a demanding tone. He was a bit tired from having a restless night.

"Okay, here's what you need to know. Charlie saw an opportunity and took it. And with everything happening on the island, and worrying

44

about the attempt on your life, he thought it best not to tell you his plan."

"So, Charlie took the diary? Why?" asked his mother.

"No, but he read me in on his plan. It's a good one. So, I don't want you two to worry about it."

"Not worry!" Jennifer yelled. "I can't help but worry."

"That goes for me too!" William added.

"Mom, Dad, you did your part. It's now Charlie's and my job as Guardians to handle this. Trust us! Now have fun down on *Oceanic One* and say hi for me. Trust in your new Guardians; it's time you let go, Dad."

"After all these years, do you think that it—" William began.

"Bye Dad. Bye Mom, have fun." David than broke his connection, leaving his parents staring at the blank monitor.

"He cut me off!" William complained.

"He's right dear. We need to concentrate on the kids now. They need us."

Fifteen minutes later, everyone was in the kitchen eating pancakes. Still neither Helaina nor J.R. would talk to the other. While sitting at the kitchen counter, Helaina put on makeup and gave instruction to Sophia about taking care of little Peanut as the older women put the dishes in the dishwasher. J.R., avoiding any eye contact with Helaina, discussed the workings of the submersible. While down in Mason's shop yesterday, J.R. had looked at the sub's operating manual and at its blueprints. He wanted to see inside the engine compartment, but Mason wouldn't unlock it for him. Mason sent him upstairs before the boy decided to get into his tool locker.

***

As the little group ate their pancakes and bacon, thirty-five-hundred miles away, another meeting was taking place. The same two men who had met Jack Webber at the Washington airport to retrieve the little pink Dream Diary, were now about to deliver the very same book to a United States Senator. A Senator who didn't trust the Unity

Corporation and wanted to prove they had something to hide. His main objective in life was to take the Unity Corporation down. Just like they tried to do to him.

Senator Doug Webster was a man who didn't like secrets even though he had many of his own. Doug Webster was forty-five years of age, five foot nine, and very muscular due to the many hours of weightlifting he did at one of the gyms he owned. He was single by choice, not wanting to share his life with anyone who could get in his way. He had big plans for his life and didn't want a wife or kids to hold him back. But this didn't stop him from using the women who were attracted to his good looks and his money. He began his career as a small-town lawyer dealing with business disputes and bankruptcy in a bad economy. He turned to scooping up businesses that were failing for little money and making them successful by eliminating the competition—sometimes in a not so legal way. He liked using strong arm tactics and a small army of muscle men to do his dirty work. Once he tried to take over a small company, one that belonged to the Unity Corporation, but lost the fight, losing half his wealth in the process. Now he wanted payback. He had hired the best detectives to find something on the family; something he could use to uncover their weaknesses and use to his advantage. Maybe this little pink book, from one of the younger members of the family, was just what he needed. He knew teenage girls were known for revealing all their secrets and that of their families and friends in journals all the time. And he hoped that was exactly what Helaina Unity did. Soon after the two hired men left, Senator Webster began reading and researching the material that was given him.

***

Back in the Pacific Ocean, the family was now in the submersible with Jennifer at the controls and William as her co-pilot. J.R. and Helaina watched out the windows as they traveled deeper into the Pacific. Still neither of them would speak to the other. Instead, they watched as giant jellyfish swim down to the sandy ocean floor. The family traveled for two hours during which J.R. and Helaina made up a game to see who could identify the most fish, communicating only through their frustrated grandparents who couldn't figure out why they were not talking.

The family saw a school of orange Garibaldi fish which had a clown like appearance and made them laugh. They also identified some Scorpion fish, Damselfish, Cardinal fish, and a large school of Coral Hawk fish. They were most excited to see two stingrays and a mother shark with a baby swimming alongside her. The deeper they got, the less sea life they found, and soon they got bored. J.R. found the little sub's electrical schematics and studied them for a few minutes, then decided to get out his laptop. Helaina was busy taking photographs and asking her grandparents endless questions. Finally, William, who was navigating, told the kids to look out the forward window; they were about to come upon their destination.

They watched. For twenty minutes the sub and its occupants traveled about ten feet above the ocean floor. The darkness so dense that nothing could be seen, the only light came from the headlight of the submersible. Jennifer and William navigated through the darkness using their instruments and experience, for they had visited this area many times. Suddenly they came upon a cliff, and they gently slipped over the edge into what was a deep valley. Jennifer depressurized the interior a little more and took the sub on a steep dive into the darkness. J.R. and Helaina sat still, watching and waiting for what was to come. Two minutes after initiating the dive, Jennifer leveled out the sub. Seconds later, it was like a bright sun had descended into the ocean to light their way. The sub had traveled through a highly sophisticated motion detector. When the computer that operated the mechanism identified the sub, it turned on the lights to welcome the little band of sea explorers. The kids saw it! Their final destination!

There, on the bottom of the ocean canyon, stood what looked like a large snow globe with a large metal base. From the base, metal pipes extended that penetrated the ocean floor. All this was encased in what looked like a large glass dome in which swam a vast collection of fish.

"J.R., Helaina, welcome to *Oceanic One*."

"That's where we are going?"

"Sure is."

"What is that place?" Helaina wanted to know.

"That is a research station; they are trying to harness the planet's thermal energy."

"You mean there are people down here," J.R. asked, forgetting that Jennifer had said something earlier about seeing old friends.

"Sure, and they are very good friends of ours. Your grandma went to college with one of the scientists."

J.R. checked his computer and spoke up. "Granddad according to my calculations, we are in a canyon between two of the earth's tectonic plates. Couldn't the two plates come together and destroy the research station?"

"Very good young man, the plates haven't moved more than one hundred millimeters in the last 300 years. But if, or when, the tectonic plates move, the *Oceanic One* is capable of breaking free from the floor and moving to another location."

"This is what they call the Pacific Plate. It's the outer rim of what they call, "The Ring of Fire," where a lot of volcanic activities takes place below the ocean and above."

"Yes, J.R., that's right." William said, not noticing J.R. sticking his tongue out at his cousin and giving her a smug grin, satisfied he showed up the girl.

"Grandma, didn't Mt. St. Helen erupt on May 18th, 1980? Was she part of the Ring of Fire?" Helaina asked as she returned J.R.'s smug look with satisfaction.

"Yes, that's right, very good at remembering the date."

William continued, "That's the energy they are trying to harvest here so the world can have an endless supply of energy without polluting the atmosphere."

The conversation came to an end when they arrived at the dome. William radioed the *Oceanic One*. A few minutes later a panel slid up and over to the top of the dome to allow them to enter. Within minutes, the sub made its way into the snow globe-like structure and connected to its docking station. They disembarked the submersible.

CHAPTER SIX

OCEANIC ONE

LEARNING WHAT POWER THE EARTH HOLDS

The small hatch was opened, and William and Jennifer were helped out of the cramped space of the little submersible by the *Oceanic One*'s electronics and mechanical expert, John Addison.

"William, Jennifer, welcome back. Did you have any trouble with your new toy here? I will have to give her a good look over before you leave. I'm dying to see what she has under her hood."

A boy's head suddenly popped up through the hatch. Not expecting anyone else, John was surprised to see the newcomer and equally surprised to see a second head appear a few seconds later. This time it was a young girl who made her presence known. It had been years since the Unity's had brought anyone else with them. The last time someone came with them, they brought David and Charlie, right after they had turned eighteen.

"Now who do we have here?" John said as he assisted the two teens onto the platform.

"I'm James Robert Black, but they just call me J.R., and this is my cousin, Helaina Marie Unity." J.R. took it upon himself to make the introductions.

"Well I'll be. I see you brought two very good-looking young people to visit with us." John Addison addressed William and Jennifer. "I will get your bags and take them to your cabins."

John then disappeared into the sub to retrieve the bags and to investigate this new model which he had only read about. Like J.R., he couldn't resist finding out how things worked. As John descended, three people came through a doorway. The women immediately gave the older couple a hug. The men shook hands and patted each other on the back as good friends who haven't seen each other in a while do.

"Jenny, it is so nice to see you again, you too, William. Now who have you brought with you? A new generation already? And how's Charlie and David?" Olivia Golden asked all in one breathe.

Jennifer Unity laughed and hugged her old friend again. "You haven't changed a bit, Olivia. Noah, you look wonderful."

Looking over Noah's shoulder, was a young man of about twenty with a big smile on his face and the deepest blue eyes imaginable. Jennifer approached him, giving him a big bear hug.

"Samuel, what a handsome young man you turned out to be. Congratulations by the way, your parents told me you completed your studies and have received your doctorate degree." From her bag she pulled out a present for Samuel. "I remembered how much you love Swiss Chocolates. That's the biggest box I could find."

Samuel returned her hug with enthusiasm. "Thank you, Aunt Jen. Are you tired of Uncle William being home all the time?" he laughed.

J.R. and Helaina, who quietly stood next to the sub, now came and stood next to their grandparents. William put his hand on Helaina's shoulder to reassure her, because she could become quite shy when around strangers. After she got to know someone, she became her normal talkative self.

Olivia Golden was sixty-two years old. She had the same blue eyes as her youngest son, Sam, and the same thick, curly blonde hair. She smiled as she approached Helaina. The young girl and woman stood eye to eye; they were the same exact height. Noticing that the girl was a bit uneasy, she made it her mission to make her feel comfortable and welcomed. Putting her arm around the girl, Olivia gave Helaina a reassuring hug,

"Jenny, please tell me who this beautiful young lady is. We are so glad that you brought her and this very handsome young man for a visit?"

"This is my very smart, very beautiful, and talented granddaughter Helaina, and next to her is my very handsome and curious grandnephew J.R."

"Hey! I'm smart also."

Everyone laughed. "That you are my dear," Jennifer responded. William then took over the introductions.

"Helaina and J.R., I would like you to meet Noah and Olivia Golden, and their youngest son, Samuel, who likes to be called Sam. Olivia is your grandmother's second cousin and best friend from college."

In unison Helaina and J.R. greeted their new friends. Helaina, finding her voice, asked, "We're related to you?"

"Helaina, our family is much bigger and extends far greater, than you could possibly imagine," said her grandfather.

Helaina looked at the very handsome Sam. Boy, how she wished she wasn't related to him. Unfortunately for her, J.R. heard her thoughts and began teasing her, using Mind Speak of course. She blushed and punched him on the arm. William, hearing everything that they were saying, gave J.R. the, *you better behave look*, which stopped his teasing immediately.

Noah, who was a whole foot taller than his wife and also good looking was about to speak, but he was halted momentarily by the rumblings of an earthquake. J.R. and Helaina went to their grandparents, not because they were scared, but because they needed something to hold on to. The shaking only lasted a minute, and Noah, who wanted to lessen the fears of his young guests, brushed off the incident as nothing to worry about.

He told them, "Don't you two worry. We get small quakes everyday down here on the ocean floor.

"How is that for a big welcome?" Olivia laughed. "Now let's all move into the main building and give you the grand tour."

Before they began moving, an alarm went off.

"John, can you stop fiddling with that machine. Come up here and turn that thing off." Noah yelled to John who was still in the small submersible.

J.R. walked over to a workstation which housed monitors, computers, and other gadgets. "Mr. Noah, something is wrong here; it needs fixing."

"Please just call me Noah, J.R. Now don't worry about that alarm; it just saying things got shook up a bit."

"No sir! See that monitor right there?"

"Yes."

"The calculations are wrong. They should have changed when the quake happened, but they didn't."

John came over to the monitors, turned off the alarm and took a closer look. "Noah, J.R. is right; the monitor is frozen."

He turned off that monitor and rebooted the computer. All the readings changed. Noah and John looked at J.R.

"How did you know that?"

"I don't know, but I do know that the readings should have changed, and the monitor has a short in it somewhere."

"John, please check that out while we take our visitors on a tour."

"Sure boss."

Noah looked at William. "The boy is right! He is a smart one."

The family was given a tour of the *Oceanic One*. Helaina relaxed a bit, and as always had lots of questions, all of them directed to young Sam.

Sam was very patient. He made sure he answered every question as carefully as possible. Sam wasn't sure how much they knew or how much the Unity's wanted them to know, and that was important. As the elder Unity's followed behind, he looked to William and Jennifer for signs that he was giving out too much information.

"What do you study here?

"What we study here is the earth's tectonic plates and the undersea volcanos along their edge."

"Grandma says you are trying to harvest that energy, to find a way to distribute it around the world in order to preserve other national resources in a cleaner and more efficient way."

"That's correct Helaina. By the way, that is a very pretty name."

Helaina blushed and looked down at her feet.

J.R., looking for a chance to tease his cousin, told her in Mind Speak so no one else could hear, "I think he likes you."

Before she could stop herself, she turned around and fussed at him. "You shut up; stop teasing me!"

"Helaina, J.R. didn't say anything," her grandmother scolded.

Realizing her mistake, a sense of panic rose up inside her. Her cousin quickly came to her rescue.

"I'm sorry, I was whispering to her and made her mad," admitted J.R.

Helaina gave her cousin a silent thank you.

William, who was following behind with Noah, smiled. "Okay then. Let's go see the lab."

William and Noah lagged behind the group speaking in hushed whispers.

"William they are very young, have they become *connected* already?"

"I am afraid they have. They've also developed advanced skills and can do things I can't explain."

"Have there been any other teens who exhibit this? Do you think it is a concern?"

"Charlie and David are having this type of thing investigated, looking for others, and yes, it is a great concern to everyone. Could it be that our genes have mutated? I don't know. I just don't know! And it worries me," William told his old friend.

As they began their way down the long corridor, it was now J.R.'s opportunity to ask a few questions and take the focus off his cousin.

"When a volcano erupts under the sea, doesn't its lava produce toxic waste and pollute the sea?"

"You are right, it does." Sam went on. "People also pollute the oceans. But what is causing the most damage is volcanoes. A volcano will build up extreme pressure, and when it can't contain it, it erupts, and the lava is its by-product."

"Volcanoes are destructive. However, after the lava cools and decomposes, it produces some very fertile soil, so it's not totally a bad thing."

"You're right. It's part of the cycle."

J.R asked: "How can you possibly use a volcano to bring power to the world?"

"A volcano can also use vents to dispel its excess pressure in the form of super-heated water and acids hot enough to melt lead. It's that power we want to harness."

Helaina wanted to know. "The acids you mentioned, and the hot water, couldn't that cause damage to the earth's plates?"

Here is where Olivia stepped in. "Yes, but not as much as you think. The lava builds up, cools down, and then provides nutrients to the plants and sea creatures. The earth uses its own material to heal itself and to rebuild what was lost. It's like when you break a bone. You heal yourself with time, making that bone stronger, in some instances."

Now Noah stepped in. "The problem we have now is too many eruptions. We need to harness it and use it. Too many eruptions are causing the oceans to warm up, and it causes the death and extinction of millions of different kinds of sea life and plants. Sea life and plants that have potential to provide medicine and food are just now being realized. That is another thing we are studying. Soon we can introduce our findings to the population of the world."

"Wow! You are doing important work!" exclaimed Helaina.

"That they are. That is why we brought you down here, to show you the good things Unity is doing. What *we* are doing. Now let's go see the amazing collection of sea plants that they have collected. Then can we get something to eat? I am starving," said William with pride and a rumbling stomach.

"Jenny, I think your next generation of Guardians is impressed with what we do." Olivia whispered to Jennifer Unity so the kids couldn't hear her.

"That they are, just as much as we are impressed by them. Now, do you have some of that cherry cobbler you make? You know it's my favorite. I look forward to it every time I visit. You make it better than anyone. One day you will have to give me the recipe."

"Never, my dear friend! That's one recipe I won't share with you. But yes! I did make two very large pans of cobbler."

"Now let's catch up on all the family news," said Olivia.

CHAPTER SEVEN
TROUBLE UNDER THE SEA

The family spent another hour exploring the immense science lab and meeting the other members of the team that worked and lived there. They looked at some of the experiments that were taking place. Afterwards, they went to the dining hall where they were served a five-course seafood dinner with Olivia's cherry cobbler for dessert.

After dinner, Helaina, who was interested in the live animal and plant specimens that were being studied by the science team, asked Sam if he could escort her back to the lab. J.R. went with John to help fix the computer system in the submersible bay. It was obvious they were still angry about something, but the excitement of visiting such an interesting place was temporarily distracting them from their issues.

William and Jennifer stayed in the dining hall with their friends to enjoy an after-dinner coffee and some more cobbler while they caught the Golden's up on all the family news. The rest of the staff, and scientists retired to another part of the lab where they had private accommodations, and enjoyed all the comforts of any land-based home. An hour later disaster struck.

The earthquake was stronger and lasted longer than the previous one. It caused the security doors to shut between the living accommodations and the labs. The lights went out, but the emergency generator immediately began operating, and the lights promptly came back on. Unfortunately, the security doors remained shut.

Noah rapidly got on the intercom to check if there were any injuries. Luckily none were reported. Next he radioed John.

"John, are you and J.R. okay?"

"Yes, we're fine. J.R was right, there is something wrong with the computer system."

"The security doors are still closed; can you open them?"

"We're working on it. Give us a few minutes."

"Noah! Please can you check on Helaina and Sam?" begged Olivia.

"Doing that now, dear." He flipped the switch which connected him to the lab. "Sam! Son, are you and Helaina all right?"

It took Sam a few seconds to get to the communications radio because he needed to climb over some debris. In the meantime, William, Jennifer, and Olivia came and stood behind Noah. Noah called again. Anxiously, the four of them waited. It seemed an eternity, but Sam finally responded to their call, and they were able to breathe a sigh of relief.

"Dad, we're fine; tell the Unitys Helaina is alright also. The security doors have closed us off from everyone."

Another alarm went off.

"Dad, where's John; is he there with you? I need him to tell me how to override the system so I can get everyone out."

"Hold on, he's in the sub bay with J.R. The four of you are separated from everyone else. Hold on a second while I talk to him."

Noah switched back to John and J.R. "John?"

"Yes boss?"

"What's that alarm?"

"Do you really want to hear this?"

"Damn it! What is it?"

"There's a crack in the outer dome." He paused and took a deep breath. "But we have an even bigger problem. The emergency shut off for the nuclear reactor is jammed shut. We need to get to it and manually open it; the stupid computer won't take my override commands. We can't open the doors. Is there anyone in the labs? Or is everyone else trapped in the living courters?"

"Only Sam and Helaina," Noah answered. "Hold on and let me think a minute."

Noah then turned to his companions as he switched off the intercom.

"We need one team to go and shut off the reactor manually, and one to repair the outer dome, but all we have available are two men."

William, not believing what he was now going to suggest, spoke, "No we don't, there are four of them on the other side of these doors."

"William, I will not put the lives of those two kids in danger."

"If those repairs aren't made, that won't be an issue."

Jennifer stepped closer to her husband, taking hold of his hand for a little reassurance.

He looked down at her. "They can do this. I know they can."

Jennifer just nodded, knowing he was right. Noah and William took a minute, and together they formulated a plan. They swiftly relayed their plan to John and Sam.

"Sam, you take Helaina and dive down through the holding tank, open the outside hatch, and go out and patch the dome."

"Dad, I can do it alone. Helaina should stay in the lab."

William stepped in. "Sam, Helaina is a certified diver. She also has special skills that might help you. It's a two-man job. Don't worry she will be just fine."

"William, I don't know about this. We should keep her protected she's next to be—"

Before Sam could say anymore, Noah broke in. "Sam, do it! Don't say anymore; just go! We are sending John and J.R. to fix the reactor. Now move it!"

"Yes, Dad"

In record time, Sam and Helaina got into the diving suits. Before they could dive in, Helaina went to the intercom.

"Granddad, can you hear me?" Helaina asked apprehensively.

"Yes, Princess. I hear you. Don't be scared, I know you can do this."

"I'm not scared. I fix broken things all the time. I take after you remember?"

"Yes, I know. Is there something you need?"

"Can I talk to J.R. for a second? Please."

"Sure, Princess. Hold on, and good luck!"

William then made the connections between the two intercoms for Helaina.

"J.R. this is Helaina, are you there?"

"Yes, I'm here. What do you want?"

"I just want to tell you I'm sorry, please don't be mad at me anymore. I don't like it."

"I'm sorry too." J.R. felt that his cousin needed his reassurance, and he was happy to give it to her. "Helaina, I promise I'm not mad anymore. I know you can do this. Just be careful."

"Thank you. You be careful too." Just before they turned away from the intercom, J.R. made a challenge to his cousin. "First one back, gets the last piece of cobbler."

Helaina laughed, "You're on cousin!"

Feeling much better, Helaina and Sam slipped into the cold water to begin their journey to the dome wall. In the meantime, Noah called the living quarters and talked to a technician to see if she could override the system from one of the laptops in the common room to open the doors. Other than that, there was nothing anyone could do but wait and watch through the windows.

First to be seen were Sam and Helaina. Together they swam towards the dome's wall. First, they had to find the crack and then patch it before it got bigger and leaked. The problem was that the dome was a mile wide and half a mile tall. It was a lot of area to cover for two people. They didn't have the water propeller units because there were only two units available, and John and J.R. needed them to get to the reactor fast. It was the bigger threat. The dome was basically a big fish tank housing the vast amount of sea life and plants that were studied with the research station in the middle. Helaina looked around, and she came up with an idea. She contacted Sam on her radio.

"Sam, I've got an idea to make this go faster."

"What?"

"Those two dolphins can help. I will send one to you, and I will take the other. Hold on to its dorsal fin. They will help us find that crack."

Before Sam could ask her how she was going to do that, Helaina had motioned for the two dolphins, taking one, and sending the other to Sam. The dolphins took the passengers around and around the dome, systematically looking for the damage. Finally, Sam found it.

"Helaina, I found it; get over here as fast as you can."

"Won't take me long with my new friend here. I think I will name her Speedy."

"You can't name her. She is a lab specimen to study, not a pet. Where are you?"

Helaina laughed. "Right behind you."

Helaina and Sam released themselves from their mode of transportation and began working.

"How are we going to fix the crack?" Helaina asked Sam.

"The dome is comprised of sixteen layers of acrylic and enforced with diamond dust; it's very hard."

He retrieved a thick, clear plastic bag, and two syringes from a bag that was attached to his belt. He handed it to Helaina.

"First I need you to inject this liquid acrylic and this diamond epoxy into that valve on top of the bag. Then massage the bag to mix the two. Don't stop, because if you stop it will harden immediately. Then we will have to go back to the station to get some more, understand?"

"Yes, mix the two, and don't stop."

"Correct, while you do that, I take the torch and heat the area. Once it is hot enough, we apply the acrylic together. I just cut a hole in the corner and use it like a pastry bag, then smooth it out using these two knives. We have to work fast. Ready?"

***

Helaina nodded and began working. As they worked on the dome, J.R. and John arrived at the reactors. They were busy trying to find the leaking valve so they could turn it off. They finally found it. They discovered that it was deep down and in a hard to reach place. John was too big to get to it, so he sent J.R. down with a wrench and a can of

59

thick nautical grease, to loosen things up. The valve was hot, and the steam made it hard for J.R. to see, but he finally got the wrench around it.

"J.R., do you have the wrench secured on the valve?

"Yes, I'm going to twist it now."

"Wait, first take the grease and apply it around the valve."

"Okay, done."

"Now take the wrench and twist it to the right very slowly. When the steam completely stops, you stop. We don't want to tighten it too much or it will break from the pressure."

J.R. used all his strength to get the wrench to move, but finally, it did. The wrench didn't have to move to far until the steam stopped flowing from it.

"I got the steam to stop," he radioed to John

"Good job. Now leave the wrench where it is, and let's get back inside. A crew will come out later to fix the valve."

John and J.R. gathered the propeller units and returned to the sub bay. As they began their journey back, Sam and Helaina were finishing up the patch work on the dome.

"Hey, Helaina we're done!" Sam said into the radio. "Think you could get your two friends to come back and take us home? By the way, nice job! You're great at fixing things."

"Thank you, I fix lots of things. I have a little sister who breaks stuff all the time, and I have to glue a lot of things back together."

"You're quite clever. I think our ride is here. Think you can tell me how you got them to help us?" he asked.

"I talk to them of course. Beat you back."

Sam was definitely curious about Helaina's last remark, but he didn't say anything. They grabbed hold of their mode of transportation and headed back to the lab. It didn't take much time before they were safely inside. Instead of going back the way they had come, they swam to the sub bay where J.R. and John helped them out of the water.

"Guess I get that last piece of cherry cobbler!" J.R. bragged.

"You deserve it!" Helaina told him. Then she gave him a huge, rib breaking hug.

"I think there's enough for the both of us," J.R. said as he pushed her away.

Sam contacted his parents and the Unitys to tell them all was well, knowing they were worried. J.R. and John went to the computer and in a few minutes had the emergency doors opened and the lab off the emergency generator and back to running normally.

William, Jennifer, Noah, and Olivia rushed to the sub bay to congratulate their heroes. Then they all went back to the dining hall to warm up with a hot cup of chocolate. When they arrived, the population of the *Oceanic One* was waiting for them. They all applauded the little band of heroes, patting them on the back. It was like a big party. Everyone wanted to know the details of what they had done.

William took John and Sam aside before they arrived in the dining hall and told them not to disclose the *special gifts* that they witnessed. He explained that the secrecy was for the protection of the two teenagers. Two hours later, after cobbler and warm drinks and exhausted from a long day, J.R and Helaina retired to their sleeping quarters to get some much-deserved rest.

CHAPTER EIGHT

OUT FOR REVENGE

As J.R., Helaina, and their grandparents were arriving at the *Oceanic One*; Senator Doug Webster was in his office, reading Helaina's Dream Diary. He read the stories from cover to cover. Then, he read them again. Senator Webster might be smart in business and getting around the law, but in other ways, he was basically an idiot. This was a good thing for Unity Corp. To him, they were just stories, the writings of a teen girl with a good imagination. But if he were to do some research and look closely at the names and dates in that book, he would see it was much more than made up stories. Finally, he called it a night, calling his secretary into his office.

"Amy make copies of this for me, send one copy to the detective agency, and see what they make of it. Send another copy to my friend at Yale; he's good at finding the hidden message in things. When you are done, put the book in the safe, and you can leave for the night." He barked those orders at his secretary as he tossed the little book at her on his way out the door.

"Yes sir."

When Amy looked at the pink diary, she saw the Unity logo on the front of it, and her heart began beating wildly. She knew that symbol! On a silver chain around her neck was a pendant. That pendant, made in silver and given to her by her grandmother, looked exactly like the logo on the cover of the little pink book. On the reverse side of the pendant was Unity's motto, "Guide with an open heart, and an open mind. A world united in peace." As soon as her boss was out of the office, she placed the book in her purse, wrote a letter of resignation, and put it on Senator Webster's desk. She then collected her things and left. She didn't know why, but she knew she had to take the book to someone at Unity. She felt that she had to protect it; she was doing this purely on instinct. Something deep inside her told her this was the right thing to do, and that's what she reacted upon. She hated Senator Webster anyway, so it was time for a new job.

***

The next morning Amy walked into David Unity's office in Maryland.

"Mr. Unity, I have something that belongs to one of your people."

She opened her purse, reached in, and as she did, the pendant around her neck was visible to David. He immediately focused on what Amy Christopher had brought him.

"Can you tell me Ms. Christopher where you got this from?"

"Two men brought this to my boss, Senator Doug Webster, yesterday morning."

"Did he read it?"

"I believe he did, several times."

"Did you read it?"

"It's funny; when I saw the Logo of Unity on the cover, I felt that I needed to protect it and bring it to you. I had no interest in what it said, but I felt it was important. Senator Webster gave it to me to copy and send out to various people before he left his office last night. I didn't make those copies. Instead, I wrote my resignation, packed up, and left. I felt it was my mission to bring it to you. Isn't that odd?"

"No, it's not odd at all. It's in you to do what's right. That diary belongs to my daughter, and it was stolen from the family home on Hope Island. I noticed your pendant. Who gave it to you?"

"My grandmother gave it to me when I was eighteen; it belonged to my great-great-grandmother. When she gave it to me, she said to always, "Remember Unity." Has Unity Corporation been around that long?" Amy Christopher asked.

"Yes, it has. That pendant means your family was one of the first to settle here. Now, Ms. Christopher, since you gave up your source of

63

income to do the right thing for the Unity Corporation, I think I can reward your actions with a job as a corporate secretary. My secretary got your resume from a friend at the Capital. I see that you are well educated and experienced in your duties. I believe that Senator Webster will be looking for you. I think it would be in your best interest to give you a job away from this area. Do you like Florida?" David Unity asked.

Amy listened closely to what David Unity had to say, and she had a few questions of her own. Like how did he get her resume without a security clearance? Where did they come from, in order to settle "here"? And finally, why did she feel she had to protect the little book, and Unity? But she didn't ask any of those things, and later wondered about that too.

"Mr. Unity, I would love to move to Florida."

"Great. I will have my secretary arrange to move your possessions and get you a flight to Ft. Lauderdale this afternoon. My cousin, Charlie Black, has arranged employment for you there in one of our smaller holdings. You will be given full title to a three-bedroom, two bath home, as a thank you gift for bringing this to us."

"Thank you. All this because I brought you a book that was taken from you; this is much too generous."

"No, Ms. Christopher, thank you. You are a wise and brave woman; enjoy Florida."

David walked her to the door, dismissing her before she began asking questions. He left her in his secretary's capable hands and went to make a few phone calls. It took several tries, but he was finally able to reach *Oceanic One* to speak to his father.

"Dad, are you having a nice visit with Noah and Olivia? Please tell them I send my love."

"We are having a wonderful time. I will tell them. Last night we did have a little situation, but it is under control now."

"Anything serious? Are Helaina and J.R. alright?"

"Yes, everyone's fine. We need to talk more about this evolving generation thing when we get home. I think I know what's happening. Now, are you calling because you have news for me?"

"You know me so well. Yes, there is news. I was brought Helaina's Dream Diary this morning by a secretary working for Senator Doug Webster. Dad, she wore our crest."

"That's great news. That man has been a thorn in my side for decades. I hope you provided this secretary with minimal information and rewarded her amply.

"Yes, I sent her to Florida. Charlie and his staff are taking it from there. He has the perfect job opening for her at one of our smaller holdings. As a thank you we gave her a new house in that housing development we are building."

"Great we need to protect our own. Thanks for the good news. We have a lot to talk about when I get us above water. I will call you tomorrow night when we are back aboard the yacht. And son!"

"Yes?"

"Great job!"

"Thanks, Dad, Have fun. Talk to you soon."

David felt guilty that he didn't tell his father everything. Just enough to ease his concerns about Helaina's diary. Now he needed to call his cousin Charlie to see what the next move would be.

***

Everyone on the *Oceanic One* slept well after their adventure the previous night. Jennifer and Olivia woke up early to help the chef prepare a huge breakfast buffet. When everyone on the *Oceanic One* was awake and ready to start the day, they arrived in the galley hungry. They enjoyed waffles, pancakes, pastries, eggs, bacon and ham, along with a lot of fresh fruit, coffee, and orange juice. The crew and visitors were still talking about the previous night's events.

That morning, two teams were organized to prepare the damage from last night's earthquake. One was to travel outside the dome and reinforce the repairs made by Sam and Helaina. A second team was to replace the damaged valve of the nuclear reactor John and J.R. shut down temporarily. Feeling that the two teens had enough adventure for a while, William sent J.R. to help John with the computer system, and

65

Helaina went with Jennifer and Olivia to the lab to investigate the sea creatures and to see some of the experiments they were doing.

William, Noah, and Sam went to look over what progress was being made in producing energy from the fissure in the earth's crust. For the next three hours, the three men worked together discussing various parts of the machinery and the different alternatives the *Oceanic One* was developing to distribute the energy that the vents produced. They agreed the first course of action was to educate the population about the value of this new way to produce clean and cost-efficient energy and to assure the world's population they could do this without having to do any renovations to homes and businesses. It would just take a few minor tweaks to their already existing equipment. In fact, Sam Golden was engineering a simple, inexpensive device to do just that, but they still had a long way to go.

In the lab, Helaina and Jennifer Unity learned about the different plants that were being studied. Olivia showed them her newest breakthrough. She'd removed the wax from sea grass and discovered its properties killed skin cancer cells. After more studies were completed, a simple lotion could be manufactured, and no one would ever have to have invasive surgery to remove skin cancer again. It could be used to cure millions, saving countless lives.

In another part of the lab they were experimenting with the common Peace Lily, trying to use it to purify the air of allergens. But what impressed Helaina the most was the collection of sea animals being raised, including her new dolphin friends she met last night. In one small tank there was a collection of various types of sea horses. When she looked into the small tank, the sea horses speedily lined up across the front of the aquarium to watch Helaina. This caught the attention of the two adults, and they stood back to watch the girl. The sea horses and the girl stared at each other for a second, and Helaina laughed. She took a finger and drew a circle in the water, and the little horses followed along. Wherever her finger went, the horses followed. When she stopped the sea horses stopped, and she applauded their performance. Thanking them, she walked over to the dolphin pool in the middle of the room. Sitting down on the edge she dangled her feet in the cool water.

"Grandma, can I swim in the pool with the dolphins?"

"Ask your cousin, it's her lab."

"Cousin Olivia, may I play with the dolphins please?" she asked.

"I can't see why not, they seem to like you, but you need to wear a diving suit and goggles, and don't go out to the dome, they are still working out there."

"Oh, thank you, I promise." She stood up and put on the suit, before diving in to play with her new friends.

"That girl sure has a way with animals. I have never seen anything like it before," Olivia whispered to Jennifer.

"I know, it's amazing, yet it scares me. We must educate her not to exhibit her talent where others could see her. It could put her in danger if the wrong people learned of her talents."

"That, it could. Have they asked why they are different?"

"No, not yet, but it is soon to come. They are so young, I believe they should learn their history and heritage a little at a time, giving them time to adsorb the information and learn to use their talent for the good. But William, David, and Charlie feel that they should speed up their education."

"I think you are right, Jennifer. They are developing abilities now at such a young age. Younger than past generations. I can't envision what that might mean to our future."

"Neither can I."

The women sat back and watch the young girl play innocently with her two dolphin friends. Both hoped that the girl and her cousin would keep their innocent curiosity about the world just a little longer. Especially, when they learned exactly who they really were and what they were destined to do. Both women agreed that J.R. and Helaina were much too young to have such a major responsibility thrust upon them. But they had to trust the Guardians.

* * *

In another part of the facility, John and J.R. finished working on the defective computer and had it running smoothly. They were now doing some test runs, making sure the improvements that J.R. suggested would work. Amazingly, they did. Finished, they turned to the submersible that had brought the family to the *Oceanic One*. John and J.R. found the plans to the powerful motor.

"John, if we could remove the computer, place it over in this console, and put in a power booster, we could have this baby moving at twenty knots easily."

"You're probably right, but the computer would need to be programmed to accept the new equipment and adjust—"

John stopped suddenly realizing that he was talking to a fifteen-year-old boy.

"Is your dad some kind of mechanical engineer? How did you learn your way around these things?"

"No, but he is a computer engineer and a mathematical genius."

"You sure are a smart one. Why is that dial pointing at me?" John asked, pointing to J.R.'s unusual watch.

"It is telling me you have ten percent energy."

"Well, I just had an energy drink an hour ago, and I am ready to swim five miles." John laughed at J.R.'s answer. "So, I think that it's wrong."

"It's never wrong!" J.R. thought to himself, not wanting to argue with the older man.

William having come to see what J.R. was up to, had heard the exchange. It wasn't uncommon to hire people who weren't of their heritage. In fact, about eighty percent of the employees were just ordinary people and not from their gene pool. Very few knew their secrets.

After what could be called a normal day for the *Oceanic One* with no emergencies or melt downs, everyone enjoyed a dinner of shellfish stew. Also served was lots of sourdough bread from San Francisco and a variety of cheese. When that was all cleared away, a special dessert of lava cake was served. It was one of William Unity's favorite desserts. After dinner, Sam, Helaina, and J.R. connected the video game to the sixty-inch Sony flat screen in the dining hall and enjoyed playing video games the rest of the evening. The adults relaxed with drinks and watched the young people compete against each other, challenging their skills in different games.

Early the next morning, before the sun rose high in the sky, the Unity family said good-bye to their friends, new and old, and returned to the yacht. They took with them stories about their adventures, to be told only to those who understood. For those who didn't, like John and a few other occupants of *Oceanic One,* they wouldn't remember the extra-ordinary skills of their young visitors. They would be debriefed by Noah, and when Noah was through with them, their memories of the last two days would be slightly altered. They would remember William and Jennifer bringing two teenagers with them for a visit, but they wouldn't remember their extra-ordinary skills, thanks to a memory altering spray that was developed by their people a long time ago. And Boy! Did it come in handy.

CHAPTER NINE
ACCEPTING THEIR DESTINY

The trip back to the *Unity One* was uneventful. Having stayed up late playing video games with John and Sam and getting up at four a.m., J.R. and Helaina were tired and slept the entire way back to the surface. They did not wake until the submersible was safely tucked back into the docking bay of the *Unity One*. They did not realize they were back on the yacht until after they were gently awoken by Jennifer and William. Forgetting their bags, they raced off in two directions. J.R. went to the galley to grab some cookies before he went to look for Elijah to tell him all about the trip to the research lab. He also wanted to persuade him to let him start up the yacht. Helaina raced to her state room to retrieve her sugar glider, Peanut, having missed her. When she arrived, she noticed the cage was open, and looking around the room, she didn't see her pet. She thought that Sophia must know where Peanut was and went to find her. She found her in the sub bay, helping Mason unload the bags.

"Sophia I can't find Peanut," Helaina said a bit worried.

"She's with me, dear. The two off us have become great friends while you were away. Look! She's safe and sound riding here in her carrying pouch."

Sure enough, there was Peanut, attached to a colorful leash, safely zipped into the pouch. The second the little animal heard her mistress's voice she began wiggling, trying to get away from her new friend to be with Helaina. Making chatting sounds, she made it quite clear she wanted out, so Sophia unzipped the pouch.

"Maybe when we get back to Hope Island, I might adopt one of these little creatures. I've come to love this one," Sophia said as she handed Peanut to Helaina.

"Paris Hilton might have a noisy little dog in her purse, but I think sugar gliders are the ultimate pocket pet. They are quiet and small, they love to be held, and they like to sleep. They make the best companions," said Helaina, as she took her little pet from Sophia.

Helaina turned all her attention to Peanut, petting her soft body, and talking to her. Sophia swore that the animal understood exactly what the girl was saying to it.

Sophia and Mason retrieved the family's bags from the submersible and stored them in their staterooms. Mason spent the afternoon giving the sub a complete going over, filling up her fuel tanks, and checking the oil. Who knew when she might be needed again; it was best to keep her, "on the ready," as he always said. Mason believed in being prepared for anything that might come up.

William Unity, chasing after J.R., went to the wheelhouse to see Elijah.

"Elijah, the *Oceanic One* is amazing! I helped fix a nuclear reactor, and they make energy from steam that comes from the earth with these fantastic machines, and—"

William interrupted him before he could continue. "J.R. you can tell Elijah all about our adventures later; we must get this boat moving."

"Can I do it this time?" He looked at the two men with eyes full of hope and anticipation; it made it difficult for the two men to refuse the simple request.

Elijah looked to William for the answer.

"I guess you can't hit anything out here, so why not."

Elijah showed J.R. which controls to use, and how to program their heading into the onboard computer—which he knew already.

"I know what's next; can I do the systems check myself?"

Elijah turned to William who simply nodded his head, giving Elijah permission to let J.R. do the systems check.

"Alright, I will be watching in case you need help."

"Don't need help. I know how to do it; I watched you after our dive."

Without saying another word, J.R. performed the twenty-five step systems check flawlessly. He turned to Elijah.

"Did I do it right?" he asked.

"You sure did; not one mistake. You learned that from watching me one time? You are sure a fast learner. Now Captain James Robert Black, are you ready to get her on the way?"

William and Elijah watched J.R. start the engines and get the large yacht on its way home.

"Great job, Captain!" William told J.R., "Now let Captain Elijah take over and you go see if your grandmother has lunch ready yet. I'm starved."

J.R. snapped to attention and saluted William. "Aye, aye, sir."

The two men laughed at J. R's antics as he ran off to the galley.

"I swear that boy can do anything he puts him young mind to," Elijah said with respect for the young man.

"That is rather evident. Elijah can you fax these calculations and diagrams from the lab to Charlie? Then I need you to fax these chemical models to our scientist in Norway. This, my friend, is the completed formula Olivia Golden has been working on; this is the cure for skin cancer."

"WOW! I will send this out first; I bet she receives the Nobel Peace Prize for this discovery."

"I bet she does too. Any problems while we were away?"

"No sir."

"Great, I think I will get a sandwich and take a nap on one of those lounge chairs near the pool. I'm exhausted."

"Have a nice nap, sir. I will get this sent immediately," Elijah said in his heavy British accent.

"Thanks, see you later."

After a simple lunch of sandwiches and chips, served with plenty of iced tea, the family settled near the pool to relax for the rest of the afternoon. J.R. worked on the ham radio set Jennifer had given him. William took a nap in the sun, getting a little red. Helaina kept Peanut, who slept comfortably in a small pet carrier, close to her as she swam in the pool and got a lesson in needle point from her grandmother.

The day went by fast; soon everyone on *Unity One* was gathered in the dining room eating spaghetti and meatballs, with plenty of garlic bread. For dessert Sophia surprised everyone with Tiramisu, layered with lots of strawberries and blueberries, whipped cream, and sponge cake.

"Granddad, I finished building the ham radio, I even improved it."

"How did you improve it?"

"Let me get it, and I will show you."

J.R. ran off, coming back a few minutes later with the ham radio. He put the radio on the table in the middle of the room. The redwood coffee table was handmade from a section of a redwood tree that had fallen in the forest, crafted by a friend, and given to the Unitys as a thank you gift. Everyone gathered around it, sitting on soft black chairs made of the best leather and beautifully trimmed with redwood from the same tree. It was a cozy area made for family conferences and business meetings.

"I fixed it so that I can call any ham radio using these stations. Earlier I called Elijah up in the wheelhouse. But I also a found a way to call any cell phone I want. First, I took Grandma's cell phone and downloaded its programming into this receiver. Then I rigged up a calculator so I could use its number pad to dial a phone number. Then I just connected it to the radio. Watch, I will call my dad in Florida."

J.R., using the calculator, dialed his father's number. Everyone heard the phone ringing, and Katie Black answered.

"Hi, Mom."

"J.R.! What a wonderful surprise. Are you having a fun?"

"Sure am, I'm calling you from my ham radio on the *Unity One*."

"I didn't know that was possible."

"It is now."

"Well I guess it is if you are calling me on it right now. How is everyone?"

Everyone answered at the same time. "Hi, Katie."

Katie laughed at hearing everyone's voice at once. "Hi everyone."

73

J.R. looked at the radio. "Mom, I'm running out of power."

"Okay, son, call us when you get back to the island."

"I will. Bye, Mom."

"Bye everyone." The radio went dead.

"I guess I am going to have to find a way to give it more power."

"I guess we are going to have to hide all our cell phones from you before you find other uses for them," William scolded him.

"Don't worry. Grandma's phone still works. I even programmed in a few special apps I thought she might like," J.R. said as he handed the phone back to Jennifer.

William just shook his head in disbelief at what J.R. had accomplished in such a short amount of time.

"Before you kids start playing games, your grandmother and I have something to give you."

William walked over to a desk in the corner of the room and pulled out two boxes. One box was bigger than the other. William handed the smaller box to J.R. and the larger one to Helaina. They held the boxes tightly, both of them feeling that this was an important moment in their lives. Why else were they here with William and Jennifer?

Jennifer spoke, "Inside those boxes is part of your heritage. Go ahead; open them."

In the box J.R. unwrapped, he found a gold I.D bracelet that look like one of those medical alert bracelets, except made of gold. The chain was thicker for more stability, knowing the abuse men put their jewelry through. On the top was the Unity symbol and his name, J.R. Black, just the way he liked it. Also, in the box was a gold chain with a gold pendant on it, with the same markings. Helaina's box had the same pendent with gold chain, and other matching accessories that included matching earrings, and a gold charm bracelet with just two charms. One was the family crest; and the other had her name engraved on it.

As the kid's put on the jewelry, William asked them, "Do you know what the symbol means?"

"It's a circle which means the planet earth. The gold in the center represents the brightness of our future. The blue represents those from above. The green, those from below. The red, on each side, means the unforeseen. The black band around the edge means the things that unite us. And the two silver lines represent the things that keep us apart."

"Very good, Helaina. Look on the back of your pendants and your ID bracelet J.R.; what is engraved there?"

"I know what that is." J.R. spoke, "That's Unity's Corporations, and our family motto." J.R. read the inscription. "Guide with an open heart. Guide with an open mind. A world united in Peace."

"Wear that jewelry with pride and keep them close to your hearts," said their grandmother. "You don't have to wear it all the time, but when the time comes, you need to hand the jewelry, or ones just like them, down to the next generation."

The kids, in unison, thanked their grandparents, giving them each a hug.

"Can we play video games now?"

"Yes, go play games."

They started walking away, but J.R. stopped and turned around, looking like he had forgotten something.

"Granddad, once I asked Mom and Dad about their pendants, they said they got their special jewelry when they were eighteen, and when they did that it was the beginning."

"Yes, that's true."

"We are only fifteen, did we get ours because we are different."

"No young man, you got yours because you are special."

J.R. and Helaina thought about this for a few seconds.

"The beginning of what?" Helaina, always full of questions, wanted to know.

"The beginning of the truth, of course," her grandfather answered.

"Are we to be the next Guardians?" J.R. asked.

"Yes, if that is what you want. You will be asked to decide when you are older."

"Okay."

Just that simply the kids accepted their destiny. Without any reservations, knowing that somehow this was what they were meant to do. Off they went to play video games with no more questions.

"Do you think they understand?" Jennifer asked her husband.

"They understand," was his simple reply.

He then picked up the John Brown novel Jennifer had given him and began to read. Jennifer turned on the television to watch her favorite channel, the Food Network, and she settled in with her needle work.

CHAPTER TEN

TROUBLE IN WASHINGTON

The same day the Unity family traveled north to Hope Island, Senator Doug Webster was becoming very angry. He came to work that morning expecting to find his secretary at her desk and his coffee waiting for him. He found neither so he just sat at his desk and waited. He was so preoccupied with his thoughts that he didn't even see Ms. Christopher's letter of resignation sitting on the corner of his desk in a plain white envelope. Ms. Christopher had never been late; he figured he would be nice and allow her to be today. One day out of two years was still not a bad record. He would deduct a half days wages to teach her a lesson.

One hour passed, then another, not even a phone call from Amy Christopher. The phone in his office rang of course; in fact, it didn't stop ringing. Not knowing how to work the multi-line phone system, he hung up on a lot of people, some he really needed to talk to. While trying to work the phones, deliveries were made and piled up on the desk. Three people waited to talk to him, and two carriers were waiting, rather impatiently, for documents he couldn't find. The last straw was when another Senator rushed into the office demanding to know why he wasn't at an important Senate committee meeting. *Hell!* He couldn't even find his day planner. He didn't know what needed to be done today or where he was supposed to be. Senator Webster kicked everyone out of the office, took the phone off the hook, and left the office, locking the doors behind him. He rushed to the Senate committee meeting which he was an hour late for. He tried to get Ms. Christopher on his cell phone while he ran down the hall without any success. He let the phone ring continually for five minutes at her home and did the same for her cell.

"I swear when I get hold of you, you are fired!" he yelled into his cell phone.

When he returned to his office with an armful of files that needed his attention, the first thing he noticed was his office door was still locked. This meant Ms. Christopher hadn't shown up for work. Getting into his office, he left the outer door locked so he could get things in control. First, he called the secretarial pool for Ms. Christopher's replacement. Next he left a message for Ms. Christopher telling her that she was fired. He sat down in his desk chair with a cup of steaming hot coffee cradled in one hand, leaned back, and shut his eyes for a few minutes. He remembered something, something very important to him, causing him to sit up far too rapidly. He spilled the hot coffee all over the front of his pants, making him scream in pain and dance around the office clutching his crotch.

After the pain subsided, he began looking for the little pink Dream Diary. For the next hour he tore the office apart, looking in every file, and in every drawer. Paper was ankle deep on the floor of his office as well as in the outer office. Books were tossed from their shelves and thrown carelessly on the couch and into the office chairs. The safe was emptied. He searched it two, maybe three times making sure the diary wasn't there. The longer Senator Webster looked, the angrier he got. Finally, a temporary secretary walked through the door.

"Where the hell is it?" he yelled throwing a book at the door, just missing the woman who walked through it.

"I don't know! I am not working for you! Find someone else to clean up this mess!"

The woman stormed out. Senator Webster picked up another book and threw it at the closed door in complete frustration and anger, breaking the glass panel. Not getting anywhere looking for the pink diary, he decided to call someone who could help. Ten minutes later two large men, whose very size and rough looking appearance could intimidate the secret service, walked into Senator Doug Webster's tornado struck office.

Without pleasantries, Senator Webster got straight down to business. "First I want you two to go to this address. Find Ms. Christopher, and force her to tell you where she put the Unity diary."

"What if she doesn't tell us?"

"Fire her, permanently, understand?"

"Yes, sir. Then?"

"Tear apart her house; you are looking for a pink diary with the Unity logo on it and the name Helaina Marie Unity printed with gold letters. When you find it, bring it to me immediately! I expect to hear from you within an hour. Now get moving! I will be on my cell."

"Yes sir!" the two henchmen snorted before leaving the office.

Senator Webster couldn't stand the sight of the mess he had managed to make. He decided just to hire someone to clean up after him and reorganize the papers and books that were thrown everywhere. This was going to cost him plenty! Just that thought made the stingy Senator even angrier. He made one call. Soon eight people arrived and began the cleanup, and he left to go home for a large stiff drink of bourbon. He was stepping into his car when he received the phone call from his two muscled friends.

"Boss, Ms. Christopher isn't here, and she isn't coming back."

"How would you know that?"

"The house is completely empty, not even a scrap of paper on the floor."

"Put a trace on her phone."

"Did that; when we called the number you gave us, the phone rang in the mailbox. Guess she got another phone. We also found something else."

Not in the mood for games, Webster yelled, "Are you going to tell me, or not?"

"We found a note. It simply said, "We protect our own." It had the Unity logo on it."

"Find her car; find anything to trace her. I will call you tomorrow with new instructions. Keep your phone close." Senator Webster drove home and got very drunk.

CHAPTER ELEVEN
NEW FRIENDS ARE FOUND

The *Unity One* arrived safely back at Hope Island early the next afternoon. Some of the household staff and a few friends met them at the dock, welcoming them back from their trip and helping to unload the baggage. J.R. and Helaina raced to the house to call their families, but William and Jennifer walked back at a more leisurely pace, talking with their friends, as they caught up on the island's latest news. By the time William and Jennifer got to the house, the two teens had called their families, changed clothes, and raided the kitchen for a snack. They also managed to call a few of their friends, arranging to meet them at the local arcade. Then they met their grandparents at the door.

"We're going to meet our friends at the arcade!" They said in unison, giving each other a dirty look.

Being teens, they didn't like when someone could read their thoughts, not even a friend, and especially not a cousin.

"But we just got home, don't you want to rest up a bit?" asked Jennifer.

"We rested all day yesterday," Helaina assured them.

"Can we have some money for the arcade and the movies?" J.R. wanted to know.

"And maybe some pizza," Helaina added.

William reached into his wallet, handing each of them thirty dollars. "Alright! You have fun and get back here after the movie. J.R., do you have your cell? You left it here while we were at sea."

J.R. checked his pocket, but he couldn't find it. "No I..."

Before he could go further, Helaina pulled J.R.'s phone from her purse. Also visible was Peanut, who had been hidden in there.

"I have it! He would forget his head if it wasn't attached. I'll be glad when mom and dad send me my new phone."

"I might forget things, but you are klutzy," her cousin teased back.

"Helaina, give me Peanut. You know they don't allow animals at the mall or the movie theatre."

"But, Grandma, she's small; no one can see her in my purse."

"Give her to me. I will take her to her cage. Besides she probably wants to rest up after such a long trip."

Helaina handed the animal to her grandmother. "Can we go now? Kellie and Mark are waiting for us?"

"Alright, come home directly after the movies."

Before William could finish this reminder, J.R. and Helaina were running down the road toward town, leaving Jennifer and him watching their fast retreat.

"Guess they didn't want to spend any more time with us old folks."

"Guess they didn't, my love; let's go get us some nice iced tea and some of my chocolate chip pecan cookies. That is if David didn't find them all."

No one worried about the safety of the two teenagers; in fact, all the residents of Hope Island felt safe and secure for there was no crime on the island. Sometimes there was a lot of arguing. Of course, there were traffic violators because of the absent mindedness of the brilliant minds who presided there, and a lot of accidents, some of them quite weird. There was no stealing, no murders, no blackmail, no cheating of any kind on the island. This was remarkable considering the islands large population, those who could be seen, and those who couldn't.

The only incident of violence was the attempted assassination of William a few weeks earlier. It had been discovered that the attack hadn't come from a gun or from anyone on the island at all. The bullet that came whizzing by William's head came from a drone operated by someone on the coast of Washington, two miles away from their island. The drone had flown under their radar and had only been detected half a second after it shot at William. Afterwards, the drone flew into the water and an explosive charge was ignited turning the drone into dust. It happened so fast that the highly advance security system was unable to stop it. But new measures were installed so that would never happen again. Humans were starting to get smart. But for now, Hope Island was safe, and all the residents felt secure.

***

As the group of ocean travelers returned from their trip, Charlie Black, J.R.'s dad, was on one of the company's private planes on his way to Grand Cayman Island in the Caribbean. Even though Unity had the capability to keep records of deaths and births of each and every one of their people, sometimes people fell from sight, like the two children at the orphanage he was visiting today.

Charlie Black was about to visit Emma and Dylan Hurley; they were twelve-year-old twins who somehow weren't registered, that is until now. They were orphaned two years earlier when their single mother was killed. A heavy rain had caused a devastating landslide which buried the school in which she was teaching. She died after rescuing twenty children, two her own, and was considered a hero in the village.

The twin's grandparents had traveled to Grand Cayman Island to help develop the region and the areas agricultural resources. The couple had no children; however, the man had an affair with a young woman soon after his wife's death. That affair produced one child, a girl. The gentleman gave his daughter a gift, the same gift his mother had given him when he was a young man, telling her she had to remember just two things. That gift was a silver pendant. Record keeping in that part of the world wasn't as precise as it should have been, and no one at Unity knew of the girl's existence, because her birth and death were never recorded. The girl grew into a beautiful woman, married and had the twins. Her husband sadly had been killed in a bar fight when the twins were just two.

After the young mother rescued her children from the landslide, she slipped off the pendant her father had given her and put it around her young daughter's neck. Before she ran back into the school for the last time, in an attempt to save another child's life, she told the twins,

"Remember my love. Remember Unity." The same two things her dying father had told her and his mother had told him. The twins understood the first part but not the second. They never saw their mother alive again.

The children were placed at St. Joseph's orphanage where they got a good education and were looked after by kind and loving people. One of the people, who volunteered at the school, was a nurse. She recognized the jewelry Emma wore, seeing it when she had treated the child for a cold. The pendant hadn't left the girls neck since her mother had placed it over her head. It was shortly after January 4th, the day the twins turned twelve, when strange things began to happen. The thing that concerned their care givers the most was the fact that the twins had completely stopped speaking. Even the doctors couldn't figure out why they had stopped talking.

Dylan began running faster and doing things with incredibly speed such as reading, doing dishes, and his homework. Emma, on the other hand, had developed a great artistic talent. Without one single day of lessons, she sculpted a bust of the nurse who volunteered at the school from a clump of clay and presented it to her for her birthday. Emma started spending time in the art room, looking at art books and making copies of the masters. Her painting of the Mona Lisa was spectacular. The children did not exhibit these talents before. They didn't understand it themselves and tried hard to keep what they could do a secret from the teachers. But the volunteer nurse saw. Not knowing why, the kids did what they could do, she did know what must be done. Because around her neck hung the same pendant as the young girls, also in silver. She "Remembered Unity."

Charles Black was met at the little airport by Nurse Chapel. Nurse Chapel was about five feet two inches tall with a few extra pounds. She was around fifty years of age. Though she was small, she possessed a big smile that reassured her patients that all would soon be well. In her hands, she carried two boxes. One held the rum cake that the island was famous for, and the second contained six bottles of the rum it was made from. She handed the welcoming gifts to Charlie and gave him a hug when he emerged from the luxury private jet, a Citation XLS.

"What a wonderful welcome. Thank you for the gifts, Mrs. Chapel."

"I wanted to give you a proper island welcome," she smiled.

"We want to thank you for contacting us about the children."

"You're very welcome. Let's go meet them. I have to warn you they won't speak to anyone."

"Did you tell them someone was coming to see them?" Charlie asked the nurse.

"No, I didn't want to frighten them. I am the only one who has noticed their unusual activity and that the girl wears our crest. They are all alone on this big planet."

"They won't be for very much longer. We have a home where they will be loved, nurtured, and where they will learn the truth," Charlie assured her.

"I am so happy you could do this for them."

"It's my pleasure. Now let's go and meet our special friends."

Mrs. Chapel drove her old station wagon up the hill to the orphanage. After she had settled Charlie in the dean's office, she went to locate Emma and Dylan who were in history class. Charlie took the chair which faced the desk and turned it around to face the door, so the children could see his smiling face when they entered the room. Charlie didn't have to wait long for Mrs. Chapel to bring the two children. Emma and Dylan came into the room, stopped in the middle, and stared at the stranger. Charlie gave the two children time to size him up while he talked to Mrs. Chapel for a second. It gave him time to watch them. Emma and Dylan had skin the color of caramel candy. Emma's hair, tied back in a neat ponytail, was a deep, dark black, as was her brothers. Both children had eyes the color of emeralds that sparkled with mischief. As expected, the two children didn't speak, but watched this stranger with interest, not knowing what to expect from him.

Suddenly Charlie heard them. They were Mind Speaking with each other. Charlie, who could do the same with his cousin David, also had the ability to read the minds of others. But only with young people, no older than twenty, who were part of their heritage. Unfortunately, he could only read the minds of those who were not related to him. He would give anything if he could read the minds of his wife, and especially J.R., but hadn't developed that skill. He now listened to the two children.

"Do you think he is another doctor?"

"No silly, doctors don't dress like that, and he don't have a white coat."

"He doesn't have a white coat," corrected his sister.

"Do you think he wants to adopt us?"

"I don't know, but he has a nice smile. I like him."

Charlie laughed and spoke to the kids for the first time. "I like you too."

"Did you say that out loud?" Dylan asked his sister.

"I don't think so," Emma said, confused.

"No, Emma didn't say that out loud. I am able to hear you talk with your minds," Charlie told them.

This scared the kids a little, and they stepped back a few steps. Seeing this, Charlie realized he had frightened them, something he didn't want to do. Charlie had to reassure them that he wasn't going to hurt them.

"It's alright; I can Mind Speak with my cousin, David, just like you can with each other."

For the first time in months, the kids used their voices. "Really?" they said in unison, and then they laughed at themselves.

"You won't tell?" they asked.

"No, I think we should keep this our secret, for now. Is that alright with you?"

Both the twins nodded in agreement.

Emma asked, "Are there others like us?"

She had a soft voice and spoke perfect English with a Jamaican accent.

"I know people who have different talents. Your friend, Mrs. Chapel, told me she thought you were pretty special."

"We wish she could adopt us, but she has eight kids already."

"Yes, I know. I have something for you."

Charlie reached into the carry all which he had brought with him and pulled out two presents for the children. They were wrapped with colorful paper and bows. He handed each child one.

"Go ahead; you can open them," Charlie encouraged them.

Dylan, always messy and impatient, ripped open his present and discovered a laptop computer.

"Thank you, this is great. Now I can write faster. Look, Emma. I am going to be the only one at school with his own computer," he excitedly told his sister.

Emma who took her time, so not to tear the nice paper, discovered a paint set with a tabletop easel and some canvas to paint on.

"Oh, thank you, thank you! This is the best paint set in the world; I saw it in a magazine in the art studio." She ran over and hugged Charlie who returned her hug.

"I have a very special family who would love to adopt both of you."

"We would like that. Are they living close by?"

"No, they live on an island called Hope."

"We have never been off this island. Are the people there Jamaican?"

"No, but the family who wants to adopt you are smart people. They have a son a few years older than you; he can't wait to have a brother and sister."

"It takes a long time to adopt kids here," Emma said. "Will we have to wait long?"

"No, I have all the paperwork with me; you can come with me on my jet plane today if you like."

They didn't have to think about that at all. "Oh, yes we would love a real family with a brother," Dylan yelled excitedly

"Great, now I have some business to take care of with Father Patrick, so why don't you go and pack your things."

It only took an hour to finalize the adoption of the two children with Father Patrick, the school's headmaster. His lawyers had done a wonderful job in a short time to procure everything he needed to take the children. Charles Black made a generous donation of two million dollars to the orphanage. He also made a promise that Unity Corporation would build a new school for the orphanage along with a baseball field. The old school would be converted into better housing for the children. With all this business settled, Charles Black, along with the twins, now known as Emma and Dylan Roberts, got on the Unity jet and flew directly to Hope Island. There they would be protected by Unity. Emma and Dylan Roberts, together with J.R. and Helaina, were proof that their people were evolving, and things were changing very quickly. These two children would be protected, loved, and watched very carefully.

The jet ride to their new home was exciting for the twins. Everything was new to them. They bounced from seat to seat, trying to get the best view from the windows. They explored the jet from nose to tail. The pilot gave them a grand tour of the cockpit. The steward treated them like royalty, fixing them ice-cream sundaes and according to both kids, the best grilled cheese sandwiches they ever had.

A few hours later, Charlie introduced the children to their new parents who welcomed them with presents and lots of hugs and kisses. The Roberts, employed by Unity Corporation, were scientists who studied genes. They were good people who loved children, but they weren't able to have any more children after their son Mark was born. Mark was one of J.R. and Helaina's best friends on the island. They would love and protect the children and guide them in learning the truth about themselves. Since he was on the island, Charlie made a quick visit to his Aunt and Uncles, and of course he had to see his boy.

"Dad, I've only been here for a week, do I have to go home already?" J.R. exclaimed when he saw his father eating a sandwich in the kitchen of the Unity estate.

"Hey, don't I get a hello first?" Charlie protested.

"Hi, do I have to go home?"

"No! I just came because I brought the Roberts their two new family members."

"What family members? And why are they new?" Helaina asked as she walked into the kitchen and gave her uncle a hug and a kiss on the cheek.

"The Roberts just adopted twins from Grand Cayman Island. You will get to meet them next time you go see them."

"Are they girls or boys?" J.R. wanted to know.

"One of each."

"I just love babies!"

"They aren't babies; they are twelve, and they are very smart."

"Maybe tomorrow we can show them our beach and the mall," Helaina said, as she started making plans in her head.

"I think that would be nice," said Charlie.

"I like getting new friends. Hey! Can I have some of that steak sandwich?" J.R. exclaimed.

"Sure can," said his father.

Charlie visited with his family for a few hours. He ate dinner with his family and enjoyed playing video games with J.R. and Helaina. When the teenagers retired for the evening, he found time to have a secretive conversation with his Uncle about Helaina's missing diary.

CHAPTER TWELVE

HELAINA'S IN DANGER

The next morning J.R. and William took Charlie to the island's airport. Helaina remained at home and was in the kitchen with her grandmother and Sophia, helping them make up a grocery list. Out of the blue, Helaina said something totally unexpected.

"Grandma, last night I dreamed there was a man who wanted to hurt me. I think he is on the island."

Jennifer and Sophia looked at each other, not knowing what to think about what the girl just said. Jennifer knew the girl had dreams of the past, but could it be possible that Helaina could dream about what was to come, the future? Jennifer thought it was best to first reassure Helaina that she was safe and then talk to William when he got home.

"Baby, it was just a dream, I am sure you are completely safe here with us."

"No, Grandma, it's different than a dream. It was like a different kind of dream story because I felt it, and I was awake."

Jennifer knew what Helaina had said could be true. Helaina knew when she felt the dream in her heart, it was special, and she wrote it down in her dream diaries. Other dreams were just that, just dreams and soon forgotten. This was the first time Helaina felt threatened, and Jennifer was alarmed, but she tried not to show her fear to her granddaughter.

"I think we will wait until granddad comes home before we go shopping this morning."

"But, Grandma, we were going to that new clothing store. They are having a grand opening today and giving away prizes."

"Don't worry; we will get there. I just want to tell your grandfather about what you told me. Maybe he can help find the man you saw in your dream and make you feel safe."

"But I'm safe with you and Sophia. I promise, and nothing bad ever happens on the island. You just said so."

Helaina really wanted to go to that grand opening, and she regretted telling her grandmother about her dream.

"They will be back in about five or ten minutes. In the meantime, help us finish the grocery list." The two women looked over the girl's head, concerned about what she had just revealed.

***

While the women made their list, William and J.R. said good-bye to Charlie. As the men spoke near the plane, Jack Webber, a helicopter pilot, and the pilot of the Citation XLS, loaded Charlie's suitcase on to the jet. Charlie nodded his thanks to Jack as he boarded the plane, not saying a single word to him. Soon Charlie was in the air on his way back home to Florida. J.R. insisted on staying and watching the jet take off. He had flown in it a few times, but he wanted to see how it looked in the air. When they couldn't see it any longer, J.R. and William drove back to the house.

Jennifer met William at the door and took him outside to the garden which was far enough away that no one could hear them speak. At the same time William and Jennifer walked out to the garden, Jack Webber got a phone call on one of his cell phones. It was Senator Webster in Washington. Jack made sure that the secret recorder in the phone was on before answering it.

"Senator Webster, how's the weather in Washington?"

"Wet! I need you to do a job for me."

"I'm listening."

"The pink Unity diary was stolen from me; I believe it was returned to the girl. What's her name?"

"Helaina Unity," Jack responded.

"Get it back."

"I don't know if it is here."

"Find it; I believe it will answer a lot of questions. Better yet, bring me the girl."

"You want me to kidnap a teenage girl?"

Jack's heart was beating fast now; this was it! He was finally going to get that no-good bastard! He would get his revenge after all.

"Kidnapping is such a harsh word; let's just say we will borrow her for a while."

"Kidnapping is kidnapping, and where do you want me to take her? Your office in Washington or your home? Jack knew those to be unlikely places to hold someone hostage, but his mind was blown by this turn of events.

"I know of an empty house; take her to this address."

Webster gave Jack the address of Ms. Christopher's old home. If she wasn't going to come back, he might as well use the house for his own purpose.

"When you get there, give me a call."

"Sure boss, I expect that I will be well rewarded for this job?" Jack asked Webster, trying to keep him on the phone as long as possible.

"I pay you enough, besides you are getting a double pay day. Unity is also paying you, remember?"

Webster was always a tight-fisted tightwad when it came to paying those who worked for him.

"I want double, or I won't do it." Jack was baiting him; he needed more on the recorder for later.

"Alright! I need this." Webster continued, "Bring me the girl, and I will give you a hundred-thousand-dollar bonus. You can keep your job, both of them. You might come across something on that island which can be useful to me in the future."

"When do you want this done?"

"As soon as possible, talk to you when you get to the house," said Senator Webster as he pushed the button to disconnect the phone.

Jack hung up the phone. He knew what he must do. He smiled. He would need help on this mission. But first he took the pages he had torn carefully from the dream diary, put them in an envelope, and addressed it. He would put it in the mail later. Jack started making all the necessary phone calls. Soon he could go home. That thought made him smile as he put his plan together in his head and quickly got to work.

***

Jennifer talked to William, telling him what Helaina had told her earlier.

"I'm worried; do you think it was just a dream, or do you think that she actually feels she is in danger? Could it be possible that she is developing the ability to see what is to come?" Jennifer piled question after question on to William, not giving him a chance to speak.

"Jenny, my love, take a breath so I can answer some of your questions. Calm down; our little Helaina is just fine."

"I don't know. She told me she felt the dream in her heart, like she did with the other dream stories. I don't know what that means exactly, but I know her dream stories in her little pink diaries are as true as there are stars in the sky."

"Yes dear, her stories of what *has been* are true. Now it is the, *what can bes* we have to worry about. We are going to watch and listen to her, learn what she can do. I think we should take this seriously. I will have a watcher with her at all times."

He was trying to ease his wife fears with a little extra security.

"She wants to go to the grand opening of that new clothing store in town. I did promise her."

"You go and keep your promise which is always important. Now go get ready; I will have a watcher with you in five minutes. Mason is working in the garage. I will go give him this new assignment. Besides, he is sweet on Sophia. He will love spending more time with her. Don't worry; remember we have always taken care of our own."

"Yes, we do! And are you playing matchmaker?" Jennifer laughed.

"Well, you can see they would be the perfect couple."

"You go from CEO to being a matchmaker, and you are perfect at both," Jennifer teased her husband.

"Go get ready for your shopping trip; I will go talk to Mason."

"Yes, dear." Jennifer kissed her husband and went back to the kitchen.

Williams's phone rang; he looked to see who it was before speaking, and he listened to the caller.

"I understand." He listened again for a few seconds. "I understand. Give me an hour, and I will meet you." Then he hung up and went to talk to Mason.

***

The ladies did go into town and had their day of shopping with Mason tagging along with them. He watched for anything bizarre, looking for unknowns, such as people who weren't supposed to be there, but he didn't see anything unusual. The ladies made a day of it. After going to the grand opening of the new store, they went to have their nails and hair done. Mason stayed outside waiting patiently, drinking a cool, strawberry milkshake that he got next door at Wendy's. When the women finished, they decided to have lunch at the tearoom. Of course, they had to have lunch looking as good as they did. Minding their manners, they did invite Mason to join them, and he gracefully accepted. Besides he didn't mind being surrounded by such beautiful ladies. They, of course, had an ulterior motive which he learned of later when they got to the shopping center.

First stop, the meat market; Mason swore they bought a hundred pounds of meat. They handed him all the packages. The next stop, which was next door, was the farmers market. Lucky for Mason they provided shopping carts, because he was loaded down already. The three women deposited the meat into one for him, and he followed the women around. All three pushed empty carts. They kept adding things to the carts, and he followed them thinking that he should have followed them with a large truck, wondering how he would fit everything into the trunk of the car. They paid for the fresh produce and decided that they needed to stop into the grocery store, which was half a block away, for some milk, coffee and eggs. Before the three of them started walking away from Mason, leaving him with three very full shopping carts to load into the car, he stopped them.

Wanting to keep Helaina close, he suggested, "Helaina can you help me unpack these carts and load them into the car while your grandmother and Sophia run in for a few things. I think I need some help with all this stuff. I will reward your kindness with a chocolate milkshake when we're done."

"I think that would be a great idea," Jennifer said, realizing that he should stay close to her granddaughter. "Tell you what, you two go and load up the car. Sophia and I will meet you at Wendy's, and we can all have a milkshake."

"That sounds good to me. Can I get one of those apple pies? No! Two of them, so I can take one to J.R. It's one of his favorites."

"Sure, now help me with these bags please; then we can relax with our treat. I need a break from all this shopping."

Mason took one cart, pushing it in front of him, while he pulled a second behind him. Helaina took the third and off to the car they went. It took ten minutes to load everything in. It was a really tight fit. They went on to Wendy's for that promised treat. Mason and Helaina were there for ten minutes when Sophia and Jennifer arrived, pushing yet another shopping cart with at least six more grocery sacks.

"I thought you ladies were only going for milk and eggs?" he protested.

"We got those, and we remembered we needed some more tea, and flour, sugar..." The list went on, but Mason didn't pay much attention to it.

"How are we going to get that back to the house?" he asked.

"We can hold a few of the bags," suggested Helaina.

"There are already four bags for you to hold in the back seat."

They sat back to enjoy the milk shakes and thought about the problem of the overstuffed car.

"I know what we can do. You all go home, and I can walk home. I want to stop at the Roberts to meet the twins anyway," said Helaina

The three adults froze for a second, knowing that the girl wasn't to be left without her watcher. The ladies were trying to think of a solution and distraction, but the silence of the three adults made Helaina feel a bit uneasy.

"Did I say something wrong?" Helaina wanted to know.

"No, I need to stop at a friend's house," said Jennifer. "You know what I need for you to do? I need for you to go back to the house with Sophia and help put away all this food. Since Sophia doesn't drive, Mason will go with you. Then you can give your granddad a fashion show with all those new clothes you got."

Helaina though about this for a second. "I guess I can go see the twins tomorrow with J.R."

"I've got an idea! Why don't you bake some cookies or maybe a cake this afternoon? You can take it with you tomorrow. That would be extremely nice of you and a nice welcome for the twins."

"Okay, but how will you get home?"

"Young lady, I am not in a wheelchair, my legs work just fine. You know I take a five-mile walk on the beach every day. I didn't get my walking in this morning, and we didn't get much exercise when we took our cruise so I could use a bit of exercise. Now you go with Mason and Sophia and tell your granddad I will be home in about two hours."

"Alright, I think I will make peanut butter cookies."

"Great! The three of you head home, and I will follow shortly. Sophia, don't forget to freeze some of that fresh fruit when you get the chance."

"Sure will, you have a nice walk."

Mason gave Jennifer a silent, "Thank you," over Helaina's head. He had to admit Jennifer Unity was a fast thinker. She helped him avoid losing sight of Helaina which wouldn't be a good thing to do right now. Whatever assignment or job he was given, Mason always gave it one hundred percent. That included watching the young ones. His motto, "Always be on the ready."

CHAPTER THIRTEEN

THE STORY CHAMBER

While the women spent the day shopping, the men in the family spent the afternoon washing and waxing William's antique car collection.

William even let J.R. do oil changes on six of them, and for fun, they went on a little drive. Remembering that fifteen-year-olds are anxious to start driving, William decided he would give J.R. a little taste of the road. William pulled the 1966 Ford Copra from the garage. It was new when his son David was born; it was one of his favorites. He got out of the low riding car after he pulled it out of the garage and stood next to it.

"How would you like to drive today?"

J.R. had to ask to make sure he heard his great-uncle right.

"Really?" J.R. held his breath for the answer.

"Sure, come on; get in. We will go for a drive, but don't tell your mom. She would have my head on a plate if she knew I let you drive a sports car."

"Okay, I promise."

William threw him the keys, and they both got into the car.

J.R. started it up like a pro, stepped on the clutch, put it in gear, and off they went. J.R. drove that car like he had done it a million times before. He obeyed all the traffic signs and the speed limits. He yielded to bicycles and pedestrians; he even stopped and let a dog run across the street as it chased after a cat.

"Has your Dad been giving you private lessons?" William asked the young driver.

"No, I've been watching Mom and Dad all my life, and when I looked in the owner's manual to see what size filter the car needed, I found that book. You know the one, the one you have to study to get your driver's license, so I took a few minutes and read it."

"Really now?"

"Yep. Can I drive to town? I want to drive by Mark's house to show off."

"No! That's not a good idea. Your grandma and Helaina might see you and tell your mom. We would both be in trouble."

"Then can we drive—"

Before he could finish the sentence, William interrupted him. "We can take the road that goes around the whole island and be back home before the women get back from their shopping trip."

"Oh! Alright." J.R. agreed with that plan.

The two had fun driving on the outer road of the island. They passed a sheriff; lucky for them he was taking a nap in the shade and didn't see J.R. speed past doing eighty. He would surely have received a ticket if the sheriff was awake, and his parents would have learned of his misdeeds with Granddad.

J.R and William had just pulled the car back into the garage when Mason pulled up in front of the house. Lucky for them there was not a scratch on the car or its passengers.

In the evening, the family grilled some nice, thick top sirloin steaks purchased that day for dinner. While they were eating, William decided it would be a good night to tell the kids the story of where they had come from.

"Before you two disappear to play those video games, I think that it is time you hear a story."

"I like stories. Are they like my dream stories?" Helaina said as she slipped a juicy grape to Peanut who sat contently in her shirt pocket. It was dark so it was now time for Peanut to be awake.

"Yes, they are in fact."

"Do you have pictures?" J.R. wanted to know.

"I have something better than pictures."

"Family movies, great! Do I really have to see my sister's piano recital again?" Helaina asked sounding disappointed.

"No, both of you help your grandma take the dishes inside and put them in the dishwasher. Then come upstairs to the den; there's a story I want you to hear."

J.R and Helaina got up, collected the dishes on trays, and walked to the house to do their chores.

"Sweetheart, do you think they are ready?"

"I think they have been ready for quite a while now. They're smart, sensitive, and I believe they will understand."

"If you think this is the best time, then it is the best time! I love seeing and hearing the story again myself. I get sentimental, remembering when my granddad told me and my sister."

"See you in ten minutes. I will go prepare the Story Chamber."

***

Soon Jennifer, J.R., and Helaina joined William in his second-floor den, settling on the couch. Peanut, attached to her leash so she wouldn't go exploring on her own, was busy jumping from one person to another demanding attention. When she appeared tired, Peanut settled on Helaina's shoulder and tangled herself in Helaina's soft curls.

J.R. and Helaina watched as William opened a secret panel on the wall. He took out what looked like a big crystal, it looked to be about six feet tall, about four feet around, and it looked like it was one solid mass. It stood on a square, oak base. They watched quietly, except the two teenagers were having a private conversation in their heads.

"That sure doesn't look like a big screen TV," J.R. observed.

"No, it looks like a crystal statue. It's pretty."

"It's not! I think it is a machine of some sort."

"Really! Why would you think that? It has no—"

"Okay I think we are ready," William said, interrupting their silent conversation.

Unknown to the family a dark figure stood watch, just below them, standing in the garden and leaning on an oak tree waiting. William now began the story.

"This is a Story Chamber. Inside, it holds the story of the beginning. The chamber has been passed down through generations, each new generation adding to the story. One day, it will be given to one of you."

"Granddad, that looks like a tanning bed standing up," laughed the kids who spoke in unison.

"That it does but watch what it reveals!"

William didn't have to open a panel or fiddle with any controls, because there were no buttons or levers. He simply took his right hand, spread his fingers wide, and waved his hand across the Story Chamber. Immediately, the story began. An unknown male, with a deep soothing voice, began the story. The Story Chamber came to life, lighting up as thousands of colors swirled around like a tornado, coming together at the bottom. Then the color particles came together to form a picture. As the picture grew, the tornado became shorter and shorter until it was gone, and the picture was revealed entirely. It was of a beautiful city and its surroundings. The story began and William sat down next to his wife to listen.

"Hello! Those of you watching are my family. I have since passed from the world, but I know that you are keeping our secret safe. I know it has been many generations since we lost our home on Unity. I chose that surname for our family because Unity must live on. Unity must be achieved for all to prosper; this is our goal, always. I welcome the next generation of Guardians of Unity and say that I'm proud of the elders who now pass on your heritage. They have made great accomplishments and can now rest, secure in the knowledge that you are strong and capable of continuing and accomplishing what is right. Now let me tell you our story.

This is Unity, the home from which we had to leave. For many centuries we took the natural resources that she provided us, thinking they would be replenished. We prospered and were very happy. We had green fields that grew our food, oceans that provided us with food,

99

plenty of fresh water that came from streams coming down from the majestic mountains. We had homes and families we loved and jobs that provided us with a purpose. But then things began to change, little by little. Our scientists warned us of impending disaster, but the people wouldn't listen, believing our people would live on Unity forever, just as they always have, without changing our ways.

Our scientists knew this was not to happen. They saw signs that our land was dying, and they began searching for a new home. It took many years and explorers were sent to far off places. Sadly, many lost their lives in this search. Finally, we found a home, your home. We sent watchers to study the people and discovered that they were fairly primitive, their minds young, needing more development, more guidance. We were similar to these people in all matters, or so we thought, but their sole purpose of living consisted of basic survival and finding pleasure at the time. We sent explorers. Their assignment was to help the population to develop; help them evolve into a stronger and smarter population by introducing our knowledge a little at a time. By doing this, we were preparing them for our arrival. We needed to teach them the value of their home. We planned to one day come and unite the two populations and preserve our new home for many centuries, for all of us.

One watcher had feelings for a young innocent woman, and they had a child. The watcher couldn't stay with them so told the female that she would have a special child and to nurture it. The watcher returned to Unity and told his Guardians about the child. This child would be the first child born from both of our people. We were quite concerned, not knowing how the genes of our two populations would affect the child that was to be born.

The watcher returned to Earth and stayed close to the child as it grew to adulthood. The child loved science, and nature, and she began researching and experimenting with the things around her. She was loved by many; this person was able to do things that couldn't be explained, like turning minerals into medicine and using plants to cure illnesses. Being different made some fearful of this child. This child, now an adult, showed her people how to build things with tools and used science to show them how to build great buildings for their kings with heavy stone. Being a simple woman, the men and the king took the credit for these great feats and hid the woman in seclusion. Seeing this, our watcher knew this home wasn't ready for our people. They wouldn't understand; they were too vulnerable. The watcher couldn't leave. He had to stay to learn what would become of his daughter so he could come home and tell us what he had learned of these people.

After his daughter died giving birth to her child, the watcher retrieved the body and brought it home to us. The watcher's grandchild grew up, and the generations that have followed began introducing our genes into the population as time went by. We saw this as a good thing.

It was decided that these people were strong, good people who needed some guidance. We found a wise ruler and gave him some basic laws which would guide the people until they were ready for us. Then more watchers came to observe from afar.

Every generation we sent new explorers to impart some of our knowledge to advance this culture. Our scientists worked tirelessly trying to save our home, but a Black Virus began killing everything. Finally, we had to admit to ourselves that we had to leave and make our home at the place we had chosen. We were able to save all our people that had survived this Black Death. We packed up what we could carry, all that we would need and traveled many months. We came and chose a beautiful island, and there we began our new life.

The island we called Hope, for we had hope that we could bring the two populations together as one. It had already begun to happen, but there was a long way to go. We had to evolve together, slowly, over time and become as one. That is why I chose Unity as the name to be carried on for generations. The name is to remind us of what was important. "To remember Unity," is to remember what was lost, where we came from, and where we are going. In the years to come, more will be learned. Each generation will add to the Story Chamber; one day, you will too. Each time you come to the Story Chamber; you shall learn more from those who have come before you. Now I shall leave you. Remember to always guide with an open heart and an open mind. Our Guardians of the future, your people are looking to you for guidance.

Love will always be in your hearts, given to you by your family and our people. We will forever be proud of you and your accomplishments. Good-bye and good luck."

The Story Chamber then began to swirl around like a tornado again, taking the picture away; suddenly it was gone in a puff of air. William and his wife didn't say anything for a minute, letting the information sink into J.R. and Helaina's mind.

"That was our beginning, do you understand the story that was told."

"It's a sad story," Helaina said.

"Yes, it was, but an important story," Jennifer acknowledged.

"Was Unity on the other side of the world hidden away from ancient people?" J.R. wanted to know. "Did we get here on big ships?"

William, avoiding the first question answered the second. "Our ancestors did travel here on big ships. Our mission is what's important."

"A world united in peace," the kids said in unison.

"That is exactly right. Now I think that you have enough to think about for now, why don't you go and play pool or video games and relax." William proceeded to put away the Story Chamber in its hiding place.

Helaina wanted to know, "Can't we see more stories? I really like the Story Chamber."

"The Story Chamber has millions of stories, and you will have plenty of time to see them all. The story of the beginning is an important first lesson to learn. Always learn from the past, but move forward," William said.

"Can I put my dream stories in the Story Chamber?"

"Helaina, sweetheart, your dream stories are already in the Story Chamber."

Helaina thought about this for a second. "You mean my Dream Stories are real, that I dreamed of things in the past. Is that why I feel them in my heart because they are about our people's past?"

"That is exactly what your Granddad means. That's why it is important for you not to share your stories with outsiders."

"Because they wouldn't understand how I know about the past without being there."

"That's exactly right sweetheart." Jennifer was proud of her granddaughter for understanding.

"We can't share the stories with anyone, can we?" J.R. assumed.

"That is also correct. Now go have some fun."

While Helaina asked questions, J.R took a closer look at the Story Chamber. After William stored it away, J.R started asking questions of his own.

"Is that some sort of computer monitor? Where is the data stored? Is it connected to a computer with Wi-Fi? And who is responsible for programing it?"

William sighed, "Those are great questions. Let's explore them later. I'm tired." William knew that J.R wanted to know how the Story Chamber worked and that his love for computers and figuring out how everything worked would buzz in his head until he got the answers. But there were no answers because William, nor anyone else, knew how the machine recorded their history.

"Can you come and play pool? Remember I am one game away from beating you more times than Uncle David has," J.R. reminded William.

"You all sure take pleasure in beating an old man at pool," William laughed with them.

J.R. and Helaina walked ahead of the adults on the way to the recreation room, having another silent conversation.

"Did you notice that they didn't answer all our questions? I think there is a lot more to the story. I want to know more about the place in the story."

"I want to know more about that machine! I have never seen anything like it before." J.R told his cousin, uninterested in what Helaina was saying.

"Do you think that maybe our family came from another world? That would be cool!"

J.R was still thinking about the Story Chamber and how it worked. He decided to play along with his cousin so she would get out of his head and he could think about what he thought was important.

"Yeah that would be really cool, but you know that it's not where you come from that is important, because everyone came from somewhere. It's how you live your life that matters," reasoned J.R.

"Yeah! That was a really adult thing to say! You're right, but it still would be the coolest thing ever."

"Yep, Dad told me that once. I wonder if I cut you if you would bleed green blood."

"You better not," the kids laughed out loud.

Having heard every word of their silent conversation, William had to laugh with them. *I think it will be a very long time before I tell these two that I hear them Mind Speaking. Might keep them out of trouble.* he told himself.

***

They went to the recreation room to play games, enjoying their time together. The man was still standing outside, watching. He saw the lights go out in the den. A couple minutes later he saw the family walking to the recreation room. This was located in a 1000 square foot building detached from the house. One part of the building had two changing rooms and storage for pool equipment. A much larger area housed two pool tables, an air hockey table, a shuffleboard court, and a food bar with a big freezer that held popsicles and gallons of ice cream.

"*Soon their day will end, then I can make my move,*" thought the man waiting in the dark.

CHAPTER FOURTEEN
ALL IS NOT WHAT IT SEEMS

Two hours later the Unity family went to their rooms, and Jack Webber proceeded with his plan. In no time, Jack had the young lady wrapped in a blanket and deposited into the back of a helicopter. Taking off, they headed to a private airfield in Washington State where they were to meet the two men who took the little pink Dream Diary to Senator Webster. Jack recruited them to help with this assignment. He knew he could trust these men. They had worked together many times on various assignments.

A plane was chartered to take them to Maryland where they were to turn the girl over to Senator Webster. The charter pilot didn't ask any questions. No one in this group said a word. They sat quietly writing and reading, listening to what looked like iPods, as the young woman slept in a seat next to the window, shielded from the pilot's view. It appeared that she might have been drugged.

It was arranged that the pilot would land at a small airport in Nebraska to refuel before the group continued to their final destination. As the airport personnel refueled the charter plane, the group of three men escorted the young woman to the small terminal where they used the restroom and got something to eat, not talking to anyone. They then returned to the chartered plane to continue the journey to Maryland.

An hour out from their destination, the pilot heard one of the men make a call to a limousine service. The driver was to meet the plane on the runway. An arrangement had been made with the airport authorities to let the car through the security gate. All the driver had to do was give the guard at the gate his I.D. and proceed to pick up his passengers.

They arrived in Maryland at six a.m. The air traffic controllers directed the chartered plane to a runway at the furthest corner of the complex. This was where private and chartered planes had hangers, where repairs could be made, and where they could safely be stored out of the way of the bigger commercial airlines. Here, also were private accommodations for their customers, especially those who didn't want to be seen. It was a popular airport used by many politicians and celebrities who were visiting the Washington, D.C. area. The security at this airport was the best in the world. Air Force One, and Air Force Two, the planes used for the President and the Vice-President were stored here in security hangers on the east side of the airport.

After the charter plane made a complete, stop Jack Webber gave the pilot instructions.

"We want you to remain in the plane until we leave; stay in your seat until our car leaves the area. We thank you for your services," Jack said, handing him an envelope filled with a thick bundle of hundred-dollar bills.

"That's the twenty thousand you were promised and another two thousand for the fuel. There's a card in there with the name of a four-star hotel. We paid for your accommodations plus meals until you leave tomorrow to return to Washington State. It's just a little thank you for flying us here at night. Thank you again and good-bye."

With that, the four quiet passengers disembarked the charter plane and hastily entered the vehicle that was waiting for them and drove away.

"That had to be the strangest group I have ever flown with," the pilot said out loud just to hear his voice. He was tired of the silence. "And on top of their strange behavior, they flew clear across the country and not one of them had any luggage. The girl didn't even have a purse. Strange indeed."

His passengers where soon forgotten as he secured the plane and called a taxi to take him to the hotel for a good night's sleep and a very expensive meal.

***

Jack Webber, the two men with him, and the young woman were taken to a shopping center parking lot. They paid the driver and dismissed him. Taking no chances that someone was following, they took another precaution. Jack had arranged for a non-descript gray van to be parked at the shopping center by someone he trusted. He had given his friend a list of the equipment that they would need, and he knew the things he asked for would be securely packed inside the van. Inside the gray Ford van, the group found radios, four bullet proof vests, four 357 magnum Smith and Wesson handguns, three knives with sheaves, clean clothes, food and drinks, and three throw away cell phones. They wanted to be protected in case Senator Webster had plans to get rid of them along with the girl.

When the group was dressed in clean clothes, Jack Webber gave everyone some last-minute instructions and made sure they knew exactly what was to take place. Then he made the call to Senator Webster, making sure their conversation was recorded. Blackmail might be the order of things in the future, and Jack needed all the leverage he could get. Senator Webster's phone rang twice before he picked up. Senator Webster used the caller I.D. feature to identify all his callers.

"Webber do you have my package?"

"Yes. I need the address that we are to meet you at." Webber knew the address but was trying to extend the conversation a few minutes longer.

Senator Webster gave him the instructions again. "How long will it take for you to get there?"

"We shall be there in a half an hour. Give us time to get the girl settled and calmed down. Why don't you meet us there at nine a.m.? You better have the money you promised, a hundred thousand dollars, plus twenty thousand for each of my two friends here."

"Wait I didn't tell you to hire extra help; that complicates things."

"Do you think I could have pulled this off alone you idiot? Bring the extra money or you won't get the girl or the information you want from her. Understand?"

Knowing that this had gone too far to back out now, Senator Webster agreed to get the extra money, but he insisted that they had to babysit the girl for a few days for him. Jack agreed, knowing that this wasn't going to happen. He was positive that this job with Webster would end today. He wasn't going to babysit for anyone! After the phone conversation, Jack settled into the driver's seat of the gray Ford. His three passengers were secured with seat belts in the back seat, and they began their journey. In ten minutes, they were at the house.

Jack backed the van into the driveway; everyone got out and went around to the back door. One of the men picked the lock, and they entered the empty house. Jack took a chair from the van and placed the young woman in it, securing her hands in the back and wrapping a rope around her feet.

"I'm sorry I have to do this," he told the the young women, and she smiled up at him, just before he placed duct tape over her mouth.

He left her in the empty room, closing the door behind him. His two partners were busy themselves. They were setting up the radio and unpacking the van of the food and clothes. They wanted to make Webster believe that they had settled in for the long term.

Nine a.m. had come and gone, and Senator Webster hadn't arrived. Getting nervous, Jack called the Senator. Making sure he sounded angry and impatient, he yelled, "Where the hell are you?"

"I'm on my way. I had to go to the bank for the extra money. They don't open up until nine, but I have it now. I am two minutes away."

"Fine!" Webber said and hung up the phone.

One man positioned himself in the kitchen, keeping busy by making sandwiches; the other was seated in a lawn chair in front of the bedroom door the girl had been placed in. Jack looked out the window and waited. It was a beautiful summer day; two teenage boys were skateboarding up and down the street. A woman was mowing the lawn next door to the empty house; she had long sexy legs and was dressed in very short shorts and a tank top. Across the street, a blue minivan was being washed by a young couple.

"Just another summer day in the neighborhood," Jack thought to himself, smiling.

He saw Senator Webster drive his white 350 SL Mercedes into the driveway. Webster waited a few minutes before stepping out of the car. He approached the front door nonchalantly like he was there to visit a friend. He was dressed casually in jeans and a light shirt. He made sure that he had brought a baseball cap. Webster had the cap low over his eyes and kept his head low so the neighbors wouldn't see his face. That didn't seem to matter, because the busy neighbors didn't seem very interested in anything except what they were doing.

Senator Webster knocked on the front door, and it was immediately opened by Jack who let the Senator walk past him into the living area. The Senator recognized the two men that Jack hired to help him with this job. He relaxed a bit, knowing that he could trust these two men because they were the ones who had brought him the pink diary. He just nodded to acknowledge them before getting down to business.

"Where's the girl?"

"In there."

Jack motioned for his man at the door to open it just enough for the Senator to see the young woman tied to the chair. Her head was down, looking at her lap. Senator Webster made a move to go to the room, but he was stopped by the man guarding the room when he shut the door.

"Before that happens, we have business to conduct first," Jack said, coming to stand next to Senator Webster.

"How do I know that is Helaina Unity?" *Damn the Senator was making this easy for us*, thought Jack.

"You just have to take our word for it. But since I knew you would want some proof. I have it right here."

Jack handed the Senator a picture he had taken of the girl with William Unity, sitting at a table playing cards.

"Yes, that's William Unity, I recognize him; let me see the girls face," demanded the Senator.

Jack nodded at the man standing guard at the door. Jack's partner opened the door. Going into the room, he put his hand on the young woman's head and tilted it back so the Senator could see that she was indeed the girl in the picture Jack had given him. When this was done, he came out of the room and shut the door again.

"She's the one who wrote the pink diary?"

"Yes, now our money, one hundred-forty-thousand."

Senator Webster pulled out three envelopes full of money and tossed them to Jack.

"It's going to take a few days for me to get the information I need from the girl; she is young. The way we are going to play this is I am going to tell her that the faster she gives me the information I want, the sooner she could go home."

"By now her family has discovered her missing, and they will begin searching," Jake reminded him.

"I thought about that. I will have one of you make a ransom demand; I might as well get my money back, along with a lot more. This is going to be a big pay day for us. After I get the information, then you will have to dispose of her," whispered the Senator as he leaned closer to Jack so that the girl couldn't hear him.

"What do you mean by dispose of her?" Jack baited Webster.

"Drown her, suffocate her, strangle her! I don't care. But the faster we get this done, the faster I can get my revenge on William Unity and get rich doing it. Now give me time with the girl."

Webster took a voice recorder out of his pocket and started for the bedroom door, thinking he was the one in charge. But in less than a minute, he discovered that wasn't so.

He heard someone yell, "Bring him down." Then three guns were pointed at his head.

The lady who was mowing the lawn came through the back door, and the couple washing the minivan burst through the front, all wearing F.B.I. jackets under which they wore bullet proof body armor. All pointed guns at Senator Webster, demanding that he lay on the floor and spread his arms and legs out.

Jack crouched down on top of the Senator, pulling his arms behind his back, and he proceeded to secure his prisoner with hand cuffs.

"Senator Douglas Webster, you are under arrest," Jack told the Senator as he pulled the man to his feet.

When doing so, the Senator saw that Jack Webber had a tattoo of the Unity logo on his wrist. Only having talked to Jack on the phone, and never seeing him in person until today, he couldn't possibly have seen the tattoo before. Usually, Jack covered the tattoo with concealing makeup when he was undercover.

"You're one of them!" the Senator yelled at Jack.

"Senator you were wrong; not only did you pay me, I was paid quite well by the Unity Corporation. But of course, I was also receiving a paycheck from good old Uncle Sam, doing my regular job as an F.B.I. Special Agent. Senator, we protect our own."

"The girl? The picture? The expensive trip from Washington I paid for? You scammed me?" the Senator yelled.

Just then the young woman walked out of the bedroom, she had been released from her bonds by one of the agents, and now she was also wearing an F.B.I. jacket.

"Senator Webster, meet Shannon Brewer, F.B.I. William Unity was glad to take this picture with this young agent the other day.

"Congratulations Shannon, great job on your first undercover assignment."

"Thank you, sir."

Just before two agents lead Senator Webster to the waiting car, Jack leaned in and whispered something to him that really got him angry, making him struggle with the two men and swear at Agent Webber.

"What did you say to him to make him so angry?" asked agent Shannon Brewer.

"I told him to Remember Unity."

They smiled knowingly, because hanging around Shannon Brewers neck, on a silver chain, under her vest was a Unity logo. It was given to her by her grandfather when she was eighteen. Shannon didn't know much about her family's history. She did know that Unity Corporation was an important commodity, and they represented everything that was good. Beyond that, she knew nothing.

***

Back on Hope Island, J.R. Black and Helaina Unity, along with a few of their friends, played volleyball on the beach. They were safe and sound but still being watched carefully by their watcher. Mason's phone rang, and he immediately answered it. Jack Webber was on the other end.

"Mason, all's safe."

"Thank you, I will inform William. He's waiting anxiously for news that the situation has been handled. All was safe?"

"Yes! Not one injured."

"Thank you again. Remember Unity!"

"Remember Unity!" Jack Webber responded before hanging up.

Now he could go home and get away from all that irritating sand. Jack preferred soft grass and concrete under his feet, which he would find back home in Washington, D.C. Jack had finally got his revenge on the man who took his father's business away. Jack Webber blamed the Senator for his father's heart attack and early death. Jack believed it was caused by the stress of losing the family business.

Right now, Unity was safe, and that was what was important. The elders decided that Helaina would not learn of the danger she had been in. This was to keep the two teens free to enjoy what was left of their summer, because very soon the world would weigh heavily on their shoulders. As always everyone could be trusted on Hope Island. There was never any doubt about that, and there never will be.

CHAPTER FIFTEEN

J.R. AND HELAINA DISCOVER AN NEW TALENT

The same morning that the kidnapping drama played out in Washington D.C., J.R. found Helaina outside on the patio. Last night he did something that he wanted to share with his cousin. He knew she got up early, way too early for him, but he was excited and wanted to share it with her before he showed William. There were others in the garden that morning; the watcher was still doing his job by looking after Helaina. Mason stood out of sight where the girl couldn't see him. He heard footsteps behind him but didn't turn around; he knew who was coming up behind him.

"Good morning, William?"

"Good morning, I see you relieved Carl a bit early this morning."

"I thought I might as well, since I am an early riser."

"Me too, always have been. Helaina takes after me I think," William said proudly.

Just then they spotted J.R. going to join his cousin who was busy writing in one of her dream diaries.

"That's unusual, J.R. loves sleeping in," said William curiously.

"Are you going to join the kids?" Mason wanted to know.

"I will later, you go for some coffee. I'll watch, but I think I will stay here to see what those two are up to. And thank you, I think we can cut the extra precautions now."

Mason took off to go down to the garage, laughing to himself at William's sneaky ways. William sat down on a bench about thirty feet from the kids, close enough to hear their conversation. The bench, a favorite place of his, was located behind a tree out of sight. The kids couldn't see him from where they were; neither could Jenny when he snuck off to smoke one of his Cuban cigars.

Helaina sat at one of the tables near the pool, dressed in pink shorts and a white summer top; she had her two favorite accessories, her pink Dream Diary and Peanut. Peanut was curled up in a pocket in Helaina's shirt and had just settled down to sleep the day away; this morning Peanut's accessories were a pink leash and a white harness to prevent her from going too far and getting lost. J.R. came out of the house wearing his favorite swim trunks, a large Hawaiian shirt with bright colors, and no shoes. He figured since they were going to meet some friends down at the beach later why bother with regular pants and shoes.

Now William listened to them.

"You're up early."

"Yeah I know. I have something to show you." J.R. pulled out a folded piece of paper from his shirt pocket and handed it to his cousin.

"That looks like the Story Chamber," she said, pointing at the center of the picture. She then took a closer look. "I had a dream about those four balls that you drew."

"First let me tell you my story, then you tell me yours. Okay?" said J.R., excitedly.

"Okay!" agreed his cousin.

"Last night when I first saw the Story Chamber, I knew it was a machine, but I also knew that it wasn't right somehow, that it had missing parts. So, after we beat Grandma and Granddad at pool last night, I went up to my room and drew this. I didn't know I could draw like this before."

"That's amazing; you have so many details."

"I know, right! Something told me I needed to show you, so I got up early; you haven't seen Granddad yet, have you?"

"No maybe he's tired; we beat them four times in a row last night." Helaina and J.R. laughed at the memory of last night's exciting games of pool.

"Now, my turn!" demanded Helaina. "Last night I had another dream story, but different. I was in this one, and I wasn't watching the story like I usually do. I dreamed about us. We were hiking. We were with Mark, Dylan, Emma, and Kellie. We haven't even met Dylan and Emma yet, but they were in my dream. We went hiking at our favorite place. You know, the place on the west side of the island that has the bison herd, lake, and hiking trails."

"Yeah I know the place."

"Well! We were hiking and we found this cave behind a waterfall. I just knew it was there, so we went to explore it. We found a little lake, it's only ankle deep so we walked through it. We found what looked like a grave marker; but it's not. It's a handle that we need to pull, and it opens a secret door. Inside we find two of those balls; they are inside two crystals boxes. The boxes have the Unity logo on the top, and the lever had some instructions on it."

"What did it say?"

"Don't know, because I woke up."

"But there are four balls in my drawing! What about the other two?" J.R. asked his cousin.

"Later, I had another daydream about them. They are in a cave under the water, right under the marina, and we go diving for them."

"This never happened before. You never dreamed about something that we would do, or maybe something we had to do. You never dreamed of a machine; the same one I drew. What do you think this means?"

"Been thinking about that. I think that it means we are supposed to work together, like our dads."

"Probably right, think we should tell Granddad and Grandma?"

"I think we should do this ourselves and tell them later. Maybe they will know what to do with the glow balls."

"Why did you call them glow balls? That's a stupid thing to call them."

"Because in my dreams they glowed, what else should we call them?"

"Don't know, we'll think of that later. I'm hungry let's go get breakfast. Remember we are going to meet Mark and his new brother and sister at the beach this morning. Afterwards, we can make plans to find the balls."

"Good plan; remember we keep this a secret. We'll surprise everyone when we have all four balls."

"Right! Now for some breakfast."

J.R. and Helaina walked back into the house where their grandmother was making scrambled eggs and sausage. Earlier she had packed them a picnic basket to take to the beach. In the basket she packed fried chicken, chips, and plenty of the homemade cookies that Helaina made yesterday. Jennifer thought a picnic on the beach was a nice way to welcome new friends to Hope Island. Being moderately hot for a July morning, Sophia packed plenty of bottled water and soft drinks for the kids into a rolling ice chest to make it easy to take down to the beach. With the ice chest, beach towels, plenty of sunscreen, and Peanut securely in her travel sling, they were off to meet the new members of the Roberts family.

Mark Roberts was excited to introduce his new brother and sister, Emma and Dylan, to his friends. Mark, who was six months older than J.R. and Helaina, was dressed in typical beach bum attire. It included baggy swim trunks torn at the cuff with a hole in the back pocket, a colorful tie dye T-shirt, and flip flops. Mark looked like a very young George Clooney right down to the dimples on his cheeks. Helaina had a big crush on Mark, but since she didn't live on the island like he did, she never pressed the matter. Besides Mark was a little shy, as was Helaina, and he was more interested in planning his next adventure, whether it be climbing a mountain or exploring the coral reef than in girls. Right now, he was busy adjusting to being a big brother and all that entailed. He was very protective of his new brother and sister and didn't let them out of his sight, not for one moment. Both Emma and Dylan stayed close to Mark. Having only been there two days, they were still unsure of their surroundings and all the new people they were meeting. Today the twins were dressed in identical shorts, T-shirts, and flip flops. They really didn't like dressing alike, but they weren't comfortable enough to tell their new mother that just yet.

The other member of this ever-expanding group was Kellie Garfield. She was Helaina's very best friend, and even when Helaina wasn't on Hope Island, the girls spent hours talking long distance. Kellie was a total gossip who loved to shop as much as Helaina. Kellie was a whole year older than Helaina. She had written and published four books. Kellie was two inches shorter than her friend, about 140 pounds, with pale skin that was in danger of getting sunburned. She always wore big brimmed hats whenever she was in the sun. Kellie, as well as her mother, loved hats so much that they had a whole room full of them. Kellie and Helaina once tried to count them all, but they kept losing count, so their best estimation was twenty-five-hundred hats. Kelly was a typical red head; her thick wavy hair was always in her way. She had freckles across the bridge of her nose and green eyes that looked like jade; eyes she kept hidden behind sunglasses because they were extremely light sensitive.

Emma, Dylan, Mark, and Kellie were already at the beach setting up the volleyball net when J.R. and Helaina arrived. After a brief hello and introduction, they decided Helaina, Emma, and Kellie would play against J.R., Mark, and Dylan. This didn't work out so well, because with J.R. and Helaina able to hear each other thoughts, and Emma and Dylan doing the same, it was a battle of the minds. It got even more interesting when they tried to think one thing, then do the opposite. Legs and arms got tangled, and they collapsed on the warm sand laughing.

Abandoning volleyball, they took the surf boards, which Mark and Kellie brought and paddled out about a hundred yards so they could swim in deeper water. Something bumped Emma's leg and she screamed. Everyone turned and saw a gray shadow in the water. Dylan yelled to his sister. "Emma, stay still and stop splashing."

Helaina swam closer to Emma. "Don't worry; she won't hurt you. Look! It's just a young sea lion. She wants to play."

Sure enough, the head of the young animal broke the surface of the water. The sea lion looked around, seemingly curious about the fuss. There was a bright red surfboard floating just a few feet from her, and she headed in that direction. The little sea lion made several attempts to get on the surfboard but failed. Each time she would slide off. This made the kids laugh. Finally, she figured it out and managed to stay on the floating board.

The kids watched and cheered her on and decided to have a bit of fun with her. First, they pushed her around, giving her a ride; which, according to Helaina, the little sea lion thoroughly enjoyed. She loudly barked out her appreciation. When tired and wanting their board back, the kids surrounded the board and tipped the little sea lion off. The sea lion swam around the surfboard, trying to find a way to get back on, but there wasn't any room for her because now the girls took her place. Helaina reached out her hand, palm down, and the animal came to her. The little sea lion rubbed her slick head against Helaina's palm and swam around to the back of the surfboard, pushing them to shore. The three boys had to swim back. The girls had their lunch all laid out by the time the boys returned.

"What took you so long?" Kellie laughed.

"We didn't have help, like you did," remarked Mark.

"Mom packed us some ham and cheese rolls, watermelon, and chips and salsa, what did you bring?" asked Emma.

"I brought some grapes, egg rolls, and jalapeño poppers," said Kellie.

"Grandma made fried chicken, and I brought some cookies I baked yesterday," chimed in Helaina.

Everyone ate the feast of a lunch until nothing was left but the watermelon slices which, they decided to save for later. They sat back on the beach towels to let their lunch settle and soak up some sun. The boys complained about the sand they managed to get in their food and discussed their favorite video games. The girls woke up the reluctant Peanut and were having fun petting the little animal as she jumped from one pair of hands to another, getting different bits of food from each girl. It was J.R. who brought up hiking to the group.

"Me and Helaina—"

"Helaina and I," corrected Kellie who by age fourteen could speak five different languages.

118

"Okay! Helaina and I, smarty pants. Well, we were thinking about going hiking tomorrow. We can ask Granddad if we could use the ATVs, and we can hike around the lake."

"That's a great idea; we haven't taken Emma and Dylan to the hiking trails yet. Do you think that tire swing we put up over the lake last year is still there?" Mark asked.

"Bet it is."

"We can pick blueberries, and we should also remember to bring along our cameras. Maybe we will see the bison, but who knows what we will find."

Helaina and J.R. glanced at each other, and smiled knowingly, glad they were able to get their friends to go on an adventure with them.

The group made their plans for the next day. They decided to meet at the Unity's house the next morning and travel by ATVs to the Nature Park about two miles from the house. The old service road behind the Unity estate would lead them straight to the area. With their plans made, they broke out the watermelon. When they had finished the sweet treat, there were watermelon seeds all over the place. The boys had to see who could spit the furthest. Dylan won, with Mark and J.R. coming in second and third. Around four, the group broke up, and everyone returned home to tell their parents, and grandparents of the plans they made for the next day.

They hoped they would be allowed to go.

CHAPTER SIXTEEN
WORKING TOGETHER

At eight the next morning, the six teens met in the garage at the Unity home. Everyone wore jeans and T-shirts, with bathing suits underneath. Each carried a backpack with towels and other items they might need on this adventure. Sophia and Jennifer made bag lunches for everyone, and Mason and William made sure the ATVs were gassed up, the radios worked, and everyone had helmets on and cell phones in their pockets.

"Everyone stay on the trails, and I want everyone back here before dark," William told the kids.

Before they could start the engines and begin their journey to the Nature Park, Jennifer came running from the house.

"Wait! Helaina don't you think Peanut would be happier here?" Jennifer just knew that the girl had the little animal hidden away in her bag.

"Not if we find some blueberries. They are her favorite," Helaina insisted.

"You can bring them back for her. That old dusty road is kind of bumpy, and I don't believe she would like the ride much. She will be more comfortable here," Jennifer insisted.

Helaina thought about this for a second, being protective of all her pets and their welfare, but she saw her grandmother's point.

"You know, I think that is best." Helaina pulled Peanut out from one of the pockets of her backpack and handed her to her grandmother.

"Thanks, Grandma."

"You're very welcome; now you have fun at the Nature Park."

The six teenagers were taking three ATVs. J.R., Helaina, and Kellie would drive. Dylan, Emma, and Mark would enjoy the view, sitting comfortably behind them. The three drivers pulled down their goggles, started up the ATVs, and headed down the old service road. This took them directly to the Nature Park.

Knowing what they were up to, William and Mason followed them ten minutes later, just in case they came across any danger. Not because they didn't trust them or their ability to drive the ATVs, but because they were curious about a waterfall they didn't know existed.

It took ten minutes to get to the gate of the Nature Park. J.R. got off the ATV he was riding and opened the gate, letting the girls drive their ATVs through. Then he got back on and drove through as Mark closed the gate behind them. The fence and the gate were not to keep anyone out, because all were welcomed to come to the park; it was to keep the herd of Bison from getting out on the roads and getting hurt. The park raised Bison so that one day they could be removed from the endangered species list. Other such projects were taking place at the islands Nature Preserve. These animals included Bald eagles, Iguanas, Beach mouse, Musk Deer, Soft-shell Turtles, and Black-neck Cranes, were just a few of the animals being studied here. None of the animals were in cages, and all ran free at the Nature Park the kids now visited. Luckily, none were dangerous.

J.R. pulled his ATV, with Dylan on the back, up next to his cousin.

Using Mind Speak he asked, "In your dream, where do we start looking for the cave?"

"The cave is behind a waterfall, so I guess we go to the lake. Then follow the river that runs to it towards the mountain. We should be able to find the waterfall that way," reasoned Helaina.

"The lake has a picnic area where we can park the ATVs, and we can hike from there."

So, everyone else could hear him, J.R. shouted, "The lake is this way, follow me."

Everyone followed J.R. to the picnic area where they abandoned the ATVs.

Wanting to have plenty of time to find the cave and the mysterious balls, Helaina suggested, "It's too early for lunch, and the sun hasn't heated the lake yet, so why don't we go hiking first."

"Good idea!" Kellie agreed. "After lunch we can pick berries, and I also saw some apple trees. We can pick some of those to take back with us."

"Our new mom made some wonderful apple turnovers for us. We could bring her some fresh apples as a surprise," Emma said, adding to the conversation.

"Everyone, let's leave the lunches here, so we don't have to carry extra weight," suggested Mark, who had climbed mountains all over the world with his father. This included Mt. Everest and some of the tallest peaks of the Andes. Both father and son were very accomplished hikers and survivalists, and J.R. was glad to have Mark along for this adventure.

After storing any unnecessary items in the small trunks of the ATVs, the group began their hike, starting at the lake. But first the boys had to look at the tire rope swing that they had brought there last year. They found it still secured to a strong tree limb that extended over the lake. They told Dylan about the fun they had on it last year as they hiked. They promised the younger boy that after lunch he could be the first to swing over the water. Emma could be second; since they were the new kids, they had the honor of going first.

They hiked along the river for an hour, taking note where the blueberry bushes where, so they could pick some on the way back to the lake. Helaina walked up front and took the lead. Even though the other girls were with her talking and making plans for a shopping trip to the mall, Helaina made sure she kept her eyes opened for things she remembered in her dream. J.R. worked his way up to Helaina.

"Do you think it's close?"

"I don't know. I keep listening for falling water, but I don't hear anything. How about you?"

"Nothing. Think that maybe we should turn back?" he asked.

Just then Helaina saw something, and she knew they were close.

"No! Look there's the bison and the sunflowers We are close; I just know it."

She got excited and ran up ahead.

"Helaina wait for us," someone yelled.

Now the other kids, picking up on Helaina's excitement began running after her. Suddenly Helaina disappeared around a bend in the river, and a grove of trees hid her from view. When everyone caught up to her, they discovered what she was so excited about.

They stood looking at a striking sight. There before them was a waterfall, about three stories high, with water falling on moss covered rocks directly below the wall of water. A family of deer was drinking peacefully from the narrow river and birds were chirping in a sweet melody, stopping only to take a cool drink, making the scene before them a paradise of nature. On either side were trees so old that they were taller than the waterfall itself. Their branches reached out meeting over the river. The tree's leafy green canopy provided a natural cathedral, hiding the fact that the waterfall existed at all. It was extremely beautiful and peaceful; it was perfect. The kids stood and took in the sight, not saying a word, and marveling in the tranquility of the scene. No one wanted to disturb the scene, not with movement or the spoken word. Helaina used Mind Speak to talk to her cousin.

"This has to be the most beautiful place in the entire world," she commented.

"And we are the ones who found it; the trees must have hidden it for a very long time."

"Think anyone else knows about this place?"

"I don't know! If they did, they are keeping it a secret."

"It looks like there's nothing but solid rock behind the water."

"There's a cave there!" Helaina said with conviction.

"Let's go take a closer look."

In a hushed whisper, because he believed that talking, or yelling seemed the wrong thing to do in such a devastatingly beautiful place, J.R. told everyone, "Come on everyone. I think I see something behind the waterfall."

"Cool, let's go!" said Mark, always the adventurer.

***

As the kids made their way towards the waterfall, William and Mason watched from binoculars. They were completely taken by surprise at the kid's discovery.

"Did you know this place existed?" Mason asked William.

"No! There's a much larger fall higher up in the mountains, we assumed that was the source of the river. Being born on the island, I thought I had explored every inch or it. I should have found this place ages ago."

"My family didn't move here until I was eighteen. But I did spend my summers here, and I did some exploring. I don't think anyone knows of this place," said Mason, wondering how such a place could remain a secret.

"It's breath taking."

"A hidden treasure! Maybe it was supposed to be hidden and has been waiting for just the right people to discover it," mused William out loud.

"They're headed toward the fall," Mason pointed out to William.

"Let's stay here; if they need us, we will be close. They need to do this themselves."

"William, you are a wise man, letting them make discoveries on their own."

"That's what they were meant to do," William said simply. Mason and William sat down, listened, and waited, as they took in the magnificence of the secret waterfall for a moment.

"William, have they discovered who tried to kill you? Do you think it could have been one of Webster's men?"

"It was impossible to trace where that drone came from. Our people are trying to retrace its radio transmission, but whoever it was covered their tracks well. It could have been Webster; he's tried to get a man on our island a few times."

"It was a genius idea to let him think he did," laughed Mason.

124

"Jack Webber is a good friend of David and Charlie. When Charlie saw Helaina's pink dream diaries he came up with a plan. He had Jack take it from the house. He gave it to agents who made an exact duplicate of the cover. Charlie had false information written into the fake book. Just enough to get Webster's interest, and he put a tracking device in it, hoping it would lead us to others out to find our secrets. But unfortunately, Webster's secretary was one of our people and took the diary and returned it to David instead. Charlie thought that was the end of his plan until Jack called him and told him of Webster's plan to kidnap Helaina.

When Charlie brought Emma and Dylan to the island, he told me everything. Later he called about the kidnapping plan and had me pose for a picture with that young FBI agent. I was so worried! But everything went as planned."

"What happened to Helaina's diary?"

William laughed, "It was returned to David. Jack had the foresight to remove a few pages of the diary, and he mailed them to David."

"Why did he do that?"

"The pages that he removed told of a story that concerned his family. He didn't want that information in the wrong hands. Just in case Webster had his own agents in the FBI."

"I'm sure glad everything worked out. Where is Webster now?"

"Awaiting his trial for treason and kidnapping and a whole lot of other charges, in jail. He's never going to be a free man again."

"Other's will try to infiltrate us."

"I know, but we always stop them," William reminded his friend.

***

J.R., Helaina, and their friends made their way to the fall. They felt the spray of the water on their bodies, cooling them down, from their long walk. They were able to walk directly to the back wall of stone. The water fell straight down, touching nothing as it fell into the river below. Large boulders had fallen on either side of the river.

"I don't see anything but a stone wall," said Mark

"It's here; I know it. We just have to climb over those rocks."

"What's here?" asked the twins in unison.

"A cave," Helaina told them, before she started to climb up on the large boulders, but J.R. stopped her.

"Wait! I will go first. But first we have to do something." J.R. put his backpack on the ground and opened it, taking out a rope and two flashlights.

"Mark, you brought that climbing stuff, right?" he asked.

"Sure, I know what you are thinking.

Helaina and J.R. looked at each other in surprise, before they realized Mark couldn't possibly know of their Mind Speaking.

"We are going to tie one end to you and take the other end and secure it to one of these boulders," said Mark as he began tying knots.

"That's right, and each of us will put one of the karabiners on our belt loops and hook ourselves to the rope."

"That way we can't get lost. Good idea!"

Kellie placed her big floppy hat down on her backpack and began helping. She tied the rope securely to J.R. as Mark used his climbing ax to put a hole into one of the boulders. He then secured an anchoring screw into the rock and clipped the rope on to it. Once all the knots were tied, J.R. began to climb over the large boulders so he could get behind the wall of water.

"Please be careful," Kellie told J.R. as he began moving towards the waterfall.

"I will, stop worrying," J.R. told her.

First climbing on top of one of the smaller boulders and hoisting himself up and over a much larger one, J.R. proceeded with caution. He placed his back against the wall and inched his way behind the water, carefully avoiding slipping on the small pebbles. Then he saw it. Hiding just behind a wall of thin long roots, which had grown over the opening, was the cave they were looking for. He retraced his steps.

"I found it. I found the cave!" J.R. yelled when he was close enough for the others to hear him.

As J.R. made the return trip, he thought of a plan. When he made it safely back to the group, he told everyone what he had seen and what he thought they should do.

"Helaina and I will go into the cave to explore and see if it is safe."

"I think I should go with you, being an experience climber and all," Mark pointed out.

"Good idea. Kellie, you stay out here, and if we get into trouble you can call someone."

"What can we do?" asked the twins.

"You two have the most important jobs of all. You are our safety monitors. Dylan, you make sure that the rope doesn't come untied and watch to make sure that the rope stays tight. If it falls to the ground, we are in trouble. Understand?" asked Helaina.

"Sure do," Dylan responded with a grin.

"Emma do you have your drawing pad and pencils with you?" J.R. asked his new friend. Emma nodded her answer.

"You need to draw the waterfall, exactly as it is. That way we can document this place. Show the path through the trees. Just in case we have to find it again. I also want you to keep an eye on the time; if we are longer than an hour, go for help."

"Okay everyone has their assignments; let's go spelunking," Mark said anxiously, wanting to get started.

"Spelunking? What's that?"

"Helaina, that's just a neat way to say, 'Go cave exploring'."

"Alright! Let's go."

J.R. took the lead, and they made their way over the boulders. When the three of them were safe and sound on the other side, they checked the rope. Making sure they were attached with the karabiners, they put their backs against the solid wall of stone and made their way to the cave.

Using mind speak Helaina told J.R., "This is exactly like my dream. Careful you are going to slip—".

Before she could finish, J.R. slipped slightly on a small slippery pebble.

127

"You knew I was going to do that, didn't you?"

"Yeah, it was in my dream," she giggled.

"You have any more things I should be aware of?" J.R. demanded.

"Not yet."

They were now at the mouth of the cave. Turning on the flashlights, they entered the dark, damp cave. Inside, it was considerably cooler causing Helaina to shiver a bit; she reached out and touched the smooth flat surface of the wall. She felt something under her fingers.

"J.R., Mark, please shine your flashlights over here."

When they moved their lights, they discovered that there were carvings on the wall.

"Wow! These are fantastic," exclaimed J.R.

"They're cave writings; I've seen something like this before. They tell a story; it's how ancient people wrote their history," Mark explained.

"Like cavemen who lived during dinosaurs' times? Helaina asked.

"Don't know, but cavemen and dinosaurs here in this area would make sense. Unity is drilling for fuel just ten miles offshore on those two oil rigs."

"Only one is drilling for fuel, the other one is an energy station. Remember what we learned on *Oceanic One*?" J.R. reminded his cousin.

As they talked, they pointed their flashlights in many directions, discovering that the cave writings were everywhere. Helaina came up with an idea.

"I think we should take pictures of all of this."

"Do you think they were made by ancestors of ours?"

"Maybe, but they might be important."

During the next five minutes J.R., Helaina, and Mark documented every single drawing and carving on the wall of the cave with their digital cameras. Then they continued down the cave, walking in ankle deep water. Helaina remembered that a shallow lake was in her dream. The spelunkers heard water dripping from the ceiling of the cave. They figured that was how the shallow lake was formed. Helaina knew that they were close to what they were looking for. Taking her flashlight, she ran up ahead of the other two. She dragged them with her because they were still attached to the safety rope.

Helaina abruptly came to a standstill. In front of them was a solid wall of rock; they had arrived at the back of the cave.

"Look for a tombstone or a rock that sticks up or something like that. It opens the doors."

"I think I found something. Give me that climbing ax," said an excited J.R.

"Let me do it; you don't want to break something off," insisted Mark.

"Dig around this, it looks like an upside-down pyramid with more of the cave carvings on it."

They worked for a few minutes pushing away the dirt, until they were able to get a closer look. Helaina bent down and sat in front of it, and then she took about ten digital pictures of the front, crawled around to the back and did the same.

"These are our instructions, see. It tells us that we are supposed to push the stone down. That's you, and that's me," she said as she pointed at the two figures.

"How do you know that's us?" demanded J.R.

"Not us dummy. That's a symbol for women, and that one is for men, and that is the Unity logo, so I guess it has to be someone from our family. And since we are the only ones from our family here, then that means US."

"What happens next?"

"Two doors open, somewhere. See right here? Those look like little doors."

"She right," Mark exclaimed. "I think it is saying something about two boxes, and that they should stay horizontal at all times, one above, and one below."

"Where have I heard that from?" wondered J.R.

"Let's do it. Let's push the stone down and open the doors."

Helaina stood up, and she and J.R. positioned themselves in front of the upside-down pyramid. Putting both hands on the stone they pushed.

"I think it's moving, push harder!" urged Mark.

"I said, harder, put your backs into it!" he urged again much more excitedly.

Finally, the large stone was lying on the ground. When they took a look at the base, the exposed bottom revealed that the stone had been hinged to the floor. When pushed down, a bottom panel rose up. Then they saw them. Two little doors opened on what they assumed had been a solid wall of rock. J.R. reached into the bottom chamber and pulled out an old cloth bag, inside he found a one-foot square crystal box. Inside was a round object that looked to be green. On top of the crystal box, cut into the crystal, was the Unity logo. The three of them looked closely, admiring it.

Helaina asked, "How is that ball just floating in there?"

"I have no idea, you?" J.R. asked Mark.

"None."

"Helaina, let's put this in my backpack. Can you get the other one? We will put it on top of this one. We have to get out of here; time's running out."

Helaina pulled out the second bag, took a quick look inside, smiled and placed it on top of the one J.R. had just put in his backpack. Then following the rope, the three spelunkers made their way out of the cave and safely returned to their friends. As they made their way out, J.R. and Helaina had a silent conversation.

"I thought you said they glowed?"

"Well, in my dream they did. Whatever you do, don't lay that bag down. Keep it upright at all times. Okay?"

"Sure thing. Maybe we have to have all four before they glow."

"We have to tell Mark not to tell anyone what we found."

"That's good thinking. He's behind me, I will tell him."

J.R. told Mark that what they found would be a secret between the three of them. That they would just share the pictures of the cave drawings and carvings with the others and tell them they had found nothing but rocks. J.R promised Mark that he and Helaina would show William and Jennifer what they found later. As J.R talked to Mark Helaina climbed back over the rock, and excitedly told Kellie, Emma, and Dylan all about the drawings. She would show them the pictures during lunch. The two boys were in agreement and followed Helaina over the boulders. After taking a whole bunch of pictures of the waterfall, the group then made their way out of the grove of trees and hiked back to get their lunch and to play on the tire swing.

William and Mason had backed away, out of sight, waiting for the kids to pass them by. Since they now knew they were out of harm's way, they themselves could now go and take a closer look at that cave. They took pictures of every symbol and every marking on the cave walls too. They made notes as to where they had been placed. They found the pyramid and documented that also. Before leaving, they took soil and water samples and GPS readings. This was a place that needed to be studied by their scientists and aerologists. The two men also took dozens of pictures of the beautiful waterfall and the surrounding area. They left the kids to enjoy the remainder of their day and headed back to town with the information they had collected. Their watchful and protective eyes remained unknown to the group of adventurers.

CHAPTER SEVENTEEN

FUN AT THE LAKE

The girls walked a few feet in front of the three boys; they listened intently to Helaina as she told them all about the cave. Blueberries were everywhere, and as planned, everyone stopped. Each hiker filled an empty grocery bag until it couldn't hold one more berry. By the time they got back to the picnic area near the lake, they were ready for lunch. Everyone spread out their beach towels and sat down to enjoy the ham and cheese subs, chips, and cupcakes that Jennifer Unity had packed. They especially enjoyed the thermoses filled with ice cold lemonade. It was appreciated after their long hike on this hot summer day.

J.R. found an opportunity to ask Helaina a question that had been on his mind for a few days. Since it was a question that the others wouldn't understand, he used Mind Speak.

"Helaina, when you talk to the animals, why can't I hear you do it?"

"I don't talk to them, not with words anyway. That's why you can't hear. You know how we can only speak to each other when we both agree or are open to it. We can't read each other's mind, like those mind readers at the fair last year."

"That's just a trick! And besides, I don't think I like the idea of you reading my thoughts, and I certainly wouldn't want to read yours all the time. You think too much about fashion and makeup! So, what's it like?"

"It's like I am connecting to them on a thin wire of energy. I feel how they feel. I feel what they need. I feel what they want, and I can picture all that in my mind. And they do the same with me. Then I picture in my mind what I would like for them to do."

"That's really cool!

"J.R., I have only been able to do this since that dive down to that old wreck. That was the first time. Before then I just talked to my pets the old-fashioned way. It kind of scared me."

"Scared you! We thought you would be eaten by those sharks. I have something to tell you. I've been having dreams that I have been floating, and then I crash to the bedroom floor and wake up. Helaina, I think those weren't dreams. I think it was really happening."

Helaina thought about this for a few seconds. "Why are we changing? I think there is something very different about us, and the elders know about it. But they aren't ready to tell us."

"Not only us. Haven't you noticed; everyone on Hope Island is smart and has advanced skills? Just look at Emma. At eleven, she draws like a master. Mark is an accomplished outdoorsman; Dylan is fast, and Kelly has already written four bestselling books. I don't think we are living in the real world."

"Sometimes it feels like that! Doesn't it?" J.R. and Helaina sat quietly, finishing their lunch and thinking about the things they'd just discussed.

After she ate her lunch, Emma got out her sketch pad to show everyone the work she did at the waterfall. Emma had sketched three different scenes. The first was the view from where they first came upon the waterfall; the second the view from the waterfall looking back at the trees that hid it from those who were walking by. The third was a map to the secret waterfall that she thought might come in handy, just in case they wanted to go explore that area in the future. Each sketch was detailed and exact. Each was a masterpiece worth framing. As her friends admired her work, Emma worked on yet another sketch, this one special. She worked for about twenty minutes and closed her sketch book. She wasn't ready to show it to anyone yet.

"Look over there?" Mark pointed in the direction of the sunflower field where two deer, a buck and a doe were standing.

Knowing that his new brother was a very fast runner, Mark decided to challenge him.

"Hey little brother, I bet you my cupcake that you can't run up to one of those deer and touch its nose before they see you and run off."

"I bet you I can."

Dylan was always up to a challenge to his speed, especially on Hope Island where he didn't have to hide who he was.

"Everyone has to be quiet. Now watch."

Dylan got up and waited until the deer were looking away from them. Then he dashed through the field. Not only did he touch one deer, the buck, he had time to give the little doe a hug, kiss her nose, and run back. He did this so fast that the deer didn't know what happened; they just stood there shocked and confused for a minute before they ran off. Dylan did it so fast the kids had to watch the video that Mark took on his camera phone several times to catch all the action.

"Well big brother, I think you owe me that cupcake," Dylan bragged.

"Next time we have track at school, you really must try out. Here's your cupcake; you earned it." After giving his brother the cupcake, Mark gave him a pat on the back.

While everyone was distracted watching Dylan, Emma finished what she was working on. Everyone gathered around her to have a look. She had sketched a group portrait, even Peanut was in the picture, though she was home asleep in her nest. They stood on the beach. She added their names under their feet, and on top of the page in bold letters she had written, "NEW FAMILY, NEW HOME, and NEW FRIENDS."

"I think this is my best work," Emma said proudly.

"I think you are right, little sister," said Mark.

"I'm speechless. It's so perfect," Kellie said, choking on her words.

"We have a problem; that's one portrait each one of us would love to have."

"Well, we can have copies made," J.R. suggested.

Kellie came up with another idea. "I know something special we can do after we make copies. I can make six picture frames to put them in. Then I can take the image and put them on tee-shirts, so everyone can see Emma's work."

Everyone thought that would be a grand idea.

"When I ran out to the deer, I saw something out near the tree line; let's go see what it was," suggested Dylan.

"Cool," the other boys agreed.

And off went the boys to investigate Dylan's sighting. The girls stayed behind to talk. It didn't take long to find out what Dylan had spotted on his run.

"It's just an old motorcycle," Dylan said disappointed in what they found.

"I think I can fix it," said J.R.

"You can fix anything," Mark commented.

"I'll make it even better, maybe even faster. You guys don't want it do you? Dylan did find it."

J.R. held his breath, wanting the two boys to say no. Dylan and Mark exchanged a look that said they were thinking about it. Teasing J.R., they took their time answering him.

"No, you can have that piece of junk, but only if we can help fix it up. Then you have to teach us how to drive it," Dylan told his new friend.

"Deal! Now can you two help me drag it to the picnic area, please! Then me and granddad can come and get it tomorrow."

"Oh, alright! Then can we play on the swing? Please?" Dylan was anxious for a cool dip in the lake. Running that fast could really make his body temperature rise.

The three girls watched as the boys struggled to drag the old bike to the picnic area. They were quite content to watch and didn't offer any help. After all, they didn't want to even touch that rusty old thing, so they just sat and made fun of the boy's efforts. They finally parked the motorcycle and leaned it against a big oak tree, but not without getting extremely greasy and grimy in their efforts. It was definitely time for a cool swim.

As promised, Dylan and Emma were the first to get to use the tire swing. For the next hour and a half, the kids took turns swinging from the tree and dropping into the cool water of the lake. The boys took turns seeing who could shoot themselves further into the lake than anyone else. J.R. was able to fly off the tire and land about five feet from the buoy that marked the middle of the lake. Mark got about ten feet from it, being the heaviest of the boys. After getting the hang of using the swing, Dylan, the lightest, was able to fly over the buoy and land about four feet on the other side, and he was the clear winner of the game.

The girls preferred just swimming out and back at a more leisurely pace. They also enjoyed walking along the bank, finding small turtles and frogs. When each girl had found a frog, they drew two lines in the mud, a starting line, and a finish line. They had great fun trying to get the frogs to race, but they didn't cooperate, always going in the wrong directions. They had better luck with the little turtles they found, except they all looked the same and the girls couldn't figure out whose turtle had won, but it really didn't matter to them anyway, it was just fun to play with the little animals. Helaina, Kellie, and Emma got tired of watching the boys' antics, and the creature's they had captured had wandered away, so they decided to go apple picking. They managed to pick another six bags of apples, two bags a piece, to take home. They talked about all the apple pies they might make with them the next day and discussed entering the pies and jams in the fair. The fair was a big summer event on the island and would be arriving the next week.

Soon the boys were tired. When they dried off and put their clothes back on, the group got back on the ATVs and went to the Unity's home. The kids were loaded down with the fruit they had picked. It took all of them to take the fruit into the kitchen, putting everything on a kitchen counter. Jennifer was overcome with the amount they had brought home. She learned of the girls' plans to can some jam and bake some pies the next day. Naturally, just now learning how to cook and bake, they would need Jennifer and Sophia's help and included them in their plans which the two women didn't mind at all. Since they were not sure how to make jam and only had just learned how to make cookies and cakes the girls would need the women's guidance. Their plans made for the next day, Mason drove the tired adventurers back to their homes.

***

Soon after getting home, Helaina took the backpack containing the two balls with their cases to her room. Carefully she placed one on the top shelf of her closet and pushed it as far back as possible to keep it out of sight. She then placed a few purses in front to hide it from anyone who opened the closet. Helaina also moved the collection of shoes on the floor of her closet to one side and placed the second ball on the floor, moving the shoes again to hide that box. Satisfied with her hiding skills, she went downstairs to the kitchen.

At dinner that night J.R. and Helaina talked about all the things they did that day. J.R. was most excited about the motorcycle and discussed getting it back to the garage. He discussed how much fun it would be to fix it up with his friends and William, of course. They had brought their cameras to the dinner table, and they proudly showed them the pictures of the secret waterfall and the cave with the cave pictures and carvings. Jennifer told them she was impressed with them, being brave to go into the cave; and how smart J.R. was to use a rope, and assign jobs to everyone, just like a true leader. J.R. and Helaina told them everything, everything except about having found the two boxes with the balls inside.

The kids were very wound up about their day. Helaina and Jennifer discussed plans to make pies and jam tomorrow with the other girls. Helaina and her grandmother spent an hour looking at the cave drawings then they copied each symbol onto a writing tablet. Jennifer and Helaina made sure that each symbol and each marking stayed in the order that the camera had recorded it, starting from the front of the cave then moving to the back. Jennifer didn't tell her granddaughter that she knew those symbols. She just didn't know what they said.

J.R. and William talked about motorcycles. J.R. had forgotten to take pictures of the bike. When J.R. couldn't describe the bike with words, he sat down and drew a picture of it, exactly as he had left it by the tree. Every pipe, every wire, every dent was drawn with great detail. William was very impressed with this new talent but didn't say a word.

The two of them made a list of things they would need to get the motorcycle into shape. When Jennifer walked by the table, the list was already two pages long. At eleven p.m., J.R and Helaina said good night and went upstairs. Before going to his room, J.R. went to his cousin's room.

Helaina first took Peanut and placed her in her cage. It was time for the little animal to eat and spend the rest of the night playing on her wheel and the other toys she had in her cage.

"Let's get the balls out, one at a time of course; I want to see what they look like. It was too dark in the cave to get a good look."

"Alright, I've wanted to look all evening. First the top one, get it down for me."

J.R. reached to the back of the closet shelf and pulled the bag containing the box with the ball down. Placing it on the floor, Helaina opened the bag and took out the box.

"It looks like a blue crystal."

"How is it just suspended in air like that?" Helaina inquired.

"Don't know! I don't see any way to open the box either."

"Put that one away, and let's see what the other one looks like."

Helaina put the box back into its bag and returned it to its hiding place. Then she got out the second; this one was identical to the first but green.

"What do you think they do?" she asked.

"I guess we will have to build the machine to find that out. Keep them here. When we get the other two, we will hide them in my room."

"I'm tired."

"Me to, see you tomorrow."

"Goodnight, and don't have any more dreams about me slipping, or hurting myself."

"I'll try. And don't float away in your sleep."

Everyone slept well that night, tired from their adventures. Everyone that is, except the nocturnal Peanut. The minute Helaina was sleeping peacefully, she escaped her cage from an opening where her water bottle hung and spent the long hours of the night exploring Helaina's room. The minute the sun rose in the sky, she would return to her nest and be sound asleep by the time Helaina woke up. Helaina would not know her pet had escaped and gone exploring on her own.

CHAPTER EIGHTEEN
WHERE'S THE WATERFALL?

Blueberry pancakes and bacon were ready for the family when they woke up the next day. Being a beautiful summer morning, the kids and their grandparents took breakfast out to the patio. William and J.R. were dressed in old jeans and T-shirts since their plan for the day was to get the motorcycle and bring it back home. As William was finishing up his blueberry pancakes topped with rich whipped cream, his cell phone rang.

"William, this is George Garret at the Nature Park, you have a minute?"

"How are you George, has your wife had the baby yet. Let's see that makes number four doesn't it?

"We're doing great, and it's number five."

"Are you trying to overpopulate the island with boys?" laughed William as he walked away from the table to a more private area.

"No, this is going to be the last; my wife is finally going to have that girl she always wanted."

"Great, did you get more samples from that waterfall and cave the kids found yesterday?"

"That's why I'm calling. Are you sure you gave me the right GPS coordinates?"

"Positive, Mason and I had the same numbers. Why?"

"Because there is only a field here. There isn't a waterfall or cave."

"That can't be right. We have pictures. We saw it with our own eyes, and Mason, and I went into the cave. We have pictures of the cave art and so do the kids."

"I'm telling you, it's not there."

"Go back and check," William insisted.

"William, me and my assistant are standing at the coordinates you gave us as we speak. I am telling you there is no waterfall and no cave, just a dry riverbed going through a field of grass."

"J.R. and I have to come and pick up an old motorcycle they found yesterday. Meet us at the picnic area, and we will help you find the fall."

"I wondered who put that old thing there this morning. I was thinking about taking it to the recycling center. Meet you in about an hour; see you then."

William walked back to the family. He had to choose his words carefully so as not to let the J.R and Helaina know he had followed them yesterday. They would think that he didn't trust their judgment. They wouldn't believe he was just making sure that they remained safe.

"Hey guys, that was the Geologist I sent to the Nature Park. I told him all about your waterfall and cave. I even sent him the pictures you took and told him what an incredibly unusual place it was. The problem is he couldn't find it."

"We know where it is," said J.R and Helaina in unison, giving each other dirty looks.

They were trying very hard not to speak in unison, because they thought it was creepy. They believed if they did it too much, someone might figure out their Mind Speaking secret.

William laughed, knowing what they were thinking. "I thought before we pick up that motorbike you found, you could show George where the waterfall and cave are?"

"I want to stay here with Grandma, we are going to learn how to make blueberry jam, and she promised to show us her secret recipe for making flaky pie crust."

"J.R., you think you can find it?"

"Sure, I know exactly where it is. Can't forget; it's special."

"Great! you girls have fun. J.R. and I will show George where it is."

"Granddad why doesn't George know where it is? He's the ranger, and geologist; he should know all the cool places in the park." said Helaina.

"That I don't know." William turned to J.R, "Let's get going, we will take the ATV and the small trailer. I don't think we need the truck for an old motorcycle. See you girls for lunch, and I would love some blueberry jam on my peanut butter sandwich."

"Have fun." Helaina and Jennifer chimed together as they picked up the breakfast dishes and headed to the kitchen.

"J.R., run upstairs and get those pictures you took yesterday. I saw you used my computer to print them out this morning. You used up all my ink, by the way."

"Sorry about that, Granddad. Meet you in the garage in five minutes."

When William and J.R. arrived at the picnic area, George was waiting for them. George was an Asian gentleman in his late thirties and dressed simply in a pair of jeans and a button-down work shirt with a long, skinny towel draped over his neck that he used to dry the perspiration from his face. He greeted the young man and his grandfather with a respectful bow. The first thing they did was put the rusty motorcycle on the trailer. A few of its pieces fell off in the process, but they threw them on the trailer with the rest of the old machine. Leaving the trailer, William and J.R. followed George's ATV as they drove into the park for about a mile and a half up the river. Another ranger waited for them. A baby bison was feeding out of his hand as its mother stood watching. Getting off the ATV, J.R. went to investigate the bison and talk to the ranger. William and George spoke quietly, making sure that J.R. couldn't overhear them.

"The GPS coordinates you gave us put the fall behind that grove of trees."

"Okay! Let's take a look. J.R., is this about where you found that fall?" William said, knowing it was, because he was here yesterday.

"Yep, behind those trees over there! Come on, I will show you."

J.R. felt important because they had found a place that no one else had, and he led the three men into the trees.

Following J.R. for about ten minutes without finding the waterfall, the ranger asked, "You sure this is the place?"

"I'm positive! It has to be here; the trees hide it."

J.R. looked in every direction, but it wasn't there. Then he spotted something on the ground. The rope they used and left behind because they didn't have room for it in their back packs. The balls had taken up all the room. J.R. picked it up to show the three men.

"Granddad, this is our rope, we left it tied to a rock near the waterfall. See it still has the ring we tied it to. Did you move it?" J.R. asked the rangers.

The rangers shook their heads. "No, we didn't even see it."

They looked some more, but the group came out on the other side of the grove of trees. All that was there was the dry riverbed through the field of grass. Just as the ranger told William.

"I don't understand; it was here! I know it." J.R. was confused and ran back into the trees. He looked again but came out minutes later frustrated.

"Let me see the pictures again," William told the boy.

The four of them looked at the pictures. The river, the fall, and the cave did exist. They had proof in their hands. But why couldn't they find it? One pictured showed the grove of trees, and they compared it to where they stood. They were at the right place. That crooked tree in the picture next to the fall was the same crooked tree that stood just a few feet away.

"How can it just disappear?" J.R. wanted to know.

"That's a good question. Let's get the bike and head home. Maybe George can find it later."

"But Granddad, that crooked tree; it was by the waterfall. See." J.R. pointed at the picture again.

"I see. I'm just as confused as you are, but we aren't getting any answers. I promise I will have someone call a geologist who specializes in such things. Don't worry; we will unlock the truth about the disappearing waterfall."

The group went back to the picnic area where William and J.R. reattached the trailer to the ATV and went back home. J.R. was silent the whole trip, William couldn't hear his thoughts; he could only hear when the kids did Mind Speaking. But he didn't have to hear anything this time. He knew the boy was confused and was thinking of possible answers that made sense to him. Unfortunately, J.R. couldn't think of anything that explained this mystery, neither could William.

By the time they returned with the old, rusty motorcycle, Mark and Dylan were at the garage waiting for them to help get it off the trailer. J.R. was unusually quiet; his friends sensed that something was bothering him.

"J.R., what's wrong?" asked Mark.

"I just don't understand," J.R. said, shaking his head in frustration.

"Understand what?"

"The waterfall and the cave, they're gone."

"Gone?"

"They disappeared! Vanished! Nowhere to be found! Gone!" J.R. was really upset about this.

J.R.'s two friends looked at him in disbelief, and William assured Dylan and Mark that J.R. was right, and this was no joke. They stood there stunned at what they'd heard.

William needed to distract them. "Hey guys! Let's talk about this later when we get some expert input to help us.

J.R, Mark and Dylan stood there like statues just staring at William, wanting answers. He had none to give them. Okay, time for plan B.

"I did a Google search on this rusty pile of metal you found. You made quite a find; it's a 1970 Triumph Tiger TR6R; one of the faster bikes of her time."

That little bit of information got the job done. The boys were now excited.

"We should take her apart and rebuild her completely." J.R.'s mind was now working on the bike and not the missing waterfall.

"Why did you call it a, 'She'?" Dylan wanted to know.

"I don't know. My dad sometimes calls his Harley Davidson a she. How about painting her black with racing stripes? Then we can race her, suggested J.R.

Mark, always the practical one, said, "I don't think the sheriff would let us race."

"Let's clean her up a bit, and we can start taking her apart," William said, glad that he distracted them from thinking about the waterfall.

Everyone went into the garage to get some cleaning supplies and tools, making big plans for when they had their new project up and running. He would have to chain the thing up until J.R turned sixteen. He did know that Katie wasn't going to like the idea of her son riding a racing motorcycle. She worried when Charlie was on his Harley Davidson. Her brother had lost his life while riding on one on the way to a New Year's Eve party, and she never got over the loss. Maybe by the time J.R. turned sixteen, they could convince her of his abilities, but he doubted it; a loss like that changed a person.

The boys worked all afternoon on the bike. They got Mason and William to help. By the time lunch came around, J.R. had William ordered about two-thousand dollars in parts.

***

While the boys were busy, the girls were totally immersed with projects of their own. The first project of the morning was to wash and dry all the blueberries and apples. They divided the berries; half were to be frozen for later use. They made fast work of bagging the berries and putting them in the freezer. The other half was made into tasty jam.

As Jennifer gave them instruction, the girls did exactly as they were told. Jennifer and Sophia watched them closely as they added ingredients to the bubbly mixture, making sure it got to the right temperature while continually stirring the berry mixture so that the berries didn't burn. When the jam was ready, Sophia showed the girls how to do the canning. When the jam was made and the jars were lined up near an open window to cool, they began to peel the apples. They were still peeling apples when the boys came in covered from head to toe in grease.

"Okay, ladies, let's take a break. I think we have a few hungry men to feed. After they get cleaned up that is," Jennifer said, needing a break herself.

They fixed themselves some nice cold iced tea and sat down at the kitchen counter. Sophia moved the apples into the refrigerator and took out things to make sandwiches. Of course, they were peanut butter with blueberry jam, served with chips and dips. After the boys removed most of the grease off their hands, they came into the kitchen hungry. They were anxious to try the jam the girls made, and they weren't disappointed; the jam tasted sweet and made the best peanut butter and jelly sandwiches. Especially when it was made with Sophia's homemade bread, made fresh that very morning.

William followed the boy's upstairs. After he cleaned up, he waited until he heard them go back to the kitchen. Taking his digital camera, he went into Helaina's room. He hated being a snoop, but he had to see those balls and their cases and take pictures to document them. Not knowing what they were, or what they did, or if they posed a threat to J.R. and Helaina, he needed to see them for himself. He wanted the company's scientists to take a discreet look at the pictures so they could advise him on the situation. The most logical place to hide such items, he assumed, was the closet, and he was right. He was careful not to disturb anything, so his crime wasn't discovered. First, he found the bag carrying one of the objects back in a corner on the floor. Carefully removing it, he snapped a few pictures, case and all, making sure he got it at all angles. Then he placed the green ball back where he had found it. He did the same with the case he found on the top shelf, the one with the blue ball.

As he left the room, a thought came to him. "The colors were similar to those of the logo. Blue is for those from above, and green for those of the earth. It couldn't be a coincidence."

William joined everyone downstairs for lunch. The only witness to his crime was Peanut, who had stuck her head out from her nest. She went right back to sleep. She couldn't possibly snitch on him.

***

146

Peanut butter sandwiches with the freshly made blueberry jam made for a wonderful lunch and for a lot of blueberry stained clothes. After this special treat, the boys went back to the garage to work on their project for a few more hours. Being elbow deep in pie crust dough, and with enough apples to feed a small army, the girls worked together making pies and apple turn overs. After running out of flour and butter, the girls made apple sauce. Afterwards, the remaining apples were frozen for use later. By four in the afternoon, the smell of apple pies and turn overs filled the air, so much so that it brought everyone together by the pool for an afternoon snack.

Everyone had to clean up the mess left from their individual projects before they could relax in the recreation room and enjoy challenging each other to games. Helaina and Kellie were setting up the shuffleboard but couldn't find one of the disks.

J.R. overheard Helaina say, "It just can't disappear!" in frustration.

"Yes, it can! The waterfall disappeared," he stated.

The three girls turned to look at him. This was news to them. J.R. recounted the story of the morning's outing to the group. They knew J.R. was speaking the truth because of the frustration and confusion in his voice. They believed his story, but they didn't understand. No one did.

CHAPTER NINETEEN

RETRIEVING THE LAST TWO BALLS

Kellie, Mark, and the twins left to go home, taking two pies and a few of the apple turnovers with them. J.R. and Helaina were left alone in the recreation room, playing a game of air hockey. This was the opportunity for Helaina to present her plan to her cousin.

"I had a dream last night," Helaina said out loud.

"Quiet, Grandma and Granddad are out on the patio, use Mind Speak."

"Okay! As I said I had another dream last night."

"About the waterfall disappearing?" This was really bothering J.R. and was front and center on his mind.

"Will you stop thinking about that! There has to be some sort of explanation. I'm sure someone will figure out the mystery."

"What did you dream about last night?" J.R. swiftly scored when Helaina wasn't paying attention.

"We have to get those other balls tomorrow, very early, before the sun rises. After you told us about the waterfall disappearing, I was thinking—"

"That can be dangerous to me," J.R. teased, interrupting her.

"Stop with the wise cracks; this is important." Helaina was getting impatient with J.R.

"I know where this is leading. You think that since the waterfall disappeared after we got the first two balls, that the place where we get the second two will do the same."

"That is exactly what I was thinking! What if some force is giving me these dreams and directing us on what we need to do? But why us? Why give us the balls and not someone else like our dads?"

"Hell! I wish I knew. We aren't ready to be Guardians yet. Besides, we have to wait until Dad and Uncle David retire. I think we have another purpose. Do you think we should give the balls to Grandma and Granddad?"

"I believe you're right about us having another purpose, but first let's go get the last two balls. I believe this is something we have to do; that it is important."

"Where do we find them?"

"I told you. We go for a dive under the pier. It will only take about half an hour, but we have to do it before sunrise tomorrow."

"Okay, here's what we do. All our diving equipment is in the boat house. Mason refilled the air tanks so we're good there. We get up at four a.m., sneak down to the boat house, change, get the balls, and be back before Granddad gets up."

"We need to remember to bring dive bags and lights; it's going to be dark that early. Don't you dare forget to set your alarm for three forty-five."

"I won't; this is a test of some sort, and I think we have to pass it."

"A test?" questioned Helaina.

"Yep, I think we are being tested by someone or something."

"I don't believe it's a test. I think we are being led to something."

"Have you noticed I just beat you at air hockey. Want to play again?"

"No, I didn't notice. Let's play, "War Heroes," instead; my feet hurt."

William was outside on the patio, enjoying an ice-cold lemonade and reading the newspaper. Jennifer sat next to him doing the crossword puzzle with a nice hot cup of green tea. It only looked like William was concentrating on a news story. What he *was concentrating* on was what the two younger members of the family were discussing in the recreation room. They had so many questions and no answers. They were confused, but they were on the right track. They just didn't know it yet. He was very proud of those two but worried. He instinctively felt that J.R. and Helaina were the ones they had been waiting for.

149

At three forty-five the next morning, two alarms woke up J.R. and Helaina. It was still very dark outside, and Peanut was playing on her wheel when she heard Helaina's alarm. Peanut chattered excitedly. Helaina went to the cage, opened the door, and immediately Peanut jumped into her hand.

With one finger Helaina stroked Peanut's soft head. "I have something to do this morning, but I will be back soon to get you. I promise."

Helaina silently dressed in her swimsuit, putting jeans and a sweatshirt over them. She met J.R. on the stairway and they both slipped out of the house, neither of them bothered to put on shoes. They were going to the beach after all, and that was just past the garden. In the boathouse, they carefully put on their diving suits, and as they were taught, checked the gages, air hoses, and dive watches.

Walking out on to the pier, they were met by a familiar little friend. It was the sea lion that they played with a few days earlier. Dressed in wet suits, J.R. and Helaina looked like big sea lions. He came over to investigate. When J.R. and Helaina sat down on the edge of the pier, so they could slip on their swim fins, the sea lion joined them. Helaina sat and stroked the animal's soft skin and hugged his head to her chest.

"I think I will name him Rambo."

"Don't give him a name; he is a wild animal."

"He's a dear, and I think he can help us."

"How?"

Helaina put the palms of her hands on either side of the sea lion's head and looked directly into his eyes. It looked like she was having a staring contest with the animal.

"He knows where the door is. He is going to take us there; it's not far." She paused for a second before she continued.

"No! I'm just messing with you. I'm the only one who knows where that hatch is. Rambo just wants to go with us."

"Cool! But he is going to get in the way. Maybe you can teach me to connect with animals like that."

"I think each of us needs to have our own talents. That way we work as a team, contributing our individual talents when there is a need," Helaina said, reaching this mature conclusion on her own.

"Okay, let's go! Tell him to stay out of our way."

"His name is Rambo."

"Let's go, Rambo. Helaina take us to the door." They fell into the water, cold and uninviting as it was at that time of morning.

First, they adjusted the dive masks and turned on the oxygen and the head lamps that they wore. Seconds later, J.R. and Helaina dove into the darkness. Rambo swam a few feet in front of the kids. They got to the bottom fast considering they only had to dive thirty feet down, and they weren't far from shore. Sea urchins, starfish, and sand crabs were scattered on the soft sand of the ocean floor, and small fish swam in schools. They didn't see a door or a hatch of any kind, even when they used their hands to sweep the white sand aside. Rambo came to Helaina's side; she reached a hand out and grabbed hold of his tail. He guided her to a spot right under the pier, stopped, and took his nose, showing her where he saw a shiny metal square. Helaina rewarded the animal with a hug and rubbed his head, as J.R. pried opened the hatch with the small crowbar he brought with him. When he finally removed the cover, he saw what they had come there to get. The two boxes which were wrapped in bags were immediately visible.

Using Mind Speak, Helaina told him, "I think that hatch was made just for those two boxes. Nothing else could fit in there."

"Yep. Hey, this one is heavy, maybe it's lead. I will get this one. You get the other and let's get back; it's almost sunrise."

"Can't we stay and see if the little hatch disappears at sunrise?"

"I don't think that's a good idea; we better get these back and hidden before Granddad gets up."

"Sometimes you are just too practical."

"And sometimes you are to inquisitive; grab that one, and let's go."

***

Five minutes later, the kids were in the boat house stripping off their diving suits. Soon after that, without having been found out, so they thought, the two balls—one gold in color and the other white—were tucked safely side by side on the bottom of J.R.'s closet. Helaina remembered that they had to remain vertical just as the first two had to remain horizontal.

In the usual summertime attire of shorts and T-shirts, the kids were down in the kitchen raiding the refrigerator when Sophia came in to start the family's breakfast.

"The two of you are up early. What are you up to?"

They froze wondering if they had been caught.

J.R. silently spoke to Helaina, "She doesn't know anything; she's fishing. I'll handle this."

"We're not up to anything; we are just hungry. That's all," J.R. told Sophia.

"I have an idea!" Helaina spoke up brightly.

"And what would that be young lady?"

"I was thinking of taking some of those apples we put in the freezer, chopping some up and putting them in some waffles."

"You know that does sound like it would be good. But if we add apples, do you remember what else we should add to the batter?"

Helaina thought for a second. "Sugar and cinnamon."

"Correct! You, my love, are going to be a great cook one day like your mom and grandmother," Sophia said, complimenting the young cook.

"Really?"

"Really! Now why don't you make that batter, and J.R., since you are up, you can fry up some of those sausage over there."

"That's women's work!" J.R. said as William walked into the kitchen.

"Young man, some of the best chefs in the world are men, and besides it was my scrambled eggs with cheese and bacon that got your grandma to fall in love with me."

152

"Well, my love, there were a few other things, but I think that was one of the main things." agreed Jennifer after hearing the conversation when she walked in the kitchen behind her husband.

"J.R., it would be best that you learn some cooking skills. It's in your genes as much as it is in Helaina's; besides, it's fun."

"Alright I will cook the sausage, but if I poison anyone, don't get mad."

Everyone pitched in and soon they were enjoying breakfast and making plans for the day. For the two sleepy teens, their plans consisted of going to the beach with friends and taking a nap in the sun. For William, it meant being a snoop again and taking pictures of the two treasures found by the kids that morning and sending them down to the science team for analyzing. William was glad that J.R. and Helaina were completely unaware that he had watched them earlier as they went on their adventure this morning.

CHAPTER TWENTY
WHAT TO DO WITH THE BALLS

Later that afternoon J.R. came back to the house to ask if they could take the wave runners for a ride. He couldn't find his grandmother or granddad in the garden or by the pool. But he did find Sophia in the kitchen.

"Sophia, can we have the keys to the wave runners?"

"You have to ask your grandparents."

"But they're not here."

"Yes, they are. They're in the den."

"Great. Hey! Can I take some of those cookies back to the beach with me?"

"Sure can, you go ask about the keys, and I will pack some up for you."

"Be back in a few minutes."

J.R. ran up the stairs to talk to his grandparents. When he got to the den, the door was closed. He was just about to knock when he heard some voices. He stopped to listen, not wanting to interrupt something important.

"Can everyone hear me?" William asked.

"We're all here, Dad; how are the kids?"

That sounded like J.R.'s dad, and J.R. listened more carefully.

"The kids are great, having a great time, doing a lot of exploring."

"Yeah, we heard about the disappearing cave. We don't understand how that can be."

"Neither do we, Katie."

"I think we were meant not to understand, not yet anyway."

"What do you mean, Dad?"

"I believe the waterfall and cave were meant just for..." William paused, not knowing how to continue.

The next voice J.R. heard was his Uncle David's.

"Dad, you were going to say, 'Meant just for The One's,' weren't you?"

"Yes. We have never had Ones so talented or so in tune with nature and each other as J.R. and Helaina are. That's why I believe that to be the case."

"Maybe it's time to show them whats below?" Joanna, Helaina's mom, suggested.

There was silence while everyone pondered this suggestion.

"Is everyone in agreement?" William asked.

J.R. heard, as one by one, the voices of his parents, Helaina's parents, and the grandparents said, "Yes."

"Alright! Then it's decided. Talk to you all again soon."

The room became silent. J.R. waited a few minutes before knocking on the door so his grandparents didn't know he had been eavesdropping. That would really get him into trouble.

As he knocked, he called out, "Granddad, are you there?"

"Yes, come on in, J.R."

J.R. acted like he hadn't heard anything and that the only thing he was interested in was taking out the wave runners.

"Granddad, can we have the keys to the wave runners? Please," he asked, giving them the best puppy-dog eyes, he could.

"What do you think, Jenny? Think J.R. and Helaina are able to handle that responsibility?"

"I think they are."

"So, do I," he said, handing the keys to J.R. "Make sure you have Mason check the oil and fill the gas tank when you're done. Have fun, and no acrobatics; both hands on the controls at all times."

"Thanks, we'll be careful, I promise. See you later," J.R. yelled back at them as he ran downstairs.

He was excited that they were going to drive the jet skis for the first time, without supervision. On his way out the back door and back to the beach, he remembered to stop to get the bag of cookies from

Sophia. After all, playing with gadgets and eating sweets were his favorite activities. He would tell Helaina what he heard later. He felt driving the wave runners would be a lot more fun than answering his cousin's questions. And he knew she would ask plenty.

Having only two wave runners and six teens didn't present any problems. Helaina and J.R. took one friend at a time and had great fun racing along the beach with their friends on the back. After two hours, they had to stop. Not because they were tired, but because they had emptied the reserve holding tank. Now they would have to wait until someone called and ordered the tank to be filled again. They returned the wave runners to the boat house, and the boys cleaned them up as the girls stored the life jackets in their proper place.

Soon Kellie had to go home for a music lesson, which her mother insisted she take, and Mark, Dylan, and Emma had to go because their mom had made appointments for them to have their teeth cleaned and checked for cavities. This left J.R. and Helaina to entertain themselves for the rest of the afternoon. They decided to go back to the house and lay by the pool, maybe even take a nap. After all, they woke up way to early that morning. As they walked to the house, J.R. told Helaina about the conference call he overheard earlier.

"What do you think they meant by, 'The Ones?'" Helaina wanted to know.

"Don't know. I'm more anxious to know what they were talking about when they said Granddad could show us what's below".

"Maybe they knew about the balls that were hidden under the pier, and they wanted to be the ones to find them. Maybe we should put those two back before they find out."

"That's sounds like it could be it; we did find the balls below the pier."

J.R. thought about this for a second. "If that's the case, I think that after dinner we should give the balls back to Grandma and Granddad. I hope they understand that we didn't mean to do anything wrong when we found them."

"We didn't, we were just doing what my dreams told me. Is that a bad thing?"

"No! I don't think so. You think they know about the balls we found in the cave?"

"I think that we should give them all the balls and tell them what my dreams said to do. We should show them your drawing of that machine. We need to show them that the machine is the place that the balls and the Story Chamber belong," Helaina reasoned.

"Yeah! I think that would be best. I hope they don't get mad at us for being sneaks."

"You're a bigger sneak then me."

"Am not!"

"Race you to the pool; first one there gets this last cookie."

Before Helaina could finish saying cookie, J.R. already started running back to the house. Of course, he got to finish off the bag of cookies which was alright with Helaina. What she wanted was a nice cold drink and a nap. An hour later, William and Jennifer found the two of them sound asleep in the deck chairs. After putting a towel over them so they wouldn't burn, they left them there until it was time to change out of their swim wear and get ready for dinner.

After dinner, when everyone was in the den preparing to watch a movie, J.R. and Helaina chose to give the balls to their grandparents. It was Helaina who began the conversation.

"Before we watch the movie, we have something to give you."

"Presents, how nice."

"No, they are something we found," J.R. said.

"We didn't find them; we knew exactly where they were. I had a dream that told me to find the balls, and we did." Helaina was stumbling over her words, trying hard to explain what happened.

Playing along, William asked, "What balls? Did a dream tell you to get them?"

Helaina shook her head.

J.R., trying to help his cousin with the story told them, "Helaina had a dream which said we would find two balls in the cave and two balls under the pier. It was the same night you showed us the Story Chamber. When I saw the Chamber, I felt like it wasn't complete. That night, I drew this." J.R. handed Jennifer the picture of the machine he drew. "But I drew it before Helaina told me about the balls."

He quickly continued the explanation, "It was like we were working together to find the parts to finish this machine. We think it is something that we must do."

"Where are the balls?" Jennifer asked the kids.

"I have two in my room, and J.R. has two in his," answered Helaina.

"Can we see them?"

"You aren't mad that we took the balls from their hiding place?"

"No, we're not. In fact, we are quite proud of you for working together and coming to us with the truth. Now go get the balls."

They were about to leave the room but Helaina remembered something important that she had to tell her grandparents, and she turned around.

"There's something else. In my dream, a voice said that the two balls we found in the cave must stay horizontal, and the two we found under the pier had to stay vertical to each other."

"That does sound like it could be important, so be careful and keep the balls as your dream told you."

Helaina ran up and gave both grandparents a hug.

"Thank you."

"Thank you for what?" her grandmother asked.

"Thank you for believing us."

"Now, why do you think that we wouldn't?"

"Because we are young," was the simple answer.

"Yes, my dear. You are young, but like I always tell you, the both of you are very special."

"Come on, William; let's help them bring the balls into the den. We can each bring one and make sure they stay the way they should."

The family went together to get the four balls and brought them into the den. It was the first time all four balls were in the same place. They stacked the two balls from the cave on the desk and placed the ones from under the dock on either side of them, keeping one set vertical and one set horizontal. Something was making Helaina nervous; something she had forgotten. Then it came to her, just as J.R. and William began to take the cases out of their bags. She stopped them.

"Wait. Stop!" Helaina yelled, feeling terrified.

Seeing the fear in her eyes, Jennifer went to comfort her. "Dear, what's wrong?"

"I remembered something. In my dream, they glowed; I don't know what that means. I don't know why they do that. Or if it means that something will happen if they do. Maybe we shouldn't take them out of the boxes, not yet anyway. I'm afraid."

Helaina was shaking from fear. William went to her, trying to calm her down. "Don't worry; this is what we will do. First, we will take a look at them one at a time. Then we will put the balls back into your closets for safe keeping. Tomorrow we will take the balls somewhere they will be safe and can be studied. Someplace where the rest of the parts to your machine can be found and some of your questions can be answered."

The kids nodded in agreement, and Helaina felt safe stopped shaking.

"That sounds like the perfect plan to me. Now let's take a look at those balls and put them back where they can be safe. Then we can watch that movie. I am dying to see it," Jennifer said, trying to ease the tension she felt in the room.

After the balls were taken back to the closets, the family returned to the den and settled in with popcorn and drinks to enjoy the movie. Halfway through the movie, Jennifer looked around the room, discovering William was sound asleep in his recliner and J.R. and Helaina were sound asleep in bean bag chairs.

Well! I am just going to have to tell them the ending tomorrow, she thought, laughing to herself.

Later she woke everyone and sent them to bed. Tomorrow would be an important day in J.R. and Helaina lives. She hoped that her plans came together without much trouble. She didn't worry much about that; her plans always worked. Jennifer was quite confident about that.

CHAPTER TWENTY-ONE
UNDERSTANDING

William was up a little earlier than usual the next morning. He was curious about something, and he had asked Elijah to meet him at the pier for a brief swim. Donning wet suits and headlights, the two went looking for the small hatch that had hidden the two balls J.R. and Helaina retrieved the previous day. They searched, and as William suspected, the hatch was no longer in existence, just like the waterfall.

After a breakfast, of blueberry muffins, ham, orange juice, and coffee, William helped Helaina put the two balls from the waterfall, carefully stacked one on top of the other, in her backpack. William and J.R. carried the other two cases and placed them side by side in the back seat of the jeep. From the weight of the gold colored ball, William assumed that the ball was pure gold. Due to the lightness of the other and its pure white color, he assumed the other was a giant pearl. All the balls would be tested in a lab for their mineral content; maybe other tests would determine what power they might possess. When he saw Helaina's reaction last night, he felt it best to get the four balls, as J.R and Helaina called them, away from his precious grandkids and into a controlled environment; the sooner the better.

"Isn't Grandma coming with us?"

"Not today dear. It's her day to volunteer at the hospital."

"Will we be back before one; I promised I would meet Dylan and Mark to go fishing."

"Call them and tell them you will go fishing with them tomorrow."

As J.R. called his friends informing them of the change of plans, Helaina asked William question after question.

"Where are we going?"

"Into town, then somewhere special."

"We found the balls; do we get to keep them?"

"They're yours, I promise, but first we have to make sure they can't harm you or anyone else," he answered patiently.

"Because in my dream they glowed?"

"Yes."

"Why do you think they float in the crystal boxes?"

"Don't know."

"A couple of them are really heavy, yet they still float. Do you think there is jell in the boxes?"

"Don't know."

"Think the gold colored ball is gold? It would be worth a lot of money."

"Could be."

"Helaina sweetheart, I know you have a lot of questions. I can't answer them all but where we're going, answers can be found, so be patient Princess."

"In other words, you are driving Granddad crazy with all your questions so you should shut up for a while," J.R. said, after completing his call.

"Granddad didn't tell me to shut up."

"That's right I didn't, but you did ask me way too many questions," William laughed.

"Sorry I just have a lot of them, and I am excited, but I don't know why."

"We are all excited; this is all new to both of you. I am so happy that I am the one who is able to share this with you."

"We are too!" said the kids in unison as William pulled the jeep into his parking space in front of the large office building in the middle of town.

It was the oldest building in town and was used as one of the main headquarters for the Unity Cooperation.

"This isn't someplace new. We've been here thousands of times."

"J.R., you've been in the upper part, today you discover, "What's Below."

"But, Granddad, J.R. and I explored the basement countless times. We even played Hide Go Seek there when we were little. There's nothing down there but boxes full of old records."

"Get the balls and let's get to my office. We can get where we are going from there, and please be patient for just a little bit more."

William picked up the heaviest bag and J.R. the other. Helaina still carried her backpack carefully, making sure the two she carried stayed vertical. Entering the building, they were greeted by the receptionist who they had known them since they were babies. Then they took the elevator up to Williams's office.

"Sit down for a minute, kids. There are a few things I must tell you before we go below."

The kids sat down in the two leather, high back chairs that faced William's desk, a beautiful handcrafted piece of furniture, which had been a gift to his great-grandfather. It was made from a redwood tree. It was hand carved and sanded; the top was so smooth to the touch it felt like it was covered in satin. William sat down in his chair made from the same soft brown leather as the ones occupied by J.R. and Helaina. This was a big moment. He didn't want to scare or confuse them, but he wanted them to understand why they were different.

William began, as his father and his father's father had begun before him. "Today, you learn something about yourselves that you must not share with anyone. Not even with your friends. When their families think they are ready, they will be told. You must never talk about this place or the secrets it hides and the good things that happen there. Those who know about it are chosen. Not everyone who carries our genes has this knowledge, only a selected few. Those who work there never speak of it or talk about what they do. You are chosen, because you have something special inside you. You must promise to never speak of this, never! Do you understand this?"

"Yes, Granddad." J.R. and Helaina looked at each. A thousand more questions raced into their heads.

"This is a sacred honor. For ten generations now we have been at our new home. Many of the original travelers married and produced children with those who were here before us. Those children grew and the two gene pools mixed as our population grew. Few families have produced new generations with 100% of our gene within their DNA makeup. I have that gene, so do your fathers. And so do you two," William explained.

"That's what's making us special?" J.R. and Helaina asked in unison.

"Yes, we believe so. Sometimes, but not often, a person who carries the full gene, or the 100% as you say, and a person with let's say 50% of the gene makeup, like your Mom, J.R., can produce a child who carries a pure 100% of our gene."

"I understand. When we studied heredity in school, we learned all about how genes are shared," Helaina assured her grandfather.

"I am very glad you understand. Now that you have promised to keep our secret, we can go on our journey. Are you two ready to learn who we are?" William asked J.R. and Helaina.

"Yes, we are."

They answered in unison, but for some reason it didn't bother them this time. Helaina put a protective hand over Peanuts sleeping form. Before she could ask her question, William answered it for her.

"It's alright that Peanut comes with us. There are other entrances, but our family has always used this one when taking down a new generation. Are you two, or rather three, ready to go?"

J.R. and Helaina simply nodded, and William positioned J.R. and Helaina in front of a paneled wall, standing behind them. He waved his hand over a nearby figurine—a crystal cat that his mother had given him. A panel slid up into the ceiling revealing an elevator neither of them had seen before.

"Let's go!"

Getting into the elevator the kids noticed there were no buttons. J.R. even looked for a panel that might be concealing them, but he couldn't find anything. The doors closed, and the elevator began moving downwards with J.R. and Helaina silently anticipating what they were about to see. The elevator traveled for about two minutes, an extremely long time for an elevator, but it was still going full speed and not slowing down.

"This has to be the longest elevator ride we have ever been on," remarked J.R.

"Are you forgetting the time when we got stuck on one two years ago with Cassie and Tina and how scared they got? We had to make up stories for them for two hours before they got that stupid thing fixed. The worst part was that we missed seeing *Fiddler on the Roof.*

"I remember."

"This ride takes exactly three minutes, so be patient," their grandfather told them.

The elevator began to slow down. William waved his hand, and the solid door of the elevator folded to the sides, revealing a glass door. Suddenly the talkative teens became speechless. They had a clear view of where they were being taken. They couldn't believe what was revealed. Still moving downward through a glass tube, they were headed for the ocean floor. They saw buildings, taller than those on the island. It was like an underground city, enclosed in glass from the bottom of the island to the bottom of the sea. Hope Island sat on top of the dome; a large, but beautiful blanket that camouflaged what was below. It reminded the kids of the *Oceanic One* but much bigger. They saw moving sidewalks and vehicles flying from building to building. They saw a park where people were eating their lunch. The trees and the plants were different from anything they had ever seen before. They saw a circular building made of glass that looked like a donut. Inside the outer ring was sea life of all kinds; the inner ring looked like some sort of laboratory. Everywhere they looked they viewed new things that were somehow familiar. Instinctively they felt secure, like they were meant to be at this place.

"I want you two to look over there."

William pointed in the direction he wanted the kids to look. They looked, and what they saw didn't surprise them or scare them. In fact, they smiled and looked up at William.

Together they spoke the all-important question. "Is that how our ancestors came to Earth?" they asked, looking at the large spaceship.

"Yes, it is."

164

You would think that finding out that your ancestors came from another planet would be cause for a lot of questions, but for J.R. Black and Helaina Unity, it answered them. They now understood, and they accepted who they were. They understood completely.

A noise came from Peanut's bag. Everyone looked down and saw wiggling.

"Helaina, I think that Peanut would like to come out and see where we are taking her," said William.

"I completely forgot about her. She always likes to explore new places."

Helaina unzipped the bag, picked up the leash, and pulled Peanut to her shoulder. The little animal attached herself to the shoulder strap of Helaina's tank top and looked around.

"This place is huge!" observed J.R.

"This is one of the smaller bases our people operate. But it was the first one completed."

"You mean there are others?"

"Do you remember I told you that ten families became the Guardians of our new home? And how now, each family has two Guardians born every generation?"

"Like you and Grandma Hanna, and Uncle David and Dad!" J.R. correctly answered.

"Right! Each family built a station like this. A few are hidden in mountain ranges; a few, like this one, are under islands. There are ten total. These stations are where we make discoveries about this planet, try to make adjustments, and try to make things better for everyone. The home our ancestors came from was called, "Unity;" and the city where they lived was called, Eden. We have made Earth our home for the last ten generations. You kids are the tenth generation to be born here."

"Eden is in a bible story, it's where Adam and Eve lived, they ate something, and it was wrong." Helaina recalled her mother reading her the story.

"Yes, the book your mother read that from was written by many people. These people were known by the first of our kind to come here…"

"Watchers!" injected J.R.

"Yes! Watchers who tried to teach and prepare these people for our coming. The watchers told stories, and some were told to predict what would happen if they didn't protect their home. Those who had heard these stories wrote them down, hoping that all who read them would learn."

"Unity was the beautiful garden planet, which was destroyed because of a black virus, just like the Eden in that book was destroyed by Adam and Eve because of sin."

"Correct."

"Granddad?"

"Yes, dear."

"Does that—"

Before Helaina could ask her question, the glass elevator came to a stop. Jennifer had called yesterday to prepare the Station for J.R. and Helaina's visit, so when the doors opened, they were greeted by several of the top scientists and a few department heads that ran this base of operation. There were a few special people who had traveled all night to be part of this special occasion. Everyone was there to welcome a new generation, the youngest yet, into their hidden world.

CHAPTER TWENTY-TWO
A SURPRISE WELCOMING

John Garfield and Selena Blanchard, the President and Vice President of operations, stood the closest to the elevator doors, ready to welcome the two future Guardians—that is if the kids decided that was to be their future. They were also there to retrieve the mysterious balls they possessed and put them into a secure area. John Garfield had boyish good looks that any actor would envy. He was tall, about six foot four, and toned from using the gym three hours every evening. John was a MIT graduate, had a mechanical engineering degree, doctorates in computer sciences, and was a physicist. He also happened to be Kellie's dad; Helaina recognized him right away. Selena Blanchard was a tall woman, just a quarter of an inch from being six feet tall, about one hundred forty-five pounds, with curly dark brown hair. Selena was a graduate of Memphis State University and held degrees in Education, Business, Zoology, Genealogy, and Physics. She also baked the best bread and cakes, beautifully decorated them and gave them out as gifts to friends and family. Selena did beautiful needlework that had won her countless ribbons at the annual Unity summer fair. Both kids recognized her as a family friend who they'd visited with many times at their grandparents home.

As soon as the doors opened, John and Selena stepped forward. First William and J.R. shook hands with John; Helaina gave him a hug instead. Selena Blanchard also preferred hugs as a way of greeting and proceeded to hug William and the kids. Many others stood nearby, some wearing lab coats, some in jeans and T-shirts, others in suits and dresses. All applauded when the family stepped out of the elevator, welcoming the newcomers, for this indeed was a very special occasion.

It was not every day that an elder educated a new generation of Guardians about their heritage.

"J.R., Helaina, welcome to Station One. We have so much to show you. Isn't this exciting? We've never had anyone as young as you down here." Selena, being the talkative type, welcomed them excitedly with a huge smile that made her whole face sparkle.

John Garfield looked intently at William, not sure if he should proceed as usual in this circumstance since J.R and Helaina were so young. William smiled and gave a nod, assuring him that he could make his presentation.

"Helaina, J.R., I also welcome you. I am sure you recognized Mrs. Blanchard and I. As you step into Station One for the first time, I am proud to be the one to present each of you with keys that work on any elevator or port of entry to this station, as well as the others positioned around this planet."

John Garfield handed J.R. and Helaina each a solid gold key ring. Engraved on the two-inch round gold piece was the Unity logo; around the edge were ten little diamonds, representing the ten original families and the ten stations. On the back of each was the motto that everyone lived by. "Guide with an open heart and an open mind. A World United in Peace."

It was such a big moment and a touching sight to see J.R. and Helaina welcomed into the community of Station One. It brought tears of joy to Selena and the women who were attending the momentous occasion. William, who was bursting with pride, even let a tear escape but wiped it away before anyone could see, but a few did. No one faulted him for this because he had the right to be touched by this moment. A photographer and a video artist were present taking pictures and video of the event that, later in the day, would be broadcasted to the other stations around the world.

Standing in the crowd, the kids saw some familiar faces. There stood J.R.'s parents, Charlie and Katie Black, and his grandmother, Hanna Unity Black. Beside them were Helaina parents, David and Joanna Unity, and Jennifer Unity stood close by. After receiving the gold keys, the crowd parted, and the two young people joined their families.

"You're all here." They said in unison.

"You think we would miss this big moment?" said David and Charlie in unison, making everyone laughed.

"Grandma, we thought you were volunteering at the hospital today," said Helaina.

"That my darling was a little fib; someone had to help pick up everyone at the airfield. I would never miss such a special occasion."

Joanna and Katie, with tears in their eyes, gave their children a hug and brought them each a present. New cell phones with GPS locators, after all, they needed to be able to find them, especially now that they believed them to be, "The Ones."

Peanut retreated into Helaina's purse to take a nap.

"Dad, we are going to stay with you. We all want to see the balls," said David Unity.

"Granddad told you about the balls?" asked J.R.

"Sure did, and all about your adventures; how brave, clever, sneaky, and secretive you both have been the last few days," said Charlie.

Two people in white lab coats, pushing what looked like a metal box with glass doors that was about six feet high and about four feet wide, were motioned forward by John Garfield.

John Garfield addressed his special guests, "We would like to study the balls you found. And we have built a special case to hold them."

William said, "Two must stay horizontal to each other, and two vertical to each other."

J.R. stepped forward, seemingly taking charge of this situation. "This white ball and the gold one Granddad has must stay vertical. Helaina and I found them in a hatch under the pier," J.R. explained simply.

He placed the bag containing the ball he was holding on a shelf in the middle of the cabinet. He took the bag holding the gold one that William was carrying and placed it next to the white one.

169

J.R. turned to his cousin, "Can you turn around, so I can get those two out of your backpack?"

"Sure, be careful!"

She turned around so J.R. could get the bags containing the two crystal cases from her backpack.

First, he took the top one and placed it on the top shelf of the cabinet; the second he put on the bottom shelf below the two balls he and William carried. Being confident with his new position, he gave the two scientists instructions. "My cousin dreamed that the balls glowed when all four were out of their bags. We don't know what that means, but we think they do something together. Please don't uncover all of them when they are together."

William, Hanna, David, and Charlie witnessed J.R. taking control of this exchange and they were proud of his assurance and confidence.

Helaina, being a little shy at having been the center of attention and being around so many people, finally found her voice. "I believe that the balls have some sort of power, but they can only work for J.R. and I. Before they do anything, we have to build J.R.'s machine, and the Story Chamber has to be part of it."

Helaina turned to her Dad and Uncle. "Dad, Granddad said we can keep the balls since we found them. They are so very beautiful. Can we go to the lab so we can show you? One at a time, of course?"

David said, "I don't see why not, and they are yours but its best they stay here for a while, just to be sure they can't harm you."

Everyone followed Selena Blanchard and John Garfield to the lab, which would become a temporary home for the four crystal cases and their precious cargo. Along the way, they took their time as Selena pointed out various buildings and explained what took place within each.

"Is that a big aquarium over there?"

Helaina was now with the family she loved and was comfortable enough to come out of her shell. The shell she put up around herself when new situations were thrust upon her, or when she was with people she didn't know. It was like she pulled away until she could assess the person or the situation. When she felt secure, she became her natural talkative self.

"That's more than an aquarium," Joanna Unity told her daughter. "That is one of my favorite places in the world. Marine Biologists, and Etiologists, those who study animal behavior, work together to learn about sea creatures. It's so much fun to sit in the center and watch as the marine life swim around you."

"Is there a zoo here?" J.R. wanted to know.

"No, not down here; we have the Nature Park on the island. I believe another station has a zoo where they are able to study animals," Katie Black acknowledged.

"Is this the place where the waterfall disappeared to?"

"No J.R., it didn't come here. We really don't know where it went. We have a few scientists working on it, but they haven't come up with a logical conclusion yet," explained John Garfield.

Helaina said something that made everyone come to a complete stop. "You're not going to find it, because it was a gift from those who gave us the pretty balls. It was meant just for us."

"How do you know?"

"I don't know! I just do. If you look at the pictures we took and all the copies that Granddad made, you will discover them blank. It is like we were privileged to be in a place that only existed for a short time." To make her point, Helaina pulled an envelope from her purse and handed it to her mother. "Those are the pictures J.R. printed of the waterfall from my camera. The images disappeared, and they disappeared from my memory card also."

"Helaina's right," Joanna said, as she quickly shuffled through the blank photos.

Noting that all the attention was on her, something Helaina hated, she decided to change the subject, "Let me guess, that building over their studies babies?"

"How did you come to that conclusion?" J.R. squinted his eyes as he looked at the building, thinking the building itself gave a hint about what was inside, but he couldn't see it.

"Because it looks like a baby bottle, butt head."

Everyone thought that was funny except J.R. so he hit his cousin on the shoulder.

"Don't call me names."

"Helaina don't call names, and J.R. stop hitting your cousin," Katie demanded.

"Well, is that where they study babies?" Helaina asked again, giving J.R. a dirty look.

"You're close, Princess," David used his pet name for her. "That building there is where geneticists work. They study genes and how different traits are inherited. It also has a cafeteria that serves the best spaghetti and meatballs I've ever had and an ice-cream bar. It's one of my favorite places to visit when I'm here."

They began walking again. The two men who pushed the cart with the balls had continued without them and disappeared into a building.

"Over there is a hand ball court and gym. Behind that building there are some apartments, swimming pools, and a small golf course. We also have a few stores and a movie theatre, because there are some people who prefer to live down here, but most live up on the island. And of course, there are some people who just come to visit," explained Hanna Black.

The family, along with Selena Blanchard and John Garfield, reached their destination. Before them were three very large and very long buildings that looked like airplane hangars. On either side of the hangers were two buildings made of steel and glass. A three-story high sky bridge went across the top, serving as a passage from one building to the other. The sky bridge looked like it was built right on top of the hangers, and you could see the elevators which came from the upper floor and traveled down into each of the large metal buildings.

"This is the largest building in Station one," John informed J.R. and Helaina.

"This is where mechanical engineers, electric engineers and computer engineers work together to build new and innovative machines. They also study things to see how they work like we will do with the balls you discovered."

"Wow! I think this is going to be my favorite place."

172

"Don't we all know that?" Helaina teased.

"Well! What are we waiting for? I can't wait to get in there to explore."

"Uncle Charlie, you might want to put a leash on him; want to use Peanut's?" Helaina said, making everyone in the group burst out laughing as they went into the main office.

CHAPTER TWENTY-THREE
MORE THAN JUST PRETTY CRYSTALS

The metal chest, containing the balls in their crystal cases, had been at the electronic science lab for half an hour before the Unity family finally made their way to the lab. A scientist was replacing one in the chest when the group approached him.

"Dr. Garfield, we haven't yet begun to analyze the balls. We have a problem."

"I know what the problem is; you can't open the crystal boxes."

"That's correct, Miss Unity, we can't. Do you have the solution?" the scientist asked Helaina.

"Yes, a dream story told me two nights ago. But I was afraid to try it."

"Would you like to show us?" asked William.

Helaina thought about this for a minute, wondering if it was safe. J.R. heard her, because she had let him in.

With Mind Speak he tried to reassure her, "If we only opened one at a time, and let the scientists take a few tests, it should be okay. We'll make sure that each is back in its case before they open the next. I think that will be a safe way; in fact, I know it will. Please trust me."

Helaina nodded her head in agreement. William, having heard the silent conversation, understood his granddaughter's hesitation. Whatever she had seen in that vision had scared her. William was very impressed with how J.R. reassured his cousin and how well they worked together.

Helaina took a deep breath before speaking as J.R. took the blue ball's crystal case from the containment chest. "In my dream, only J.R. and I can open the boxes and only one at a time."

"When you open the box may we take a few scrapings so that we can run a few tests?" asked the scientist, being respectful of their ownership.

Knowing his cousin's shyness around strangers, J.R. answered this question. "Of course, but please don't hurt them or change them in any way."

This statement was straight out of his cousin's mind. J.R. heard her tell him those words only seconds before.

Helaina gave him a silent, "Thank You."

"Do you have the test ready?" J.R. asked the scientist.

"Yes sir! I do."

"Ready Helaina?"

She answered with a soft, "Okay."

Helaina was uncomfortable around all these strangers; William and J.R. both sensed it. William saw his grand-daughter shiver slightly in fear and came up with an idea.

"Helaina I want you to look around the room, then tell me who you see."

The nervous girl looked around, then answered her Granddad.

"I see my family, I see Kellie's dad, and Grandma's friend Selena. And a whole lot of people in white coats looking at me, they're making me nervous."

"I know Princess. Can you tell me this, are there more family and friends in this room than there are strangers?"

Helaina counted each group of people then smiled. "There are more family and friends."

"Do we make you nervous?"

"No."

"I want you to pretend the scientists doing the test are Sophia, Mason, and Elijah, can you do that? Then show us how you open the crystal boxes, its safe here. I promise!"

"Okay, Granddad." She took a deep breath, looked at her mom and dad's smiling faces, realizing they were there for support and began.

"In my dream, only J.R. and I can open the boxes." Helaina faced her cousin.

"First, I extend my hands palms down over the box. J.R., you do the same except your palms are face up right under mine."

J.R. positioned himself across from Helaina with the box between them and did as he was told.

Helaina continued to instruct him on what to do, "Stay about six inches away from my hands. Look into my eyes and feel the power coming from the box. Do you feel it?"

J.R. nodded, feeling a tingling sensation throughout his body.

"Now when I shut my eyes, you do the same. Then without looking our hands come together slowly. Next we open our eyes, but we keep our hands together. The box will open for us when we turn our hands over while they are still together. Ready?"

J.R. nodded again. The room was silent, and everyone stood watching. When they opened their eyes, they instinctively looked down at the box, hands still together. From the middle of the blue ball, a tiny light began to grow and grow until it filled the box. Using Mind Speak, Helaina told her cousin not to move, and he told her not to be afraid, because he felt her hands trembling. The box became so bright that the blue ball inside couldn't be seen. The top lifted; the sides fell gently to the table, and the light disappeared back into the ball.

"That was mega cool!" J.R. said excitedly, being the first to break the eerie silence that hung over the room.

One of the scientists moved closer to the blue orb that was now sitting on the bottom portion of the open case. "May I take a closer look? Please!"

Everyone watched as scientists took cotton swabs and rubbed them gently on the blue ball, taking cell samples. They took the surface temperature of the ball, and of the box. They looked at the ball, and case under a magnifying glass and under a very large microscope, where they were able to take pictures of the cells. One scientist did a light scrapping of the case. For five minutes they worked fast and efficiently. They didn't want to take too much time with this specimen, but they did want to be meticulous and get all the information they could. When they finished, they stepped back from the ball.

"How do we close it?"

"Simple; we reverse the process."

As everyone watched, J.R. and Helaina put their hands together just as they had before. When they did this, the case began to close its walls. When the top was replaced, the crystal box turned into a bright lantern.

"J.R., now we pull our hands apart, slowly, while we shut our eyes."

They shut their eyes. When they opened them again, the light was gone, and the box was sealed tight.

"Thank you for letting us examine your precious jewel. Would you like to know what we already discovered?" asked the scientist who was overseeing the tests.

"You know something already?" They asked in unison.

Everyone was staring at the scientist, waiting to hear the results of the test.

"What you have in that box is a very rare, perfectly round, blue diamond. About 20,000 karats I would guess."

"That would make it worth about thirty million dollars," said David,

"No," said the scientist. "It's rare, and round, I would say more in the range of a hundred million dollars, maybe even priceless. I wouldn't know how they put a value on something like gems. You would need to let a geologist examine it. Let's examine the remaining three and see what we find, shall we?"

After the blue diamond was placed back in its place, the other three crystal cases where opened one at a time, examined, and placed back in the containment chest. When they finished, the family was given the news. The green ball turned out to be a giant round green emerald, the white a giant pearl, and the gold ball turned out to be just that, a perfectly round, one hundred percent solid gold ball. From the tests they performed, they discovered each was also equipped with an energy shield. The four jewels contained some kind of energy that radiated from within the jewels themselves. They would do more tests on the samples they took before they could give the Unity family a complete report.

"I think that the jewels should stay here for safe keeping, and we can see what they do after I build the machine," J.R. said, breaking the silence of the stunned adults.

"That's a very practical idea," William agreed.

"Granddad, you said that the jewels belong to J.R. and I. Does that change now that they are worth so much money?"

"Helaina, they have monetary value. That is quite obvious, but I have a feeling that they have more value than just that. I believe they hold some sort of power that will be revealed later. After we discover what it is, and they've served their purpose, you can do what you want with them."

"Just think, Dad, with those jewels we can feed all the hungry people in the world and build houses for all the homeless people. And still have enough for Helaina and I to get a sports car when we turn sixteen, maybe even a whole garage full," J.R. said, excited at the prospect.

"What about building shelters for all the animals and planting trees in the rain forest and cleaning up the air, and—"

"Those are all noble ideas, but we are getting ahead of ourselves. Be patient and one day the jewels will tell you their secrets; I'm sure of it," said the always practical Katie. "You two are very unique and generous teenagers. That is excluding the idea of a garage full of sports cars."

As the Unity family talked about the jewels and the power that they held, John Garfield was handed a few sheets of paper. He studied them for a while before saying anything.

"Mr. Black."

"Yes," said Charlie.

"I'm sorry. I'm addressing the young Mr. Black."

"Me?"

"Well of course, you are a Mr. Black after all." John smiled.

"Did I do something wrong?"

"No! Mr. J.R. Black, you did something amazing with the drawing of the machine you made. Can you come over here to the table? I will show you."

John went over to a table and pushed aside everything that was on it. He laid out the paper he had in his hand and began to explain. "Mr. Black, here is the drawing you made. Am I correct?"

J.R. just nodded his agreement.

"These four pictures here, take a close look at them," John Garfield said, pointing at the four pieces of paper he had laid at the top of the table.

J.R., David, Charlie, and William gathered around the table. The women were busy looking at the jewels and talking to the scientist about what kind of test they planned to do on them, and their crystal boxes. They were uninterested in the mechanical drawings.

J.R. was the first to see what John was trying to show them.

"Those are the arms to the machine; see they match the ones I drew."

It took William, David, and Charlie a few seconds, but they finally saw it.

"You're right! But they look like they are attached to different machines, and according to the text under each picture, each arm, and the machine it is attached to, are located in different stations."

"That is exactly what I want to show you. This one is in Antarctica; this one in the Caribbean; this one in China and this one here is in our very own basement."

J.R. was excited. "That means we don't have to build the machine from scratch."

"That's right!" said his Uncle David.

Always the organizer, Charlie started thinking out loud. "We just have to bring all the parts together. I will get the paperwork done and have the parts brought here."

"There's something else I need to show you." Everyone's eyes were now on John again, wondering what other discoveries this day might have?

"This is J.R.'s drawing; he did this without ever seeing the existing papers. In fact, these haven't been seen in over two hundred years. Lucky for us all, the old records are now in our organic computers."

"Well, are you going to show us or not," J.R. demanded.

179

John put the piece of computer paper on the desk. Four pairs of eyes looked at the same exact drawing that J.R. had produced with the same details.

"You sure there wasn't a mistake, and this is J.R.'s?" Charlie asked, wanting to make certain that somehow J.R.'s drawing didn't get produced twice.

"Positive, look at the date it was put into our computer. June 1920. It was then downloaded to the organic computer on May 2001. And it was in the classified files, which no one can get into without a security clearance."

"You mean I drew something very old that was forgotten?"

"That's exactly right."

All J.R. could say was, "Mega Cool."

A box filled with old gears, wires and computer chips, and other cast-off things, caught J.R.'s eye so he went to investigate, losing all interest in the papers on the table. There were just too many new things around, and J.R.'s mind was racing from one thing to another trying to absorb everything.

"Dad, can I have this box of junk please?"

"What do you want to do with that stuff?"

"I want to see if I can use them on my motorcycle."

Now this part of the conversation Katie heard, and she wasn't too happy about it.

"William did you give J.R. a motorcycle?" she yelled, really upset about the idea of her young son driving such a vehicle. "You know how I feel about them."

"William, how dare you do that without asking Katie?" his sister Hanna scolded him.

"Wait ladies, I didn't give it to him, he found it."

"That doesn't change things; he is too young to drive that thing," said Joanna, J.R.'s aunt.

"Ladies, stop ganging up on Dad." David stepped in before the ladies attacked William.

"Mom, I have to fix it up before I can ride it."

"We will talk about that when it happens, young man," said his mother.

Helaina thought it was funny that everyone was ganging up on William and J.R. about the motorcycle, something that was still in a million pieces on the garage floor. Knowing her cousin, he will have it put together and running in a week, if that long, Helaina laughed to herself.

An hour later everyone in the family, except William, J.R., and Helaina, and little Peanut went back up to the island, to prepare the celebratory barbeque for that evening. William wanted to show the kids a few more things, before they returned home.

CHAPTER TWENTY-FOUR
VALUABLE DISCOVERIES

Looking at his watch, J.R. noticed that it was almost eleven thirty. He was thirsty as well as a bit hungry.

Selena noticed the unusual watch, and the strange meter on top. She asked, "Mr. Black—"

"Just call me J.R.," he insisted.

"Is that the watch your Grandma Hanna told me about?"

"I made two, one for Grandma for Christmas and one for me; I had leftover parts."

"Can you point it at Dr. Garfield; I want to see what the meter tells us about his "energy" as you call it."

J.R. held the watch up to Dr. John Garfield. Based on what Hanna Black had told her, the meter should read between seventy-five and eighty percent because she already knew what his gene makeup was. She looked; it accurately measured John's heritage. She wanted another test so she chose the two scientists and herself to test it on.

"Can you point it at Dr. Green and tell me what it says, please?"

"It says that she is fifty percent."

"What about Dr. Rains?"

"It says he is eighty-seven percent."

"And me?"

J.R. looked again, "Ninety percent, is that right?"

"That is one hundred percent right. I was wondering, could we have one of our mechanical engineers and one of our geneticists take a look at that watch? You can go have some lunch at our special cafeteria and get the rest of the tour while we see how this thing ticks. I promise to get it back to you before you go back home."

J.R. saw the opportunity for a tradeoff. "I will let you, if I can have that box of spare parts over there?

"Selena, it looks like we a savvy businessman in our midst," laughed John.

"I think so, and one who gets the better end of the deal. I think we could give him the box; I will even throw in a few things we have no use for. What do you think of that deal, Mr. Black?"

"Sounds good to me. After lunch, can I come back here and see what other things you are working on?"

"But I want to go to the aquarium," Helaina demanded.

"You each can go explore any area you want after lunch." William stepped in putting an end to that argument before it went too far.

J.R. handed the watch to Dr. Green and went to get the box.

"Why don't you leave that here for now? We will be back later to pick it up. Let's go get some lunch!" advised William.

J.R. reluctantly left his box of treasures and followed Helaina and William to the cafeteria to get some lunch. They were expecting a place that looked like the cafeterias in the private schools they attended, with folding tables and chairs, and a long counter of food to choose from, but this was truly unexpected. They were met by a hostess who led them to William's private table already set with utensils, glasses, a basket of bread and crackers, and bread sticks, accompanied by a dish of two kinds of pesto, humus, and butter. The chairs were pulled out for them and napkins placed in their laps. Before leaving, she introduced the waiter and took their drink orders. In the center of the table was a bowl of fresh flowers.

"How can they take our order when we don't have a menu? I thought you said we were going to the cafeteria. This is a fancy restaurant; it doesn't even have a buffet table," said Helaina.

"This does look like a fancy restaurant!" Agreed J.R.

"In a restaurant you have to order from what's on a menu. In a cafeteria you can get what you like and as much as you like. Here, you can order anything, and they will make it for you," William explained.

"I can have all my favorites?"

"If that is what you want. Try it! Here comes our waiter with our drinks."

"Sir, are you ready to order?" the young waiter asked and patiently waited.

"I think we are."

"Miss Unity, what would you like?" Waiters always took the ladies order first.

"I think I would love a big plate of peeled shrimp with tartar sauce and cocktail sauce, boiled of course, two big artichokes with lots of mayo on the side, and onion rings. For dessert, I would like strawberry shortcake."

"Very good choices, Miss Unity. Mr. Black, have you decided?"

"How did you know our names?"

"Because, Mr. Black, today is yours and Ms. Unity's special day; everyone knows of your visit. May I take your order sir?"

"I would like two big quesadillas with salsa on the side and sour cream. Also, I would like a big plate of nachos with lots of jalapeños. For dessert, chocolate pudding pie with whipped cream."

"Very good, sir, and, Mr. William, what would you like?"

"I think I will have a mixed salad, baked salmon, and asparagus with parmesan cheese sauce, with apple pie and vanilla ice-cream for dessert."

"Very good, sir. I shall return shortly with your order."

When the waiter left with their orders, J.R. pointed out, "Did you hear what the waiter said? We are famous! This is the coolest of all places. Can I go explore the machine shops to see what they are building?"

"Sure, you can, but not alone, I will go with you."

"But, Granddad, I promise I won't—"

Before J.R. could finish arguing he was interrupted. "I know! But this first time, I think it's best that someone is with you to show you around. It's for your safety, not because we don't trust you."

William felt he needed to put that last part in, because like it or not, the boy was going to have a watcher with him until he became of age. Just ten minutes after placing their order, the meal arrived, and it was everything they wanted. Just like on their birthday when their moms made their favorite meals for dinner. Peanut smelled the sweet aroma of the bacon wrapped around the asparagus that William ordered and came out to get some lunch herself. The kids ate so much that William wondered if they would be able to continue the sightseeing tour. But he needn't worry, because both J.R. and Helaina were fueling up and getting ready to conquer this new world. While eating dessert, William called and arranged for a marine biologist to come and escort Helaina to the donut-shaped aquarium.

Dr. Marlo Turner met the group outside the cafeteria. Marlo was a little above four feet tall; she was one of the youngest junior scientists at Station One. She was twenty-three and already had a doctorate in marine biology. She was presently studying geology. Also waiting for the family was Dr. Blanchard; both women had a surprise for the two new Guardians in training.

Dr. Marlo Turner greeted them, "Mr. Black, Miss Unity, it is nice to meet you. Mr. William, it is very good to see you again. I presume the little sugar glider on Miss Unity's shoulder is Ms. Peanut. I heard all about her from my new cousins, Dylan and Emma."

"It's nice to see you also. My wife tells me you will be getting married soon. Congratulations." William gave her a hug, having known the young Dr. Turner since the day she was born."

"Thank you very much, William. Your grandchildren are beautiful. I hear they are very intelligent and talented, more than those that preceded them."

"That's true, my dear, I see you two ladies brought the air cars. I think these two would love a bird's eye view of Station One."

"We thought the same way."

"Helaina, you travel with Dr. Turner here. She will take you to the aquarium and return you to the electron science lab around four. I bet you girls find that you have a lot in common, so you have fun."

"We will, thanks, Granddad."

Helaina jumped into the passenger seat of the air car, and Dr. Turner took the controls. Everyone noticed that J.R. was already strapped into the air car before anyone could invite him, excited to be riding in something he had only read about in comic books or seen in science fiction movies.

"You look so young to be a marine biologist." Helaina told her new companion, trying to shake away her nervousness.

"Thank you, on my next birthday I will be twenty-four," said Marlo.

"First let's buzz the park; then we will make circles around the different buildings before we head for the aquarium. Maybe you can help with something we are having a bit of trouble with."

"Really that would be cool."

"Look! See the guy in the red shirt and jeans with the ice-cream cone?"

"He's cute; is he your boyfriend?" Helaina asked.

"Yep, I think he is quite handsome. See those trees in the park?"

"I have never seen trees with red trunks and white leaves. Is that an experiment?"

"It used to be a long time ago," laughed Marlo. "The doctors who work with genes had a warehouse full of gene samples taken from the planet of Unity and started experimenting with plant material. That was supposed to be a fruit tree of some sort, but no fruit has ever been produced from it."

"It would be cool to eat the fruit our ancestors ate when they lived on Unity."

"I agree. I just love trying new fruits and vegetables. Two weeks ago, one of the botanists produced a fruit that stunk up his whole office after he cut into it. It was really funny. No one could work there until the smell disappeared."

"Can we fly over to the ship; I would love to take a closer look."

"Sure, that's not a problem!"

As they approached the ship, they noticed that J.R. and William had arrived before them. The air cars looked like specks of dust next to the large space craft. J.R. and Helaina were close enough to use Mind Speak.

"You beat me here."

"You probably figured I would want to come see this first. But unfortunately, they won't let us go inside."

"They are probably afraid you would get the thing working and fly off with it," said his cousin.

"That crossed my mind. Wouldn't it be cool to be in it, traveling through space?"

"We might do that, I think."

"Another dream?"

"Yep, but different, and we travel through space, but not for a while, maybe next year. We have to do something first."

"You can tell me later. I am going to see if they will let me fly this air car."

"Bet you they won't."

"No bet! I owe you money for the video game tournament; I still say you cheated. Oh! Have fun with the fish. They have a giant star fish on the city wall. Have you seen it yet?" J.R. asked, trying to divert his cousin's attention from the money he owed her.

"No, but we are headed that way now. Don't blow up anything."

The two vehicles separated, one taking J.R., William, and Dr. Selena Blanchard to the mechanics shops, and the second taking Helaina, Peanut, and Dr. Marlo Turner to the aquarium.

Helaina wondered what kind of adventures awaited them today as she waved good-bye to J.R. and her grandfather.

It didn't take long before she found out.

CHAPTER TWENTY-FIVE
THE HOKEY POKEY

As Marlo Turner turned the air car in the direction of the aquarium, Helaina turned to her and asked to see her sugar glider.

"Your Granddad did mention that you could communicate with animals, but how did you know I had mine with me? He has been a sleepyhead all day."

"I know because you snapped your jacket pocket shut and he can't open it. See?"

Helaina was laughing at the little sugar glider who had only just managed to get his little head through the opening and was now stuck. Marlo looked down and saw that her pet was in distress; she quickly unsnapped the jacket pocket. Then her friend climbed up her arm. Marlo's pet began chattering quite loudly which attracted Peanut's attention. Helaina and Marlo laughed at the antics of their two little companions.

"Why did my Granddad tell you about me communicating with animals? Did he tell everyone? I don't want everyone to think I'm weird or something!

"He didn't tell everyone, just me. We have that in common; and if you are weird then so am I."

"Can you hear them in your head?"

"They communicate with you using their minds. That is different than what I can do. I can feel their emotions; right now, I feel that our two little sweethearts like each other very much." This made both young ladies giggle.

"What is his name?" Helaina asked Marlo.

"Why don't you ask him?"

"May I hold him?"

As Helaina said this, she held out her hand and Marlo's little black sugar glider jumped to her. She rubbed his soft fur with an extended finger as he and Peanut got acquainted with each other.

"His name is Shadow, and he likes my Peanut and thinks she is beautiful."

"That's right, I am impressed. Did he really tell you his name?"

"Not actually. When I touched him, I saw a shadow. I figured out that must be his name. And it is obvious that he likes my little Peanut."

"That's very impressive."

Just then their air car approached the aquarium. Before parking the vehicle, Marlo flew over the top and around the facility to give Helaina a look at the outside of the glass donut. The place was massive. From the outside you could watch the sea life swimming and playing. Inside the tank there was also coral and plant life as well as a sunken boat, massive rocks, and caves in which the inhabitants could find shelter. Helaina was able to look down from the top and see divers hand feeding fish, sharks, and a baby whale. It was absolutely mind blowing! Fantastic!

"How big is this place?" Helaina questioned.

"It's three miles in diameter. It's the biggest aquarium in the world. It is a small ocean inside an underwater city which is an amazing engineering accomplishment; it took us five years to build. It was finished in the year 2000."

"Is this..."

Before Helaina could finish her question, she saw something that looked like it was connected to the outside of the underwater city's dome that left her speechless for a moment. It was about two miles away but big enough that she could see. She pointed it out to Marlo.

"Dr. Turner."

"Please call me Marlo; may I call you Helaina? You look much too young to be called, Miss Unity."

"Sounds good to me! What is that over there? It looks like it is stuck to the outside of the city."

"That is the little problem I was hoping you could help us with."

189

"It doesn't look small."

"No, in fact it is the largest starfish on record that we know about. She came about a week ago for a visit and attached herself close to the aquarium on the outside wall."

"Did you feel that she wanted something?"

"When I get close, I feel she is sad and scared. That's about all; she won't let us get near her. I was thinking that maybe you could help find out what her situation is."

"I can't do that unless I get close to her."

"I was kind of hoping that if we got you close enough, maybe she would tell you or show you what she wants."

"I don't know. We can see if it works. Is there a way I can swim outside?"

"Let's park and go inside, then see what happens. If it doesn't work, I will have to call your Granddad to see if we can take you outside. We don't want to put you in danger."

Marlo Turner parked the air car at the closest entrance to the giant starfish. Getting out of the air car the two young ladies pulled the sugar gliders by their leashes, placing them back into their pocket carriers. This was done with much protest from the animals. Taking the outer path, the two young women walked around the aquarium and past the sea creatures that made their home in the aquarium. They entered the building and took a glass elevator to the fourth floor; from there they went through another glass door to the outside of the building. Here, Helaina and Marlo came face to face with the starfish underbelly as seen from the inside of the dome. The starfish was large, measuring twenty feet wide, starting from the tip of one tentacle to the tip of another on the opposite side of its huge body. A few people with clip boards were standing close by, taking notes about the giant starfish's behavior and its characteristics.

"She's amazing!" Helaina was mesmerized at the sight before her.

"That she is! We think she is one of a kind. She hasn't caused us any problems, so far. We would like to know why she is here; can you help?"

"I'll try!" Helaina told Marlo.

Helaina walked up to touch the thick glass wall of the dome, it felt cool to her fingers when she reached up to get closer to one of the massive tentacles. As she did the starfish moved down; it looked like she was reaching out to Helaina. Helaina stared at the animal's underbody, not exactly knowing where its eyes were for a few minutes. Those around her didn't move or make a sound. She let out a long sigh and put her hand down.

"I feel her sadness; she does want something I saw brief flashes I didn't understand. If I could get outside the wall to touch her, I know the two of us could connect. Then she could tell me why she is here."

"I don't know. It could be too dangerous."

"She won't hurt me," Helaina assured her new friend.

"I've been told you are quite the accomplished diver. But still, let's call your grandfather he will make the decision. Call him and explain to him what you want to do and let me speak with him."

Helaina got out her cell phone. When the bag opened, Peanut tried to get out. Unfortunately for her, she wasn't fast enough. Helaina gently pulled her back into her pouch and zipped it closed. Then she called her grandfather and did as Marlo instructed her.

"William, this is Marlo, what do you think of this plan?"

"I think our new friend out there needs something, and the only person who can find that out is Helaina."

"Yes, I agree."

"She has the diving skills, and I believe she will be safe. Helaina instinctively knows when an animal is out to harm someone or something."

"Then you approve?"

"Yes, on a few conditions. Helaina must be protected at all costs. Do you understand that?"

"Yes, William!"

"I want you to go with her, and I want you to take two other divers with tranquilizer guns."

"That is a given; I had that in mind also."

"Take care of our girl and yourself. Call me the second you get back into the dome."

"We will; and thank you, William."

"Good luck!" William and Marlo disconnected.

"Well, it looks like we are going for a little swim," Marlo told Helaina.

"Cool! How will we get outside?"

"There are several ways, but we will take the acquisition tunnel."

Dr. Marlo Turner made a call down to the tunnel personnel to have them prepare the equipment they would need and to get two companion divers suited up with prepared tranquilizer guns.

"That's not necessary; she won't hurt us!" insisted Helaina.

Marlo bent closer and whispered to the young girl, "We know that, and she knows that. We have to convince everyone else; especially your granddad and family. They will worry if we don't take along a little protection. Let's just humor them. Okay?"

"Okay!"

Using one of many elevators, it didn't take them long to get to the lowest level, and they took a rail tram to the acquisition tunnel. The acquisition tunnel was used to launch transport subs to the surface; it was one of the tunnels used to bring in supplies for Station One. It was also used to get outside when it was necessary to make repairs to the outer wall or to acquire the occasional sea creature that traveled by needing first aid.

With help from the personnel who worked the tunnel, it took no time at all to get dressed in the wet suits, check their equipment and helmet radios, and dive into the cool water. Dr. Marlo Turner's dive suit had been made specially for her very small body. Being of small stature, the young Asian woman had to wear equipment made for children; even her size two swim flippers were custom made to fit her small feet.

The four swimmers moved upward. The two young women swam ahead of the two bodyguards who were equipped with helmet cams to take video of this event. The starfish was four stories above them, so every twenty feet they had to stop to adjust to the water pressure. Finally, they arrived at their destination.

"Helaina, are you ready?" radioed Marlo.

"Sure am! Look she wants to meet us."

The giant starfish disconnected herself from the dome and slowly made her way towards the group of divers. Not sure about the two with the underwater tranquilizer guns, she didn't get to close. Just close enough to see who had come for a visit.

"Can those two stay back? They are scaring her."

Marlo motioned the two other divers to turn on their radios.

"Can everyone hear me?" she asked.

"Roger that," three voices responded.

"Good. Guys, you two stay back. You are scaring our friend here."

"Understood!" replied the two divers. Because of the species nature, the two support divers really didn't believe that a giant starfish was a serious threat.

"Helaina this is what we will do. Let her approach us. I am staying here with you; maybe I can make contact with her also. We will work as a team."

Just then the giant starfish reached out one of her tentacles and tapped Marlo Turner on the shoulder. Having recognized the young woman's voice vibrations, she was comfortable enough to come closer and say hello. This act made everyone laugh, making everyone more relaxed around the very large creature. Without a word, Helaina swam confidently up to the creature, took off her swim gloves, which were way too thick to feel the rough exterior of the creature's skin, and placed her hands out. Reaching out, palms down, she waited for the starfish to respond. It didn't take long. Ever so gently, the giant starfish reached for Helaina. At the same time, she allowed Marlo to rub the underside of one of her tentacles.

"She is sad," Marlo confirmed.

"Just a little, but we can fix that."

"How?"

Helaina rubbed her fingers on the starfish, concentrating and connecting with the giant sea creature's nervous system.

"She has a friend who was sick. A dolphin. He came to you for help, and you took him in."

"That's right. One came to us about three weeks ago."

"She misses her friend, and she wants to know if he is doing better?"

"Tell her, or show her. He is doing great, and we plan on releasing him in a day or so."

As they spoke, Marlo took her hands off the starfish.

"Marlo, put your hands back on her, can you feel that?"

"Yes, I do; she is excited."

"She wants to know if it is alright if she stays here so she can wait for her friend."

"Can I try to answer her?"

"Sure, just look at her. Feel her with your hands and your heart and speak with your mind; picture releasing the dolphin."

Marlo followed Helaina's instructions. She felt the connection before she said the words in her head. "You are welcome to stay."

She then perceived a very faint, "Thank you."

"Helaina, did you catch that?"

"Yes, of course.

"That's the first time that has happened to me; it's amazing."

"Pretty cool isn't it?"

"Did she just say the word *play*?" Marlo asked, trying to listen for more.

"Yes, she showed me that she has no one to play with; she wants us to play."

"Helaina, how do you play with a giant starfish?" said a curious Marlo.

Thinking for a few minutes Helaina came up with an idea. "Animals like following one another, don't they?"

"Yes."

"We play a follow me game. It's just that simple."

"And what game would that be? We only have thirty more minutes of air left."

"The Hokey Pokey of course. I will picture in my mind that I want her to follow my actions. Come on; this will be fun."

Helaina and Marlo swam back a few yards so their new friend could see them and follow along. Helaina started singing the words and moving along as she sang. Amazingly, so did their giant friend.

"You put your right hand in, you put your right hand out, then you shake it all around, you do the Hokey Pokey…"

The giant starfish moved one of its arms just as the two young women did, even shaking it and then spinning its body around like they did. Then, repeating the action again, with another arm. What a sight that was! Two women playing a child's game with a giant starfish. Luckily it was all caught on the video recorders the two other divers attached to their helmets. Otherwise, no one would have believed them if they hadn't recorded the whole event.

Helaina and Marlo played with their friend for about twenty minutes before they had to say goodbye. Marlo promised to come out the next day to keep her company for a bit. Of course, not being as skilled as Helaina in communicating so much information, she let the girl have the privileged.

"She said thank you and is glad she will have her friend back soon. She would love for you to come see her again."

Marlo reached out one last time. "No, my big friend, thank you. Good-bye."

"She understood you," Helaina assured Marlo.

The starfish attached herself back on to the wall of Station One and took a nap. The group of divers made their way back down to the acquisition tunnel. When they broke through the water, they were welcomed back by a round of applause for the two underwater dancers. When the two dancers got up on their feet they bowed to their audience, thanking them for their show of appreciation. Marlo gave Helaina a big hug as a way of saying thank you. It took a few minutes before Helaina remembered she had promised to call her Granddad. Excited about her new friend, she spent the next ten minutes telling him all about the starfish and what fun it was to play "The Hokey Pokey" with her. She told William that soon the veterinarians would have her dolphin friend well enough to release. That all she wanted was just to have her friend back. Sometimes that is all it takes to make someone, or something, happy. Just one very true friend.

Soon it was time to return Helaina to William and her cousin. On the ride back to the science and computer engineering building, Helaina, who now counted Marlo Turner as a friend, began her onslaught of questions.

"I've been thinking about the Unity logo and its colors. Does the blue represents those from above and the green those from below?"

"That's correct," Marlo assured her.

"Are we the ones from below, because our ancestors built places like this?"

"No! Even though the original settlers from Unity are gone now, and only their genes live on within us, we are the ones from above. From a place above Earth. Those whose ancestors were here, on this planet, are those from below."

"That makes sense; I guess I had it backwards."

"I did too for a while. That's why our elders teach us about our heritage with short lessons so as not to overwhelm us."

"I guess they know better."

"Yes, they do. Be patient; the knowledge will come."

"Do you come up to the island?"

"Sure, I do. They don't keep us prisoner here, silly."

"When you do, maybe we can go shopping or something."

"I would like that, Helaina. Maybe we can even get my husband-to-be to take us to the movies; I'm dying to see that new one about aliens."

"That's so funny."

They were laughing when they arrived at their destination. Marlo and Helaina exchanged cell numbers. Marlo, wanting to get back to the aquarium and back to work, left Helaina with a friend who escorted her to where she would find her cousin and granddad. After all, Marlo wanted to make sure a certain dolphin knew his friend was waiting for him and had missed him. She also thought that this would be a great opportunity to practice her new skill. A hidden talent she'd possessed but didn't know how to let come to the surface, until now. Thanks to

Helaina Unity. She'd just needed a little confidence and a little coaxing to release her inner talent, just like we all do.

CHAPTER TWENTY-SIX
WHAT'S WITH THAT WATCH?

While Helaina was with Dr. Marlo Turner, J.R. and William explored the mechanical and electric engineering facilities with Dr. John Garfield. While J.R. was watching an experiment, John got a phone call. After his conversation, he took William aside to talk so J.R. wouldn't hear.

"William, that was one of our researchers in the archives. Working from J.R.'s elaborately detailed drawing, she was able to find out more information. The machines arms, the Story Chamber, and the jeweled balls all came from Unity. The story goes like this, the jewels were brought here on the main ship which, as you know, is here. The machine was dismantled and brought here on separate ships. Together they were said to contain certain powers that our ancestors believed should be hidden until a time when the right ones would be able to solve the puzzle. When they arrived, the four arms of the machine were taken to their present locations, and the jeweled balls were hidden. The rest of the parts needed to rebuild the machine are right here in our storage facility."

"So, what you are saying is that those jeweled balls were waiting for J.R. and Helaina to find them?" William summarized.

"That's what I believe. How many ships were there? Ten. How many families agreed to keep their genes as pure as possible? Ten. How many secret communities are hidden? Ten. Now, for the big question, William how many generations have been born on this planet that we now call home?" John waited for William to answer.

"J.R. and Helaina are the tenth generation. Yes! I now understand. Do you believe that these two grandkids of mine could possibly have the gene that is pure? I didn't believe that could be possible any longer."

"I believe so, according to the researcher, 'The jeweled balls would only be revealed to the pure of heart, the pure of Unity.'"

"Do we have a pure DNA sample from each of the ten original families?"

"Yes, we do. What are you thinking, William?"

"I'm thinking that we should compare J.R. and Helaina's DNA to those samples of our ancestors. I want you to very discreetly take a sample from each of the kids before we leave today."

"I think we can do that. What will we tell J.R. and Helaina?"

"Nothing for now."

"I think that's wise. They are still very young. Besides, they are dealing with a lot of changes and new idea's right now. There is plenty of time to tell them later."

Just then J.R. approached the two men. "Granddad, can we go back to get that box of stuff? And I want to see if they figured out my watch. I bet they haven't figured out what makes it work."

"I bet you that they have, after all they are very smart scientists, what do you want to bet?"

"I bet you that if they figured it out, I will do one of your chores. If they didn't, you have to do one of mine?"

"I don't know. What chores are you thinking of?"

J.R. thought about this. "I will mow the lawn, and you do the dinner dishes for a week."

"What do you think, John; does that sound like a good deal to you?"

"I know I would take that bet. I hate mowing the lawn."

"Okay. Deal!" William and J.R. shook hands, since they were gentlemen gamblers.

During the tour, they traveled quit a distance from the lab they visited that morning. J.R. insisted on seeing every new machine they worked on. Every gadget he hadn't seen before had to be investigated, examined, and asked about. J.R. could not contain his excitement when they went to the robotics lab. When he came upon a robotic arm that was not correctly performing its task, he asked if he could take a look at it. With a little hesitation from the engineer, J.R. took over the controls and within seconds, diagnosed the problem. He showed the engineer why the connecting wires needed to be of a higher gauge and what circuit board wasn't getting the commands. J.R. even made the repairs to the circuit board himself, telling the engineer that they really should build a new one. After the repairs were made, the robotic arm performed flawlessly. The embarrassed engineer was stunned that a fifteen-year-old had figured out a problem he had been working on for a week. A few of his fellow engineers watched the young man solve the problem. They teased him relentlessly and let him know it would take a long time before they let him forget it.

On the way back to where they began, J.R. drove the air car they used to travel between the different parts of the complex. Well drive isn't really the right word, for all anyone had to do was to sit in the golf cart style vehicle, tell the computer their destination, and it would take them on to their next stop automatically. It was one of the inventions J.R. was most impressed with. He sat in the driver's seat that had the usual steering wheel, brake, and accelerator just in case something happened and an actual driver was needed. Since it would take about ten minutes to return to the lab, J.R. thought that it was a great time to ask a few questions of the two men in the back seat.

"Granddad, we have been diving around the island for years. How come we didn't see this place before?"

"Remember all those Star Trek episodes you watched, when a Star Ship didn't want to be seen, what did it do?" asked William.

"It cloaked itself, making it invisible."

"That's correct. Did you know one of the writers on that show happened to be one of our people?"

"Really? We can really hide here, and no one could find us, not even with radar? But why did he give away a secret?"

"Yes, outsiders can't find this place, or the nine others hidden around the world. And no, he didn't disclose a secret. By writing that into a script for television, millions and millions of people watched. In a subtle way, they learned about advanced technology we are capable of bringing to them, getting them used to the idea that something like that might exist one day."

This is where John Garfield took over. John loved history, especially their history, and there was nothing he liked better then sharing it with young people. His daughter, Kellie, was like him and had developed the love of words, written or spoken. It prompted her to write marvelous stories.

"You see, J.R., when our ancestors came, the people here needed to be educated slowly with knowledge that would benefit all. They were like babies and needed to learn by taking one step at a time."

"Are you trying to say that if our ancestors gave them too much information too fast, they would short circuit like a computer that's overloaded?" asked J.R.

"William, I do believe this young man is a genius."

"I know I am a genius, but I still got a D in English, and a C- in History."

"We all can't be good at everything! Look, we are here already. Let's go see who won our bet."

***

As they walked into the lab, William got a call from Helaina. He didn't say much, listening to her tell the story. Helaina was much too excited to give her grandfather time to say anything. He talked with Dr. Turner for a minute before he hung up the cell phone.

"Looks like your cousin went on a little adventure."

"Yeah, it figures. I figured she couldn't help but go out and help that poor sad giant starfish. She does have a talent with creatures big and small."

"Yep, she will tell us about it later, now let's go see who won; sure, you don't want to back out?"

"No way!"

Dr. Selena Blanchard, one mechanical engineer and one electric engineer had been studying and testing J.R.'s watch for the last two hours. They were ready to tell J.R. and William what they had learned about the seemingly innocent looking watch.

"Dr. Blanchard have you figured out that watch yet?" J.R asked as he entered the lab."

"Yes, and no." Pointing to the man at the table, "Adam here noticed that the wire and components used came from the normal everyday watch, except for this gauge here." Selena began the explanation.

"The gauge is made up of a new combination of metals we have been experimenting with that eventually will make automobiles stronger. This little sample here had too much zinc and titanium so it wasn't effective," Adam explained, taking over from Selena.

"But it did have practical uses in smaller devises like diving gauges," the other engineer explained.

"That's where I got it, Granddad. Dad had some broken gauges; he said I could have them," J.R. informed the group.

"Then that solves the mystery of how you got a hold of that material," said Selena. "J.R. did you prick your finger or cut yourself when you made the watches?"

"Yeah! But it didn't hurt."

"I'm sure it didn't, but look, right here!" Selena pointed to a little brown spot on the gauge.

Everyone took turns looking through her magnifying glass to see what she was trying to show them. She continued, "That is a tiny drop of your blood; your blood contains your DNA and reacted with the metal and its compound."

"And that is why your watch can tell who has our genetic background, and it's very accurate," explained Selena.

"Well, J.R., I guess you are going to have to mow the lawn this week."

"Yeah great!" J.R. didn't sound very happy about adding another chore to his already full list. "I didn't even know how it worked or what that gauge did anyway. I thought it told me who had a lot of energy and who didn't."

"This little gadget will come in handy, knowing who has our special gene and who doesn't, it will make tracking the family trees a lot easier," Selena pointed out.

"I have all the information I need to duplicate the watch, all except Mr. Black's unique blood. Would you mind if we took a little to build more watches like this one?" Adam asked.

J.R. looked horrified with that idea. But before he could protest, Selena Blanchard made a different suggestion, one that didn't involve needles. "I don't think we need to take any blood. How about if we just give you a little haircut? Your DNA is also in your hair.'

"I guess that would be okay," J.R. replied. "I like that idea better than taking my blood."

"I thought you would."

As Selena pulled a few samples of hair from his head and took a swab from the inside of J.R.'s cheek, William reminded John about the other test he wanted done. William began to think that J.R. did have a pure gene in his DNA. How else could that device react as it did? J.R. was bored with the watch discussion, he now turned his attention to something else. The box of miscellaneous parts he had his eye on. While at lunch, and on his tour, the people working in the lab had added more unwanted gauges, wires, fuses and a few unsuccessful little projects that they had worked on. His mind was going full speed on how he could use some of those things on his motorcycle. Then he thought of the project that he was most interested in.

"When can we build the machine for the jeweled balls? We can build it, can't we?"

"Yes, you can build it. I think you and Helaina were meant to build that machine," William told J.R.

"It's going to take a while to get the arms here. We have to locate all the parts. We also have to get a team organized to help you rebuild it," John told J.R.

"How did I know I was supposed to draw it? And how did Helaina know where to find the jeweled balls? No one told us anything! We just did it on our own."

"That we don't know."

"Guess we are going to have to figure that out too," J.R. said matter-of-factly.

"Yep! But not today. So, don't go worrying about it."

"Mr. Black, I have something for you. We found a bunch of tools we no longer use; we would be pleased if you would take them as a gift from us," said Adam, the young engineer who was standing next to him holding the rather large box. He now presented J.R. with a toolbox stuffed full of tools, some that were very unusual looking.

"Thank you, thank you so much! These are so cool."

One hour later, after going over the detailed sketch of the machine and discussing what would be needed to build it and where it would be safe to do so, J.R. and William left the lab loaded down with his new tools, and a big heavy box of unwanted junk. They caught up with Helaina in the snack room where they enjoyed some iced tea and cookies before they got back on the elevator to the island.

Before they returned home, Dr. Selena Blanchard and Dr. John Garfield joined them; they too needed a little break. When Helaina excused herself to use the restroom, she left her purse on the seat next to Selena. Selena took the opportunity to reach inside and find Helaina's hair bush from which she pulled a good sample of hair before the girl returned. But not before Peanut, whom she had disturbed, bit her fingers several times. Having obtained Helaina's DNA, they said their good-byes, and returned to the lab.

On the long elevator ride back up to the surface, J.R. and Helaina told each other about the things they did that afternoon. Before they arrived back on the island, William reminded them that they weren't to tell their friends about the things they saw or what was under the island.

"We understand!" they said in unison and continued telling their stories like keeping secrets was just a normal part of their lives. Of course, it was. Keeping secrets would be a lifelong chore for Helaina Unity and J.R. Black; and they were just beginning to realize this.

CHAPTER TWENTY-SEVEN
BEACH PARTY

William and the two teens arrived back at the house around six-thirty where they were greeted by their brother and sisters, cousins, parents, and grandparents. Everyone was outside enjoying the warm summer afternoon, cooling off in the pool or in the recreation room playing games. Those who had made the journey down to Station One that day acted like nothing extraordinary had occurred. With the sun setting, turning the sky into a brilliant array of oranges and yellows, the grills were prepared for the big barbeque. Thick and juicy steaks, hot dogs, and hamburgers were grilled to perfection by the men in the family.

Everyone helped prepare dinner that night. The older teens set the tables, arguing over who was best at certain video games and which sports or after school activities might be fun this year. The younger members of the family played and chased each other around the pool and gardens, argued, and mostly got in everyone's way. A typical, normal everyday family gathering.

After a big feast the teens thought it would be cool to have a bonfire at the beach, toast marshmallows, and tell stories; which Helaina was pretty good at! It took a good hour to dig a pit and gather wood. When they were done with all the work, the adults in the family joined them, having preferred to relax with an after-dinner drink as the kids set up the bonfire. Usually William, Charlie, or David would light the fire but not this time. This time they gave the honor to J.R. and Helaina, letting them, in this small way, know they were part of an elite group.

With the fire blazing, everyone gathered around, listening to the crackling of the flames and toasting marshmallows on the end of roasting skewers. Cassie, Helaina's little sister, snuggled in her dad's lap. Cassie was a miniature copy of her older sister. She had the same long, dark wavy hair, except her eyes were blue with the gold streaks permeating out from the iris There the similarities ended. Unlike Helaina, Cassie saw the world as a big canvas in which she could create beautiful and inventive pieces of art.

"Can Helaina tell us a story? She always tells good ones."

"What do you think dear? Want to tell us one of your stories?" David asked his daughter.

"Let me think." She thought for a minute.

Not knowing which story to tell, she turned to J.R. using Mind Speak. "What story would be a good one to scare them? How about the one when the shark hunter gets eaten by the whale?"

"No! How about the one with the headless horseman?"

"No, that's more of a Halloween story."

"The one with the axe murderer on the loose that my dad told last year?"

"No, that scared Cassie, she had nightmares for a week."

"How about one of your dream stories?" J.R. asked.

"I think I will just come up with one myself. Halfway through I will tell you to duck behind the rock over there. Then when I come to the part about the evil witch scaring the explorers, you jump out and startle everyone."

"Cool." J.R. agreed with this plan.

William, having heard their unspoken conversation, decided to have a little fun with the two pranksters himself. He whispered something into Charlie's ear. Laughing, Charlie went to get something out of the house. Helaina began her story. The younger kids, as always, listened as she entertained them; she had a gift that got everyone concentrating, and engrossed in the stories she told. She was very good with her young sister and younger cousins; she had spent many hours entertaining them with make-believe stories in the past. Helaina began.

"Once upon a time a group of brave explorers heard a story about a great treasure; they were told it was hidden in a cave deep in the Amazon jungle. The brave and handsome explorer, his beautiful sister, and two of their best friends decided that they would go find that treasure because their village was poor. The children needed a new school and better houses because an awful hurricane came and destroyed much of what they had the previous year. It was a long and dangerous trip, taking many days. First, they traveled a great distance on an old steam ship, arriving at the mouth of the great Amazon River in the dead of night.

"After a short rest they looked for a guide to take them to the cave, but no one would. Everyone was scared, for a witch was protecting the cave and the great treasure. Waiting! Waiting for the chosen ones to come and claim what was rightfully theirs. Many, many years had passed since a great king had a witch put a curse on a beautiful sorceress, turning her into the ugliest witch that ever existed. The King made the poor dear guard the treasure until his descendants, bearing his mark, came to take the great treasure away, using it for good. The King hid it because a selfish and greedy men wanted the treasure for himself. The only way the beautiful sorceress could break the spell was to wait for the rightful heirs of the great treasure. The king knew that the rightful heirs would come and claim what was their birth right and use it for the good of the people. He just didn't know when.

"She guarded the treasure for a thousand years, and the longer she waited, the meaner she got. People who got near and were proven not to be the chosen ones were turned into cattle or chickens and eaten for dinner. While she waited for the chosen ones to come, she wrote down beautiful stories and created beautiful paintings and tapestries as welcoming gifts for the chosen ones."

Helaina now had the complete attention of her audience. No one noticed that Charlie had come back, giving each adult something which they then hid in their laps. Then he placed something behind each of the children so they could get into the fun. Helaina continued her story, focused on the faces of her sister and young cousins. She didn't pay attention to what her uncle was doing.

"The brave explorers were on their own. First, they took the old broken-down jeeps as far as they could, running out of road and gas at the place the forest began and the desert ended. Following a map they were given, they climbed through a dense forest of trees on foot for many, many miles. They were so tired and so hungry they didn't think they would survive the trip. Then suddenly before them, the small stream they had been searching for appeared out of nowhere. Taking a well-deserved break, they sat on the edge of the stream, drinking the cool water and splashing it on their faces to cool off. They were really close now, so close that they could hear a waterfall. Behind the waterfall was the cave that they searched for.

"When rested, our adventurers continued their journey up the little stream, finding the waterfall. It was hidden by magical trees, protecting the waterfall, the cave, the treasure, and yes! The wicked witch from outsiders. The scene before them was so beautiful that they stood staring, admiring the beauty, feeling the magical spirit that was all around them."

"J.R., go hide," Helaina instructed her cousin using Mind Speak.

"Okay," he told her, ready to do his part in scaring the younger kids.

She continued her story.

"They walked slowly, cautiously towards the waterfall. Looking and listening out for the witch." She paused for a dramatic touch and to talk to J.R. "Okay J.R. when I tell them, 'When they look around the corner then...' you jump out yelling like a witch, scaring them."

Helaina's voice now became barely a whisper, and everyone leaned forward to her. At times, she paused just to make sure everyone was focused on her.

"Inch by inch, over slippery stones they went, ever so careful not to splash water as they walked. They quietly approached the cave entrance. The witch was nowhere to be seen. The only sound was the water falling into the stream below. The leader of the group took one more step and looked around the corner."

Just then J.R. jumped out of his hiding place, screeching like a witch. Everyone jumped and the little ones screamed, startled by the sudden noise. It took everyone a few seconds for their hearts, pounding with fright, to settle back down to a normal rhythm.

"Damn, you sure got everyone that time."

Everyone laughed at J.R. and Helaina's stunt.

"Can you finish the story now; I want to know; did they get the treasure?" Cassie asked after everyone had settled down again.

"Sure, I will."

J.R. sat down to listen with the rest of the family. After all, Helaina could tell a good story, and since this one was about him, he wanted to find out how it ended.

"As you know, the witch jumped out trying to scare the group away. But that didn't happen because the leader of the group and his beautiful sister were indeed the chosen ones. The witch knew it immediately because she felt their energy and their goodness. She also saw that they had the birthmark of the King. The witch welcomed the group into her cave and presented them with the treasure. With the treasure came great knowledge and the wisdom of the great kings. She gave them her stories to share with the world and the beautiful tapestries which she had made, depicting the story of the treasure and those who it belonged to. With this done the great explorer and his beautiful sister hugged the wicked witch. Before their very eyes, she turned into a water nymph and—"

"We know what happens now," Cassie interrupted, being coaxed by her dad.

"Okay smarty, what happens now?"

David whispered something into his youngest child's ear.

"Oh yeah! The explorers left the cave, and they got all wet," Cassie laughed.

Then everyone, now armed with water balloons, thanks to Charlie, bombed Helaina and J.R. with the balloons, getting them all wet and ending the story. The kids had a great time chasing the younger ones, pretending to be angry. Soon, exhausted from their day, everyone retired to bed for a good night's rest.

William, David, and Charlie remained at the beach to watch over the fire. When ready, they took buckets of sand and put out the remainder of the hot embers. Before they returned to the house, they had a brief conversation.

"I learned a lot at the station today. J.R. and Helaina are the tenth generation to be born from the ten original leaders that were last to settle here. We know that there are ten stations around the world. I believe the number ten plays a big part in this somehow. Our geneticist believes that somehow they were born with a pure gene of our ancestors, they are doing tests right now."

"Dad, is that even possible?"

"According to the geneticist, we carry the genes within our DNA, sometimes they lay dormant for generations, sometimes only part of that gene is passed down, sometimes none of it, and very rarely, the complete gene is passed on. They think that J.R. and Helaina have the complete DNA make up of our people who, of course, come with the gene that makes us unique."

"Could this happen with others? What about Tina, Paul, and Cassie?" Charlie wanted to know.

"Yes, maybe, I don't really know. If J.R. and Helaina are an example of the powers that can materialize because of this, there might be problems."

"We will take one problem at a time, like always. But we need to nurture their skills."

"Agreed!" Charlie and David answer in unison.

"Talk to your wives, discuss how we should proceed, then we will talk with the kid's tomorrow night."

The fire went out and all was calm. But for how long?

CHAPTER TWENTY-EIGHT
A NORMAL SUMMER DAY FOR THE FAMILY

William and Helaina weren't the only early birds the next morning. Cassie, Helaina's sister, and Tina, J.R.'s eight-year-old sister, and Paul, who looked identical to his older brother and was ten years old, were wide awake at five a.m. Tina and Cassie, who were very close in age, shared a room together anytime they visited with each other. Cassie was small for her age, just seventy pounds of pure energy, with long, thick wavy hair the color of dark chocolate and deep blue eyes, the color so striking it was the first thing people noticed about her. Tina, a few months younger, was taller than her favorite cousin. She had thick red hair which fell in waves halfway down her back, and she had eyes the color of jade. They both loved to see what they could get their hands into. Cooking, painting, needlework, sandcastle building, and sculpting from things they found, were favorite pastimes. The family's little artists as they were fondly known. The family learned that whatever they thought might be trash, the girls believed to be a treasure.

One time the girls horrified poor Helaina. They used her training bra which mistakenly fell into the trash in the bathroom. When it was found by Cassie and Tina, they turned it into earmuffs. No one was immune; William once found a few of his car parts, mistakenly left out on the driveway, gone. The two girls having watched the men solder things together, decided to try it themselves. They took the parts, soldered them together, and made a modern art statue for the garden. The sculpture now stood in Jennifer's garden near the recreation room. David and Charlie once found a few golf clubs missing after they left them leaning up against a garbage can for a few hours. When they returned to put them away, they had been cut up with a hack saw and used for a jungle gym for the girl's dolls. J.R.'s spare parts were used in collages. Paul's math calculations and old comic books ended up as paper in the girl's scrap books. But their hearts were in the right place; they made Jennifer and Hanna hand-carved, wooden recipe boxes and their mothers beaded necklaces from shells and old jewelry they found. It seemed that the men were their favorite targets for acquiring the stuff to make it with; after all boys have the best toys.

Helaina and William made Cassie, Tina, and Paul some chocolate milk and made them promise to be quiet until everyone else woke up. Sitting at a table in the kitchen drinking their milk, Cassie and Tina put their heads together and came up with an idea.

Cassie, the more outspoken of the two, was the one to ask her Granddad. "Granddad, we have a great idea."

"Now what would that be, Sunshine?" William asked, using the nickname the family used for her. They called her that because of her sunny disposition.

"Since everyone is still sleeping, let's surprise them by making breakfast; it would be fun."

Thinking that this would keep them busy and out of trouble, he believed that this was a great idea. Besides, what could possibly go wrong, especially if he supervised. Right?

"You know, I think that is a wonderful idea. Does your mom let you cook?"

"Sure, all the time. Remember, Helaina, I made breakfast for mom on Mother's Day."

"I remember you made some really good French toast and sausage," agreed her sister.

A discussion followed and a menu was agreed upon, and everyone was assigned a job to do. It was decided that Cassie and Tina would make French toast; Paul would fry the bacon and sausage, and William would supervise. Helaina was in charge of making scrambled eggs and setting the table.

Everything was going extremely well. The girls worked with the electric grill on the counter to grill up the French toast. Paul and William used two cast iron pans on the stove to fry up the bacon. When finished, Paul sat down at the kitchen table with William and started looking at the new comic books he brought with him. They forgot to turn off the burners to the stove and left the greasy pans sitting there. It was only when smoke started filling up the kitchen that they noticed they forgot to do something. But not before the smoke detector went off, which woke up the rest of the family.

At least the rest of the meal was completed when that happened. Cassie and Tina and Helaina did a great job on the rest of the meal and were just finishing up when the alarm went off.. After being assured that the house wasn't burning down, the sleepy heads went back upstairs to get dressed.

Everyone had been so busy making breakfast that they did forget one little detail; actually, it was a very big detail. The huge mess that they were making. Egg shells were filling empty egg cartons; grease was all over the stove and someone had spilled the milk. There were fruit peelings everywhere, and dishes piled high in the two sinks. While they waited for the others, they sat at the kitchen table surrounded by the mess they had made.

"Something sure smells good in here," said Jennifer, looking at the mess when she returned with Joanna and Katie.

"Grandma, we made breakfast. Mom! Tina and I made French toast for everyone, and Paul cooked the bacon."

"We kind of made a little mess, but we will take care of it," promised Helaina.

"Well ladies, I think we are going to have a treat this morning, it sure smells good and a bit smoky. I think we can help our little breakfast cooks and do a little cleaning up."

"I think if we all worked together, we will be done in no time," agreed Katie.

In fifteen minutes, the counters were cleared, the garbage thrown away, and the dishes in the dishwasher. Even J.R. helped, by setting out the plates and cups so that everyone could enjoy their breakfast as soon as the work was finished. He was hungry and thought that it would be best to help so he could get his breakfast. Cassie and Tina's French toast was delicious as was everything else. After breakfast, everyone headed in different directions.

William took J.R.'s Grandparents, Hanna and Carl, to the airfield. They were headed to meet a cruise ship for an Alaskan adventure they were going on that week. A package, full of the motorcycle parts that William had ordered arrived, so J.R., Paul, Charlie, and David went to the garage to see what they could do to get it working. William joined them when he returned from his little trip to the air strip. J.R. had drawn out what he wanted the machine to look like when it was completed. He also made a complete parts list, drawing each part and showing exactly where it should be placed. But the first plan of action was to dismantle the old motorcycle. Charlie had convinced his wife it was a good learning experience for J.R., even though he was the one being taught by his fifteen-year-old son. After they had finished the dismantling of the bike, the men were covered with grease and grime. They cleaned up, changed clothes, and were waiting for the girls by the pool when they got back from visiting friends.

That afternoon the younger members of the family slipped away to the beach as the adult relaxed in the cabañas. The adults sat enjoying cold drinks out of the sun while they kept a close watch on the kids. They even took turns napping. After all, it had already been a very busy day and the kids seemed to have a never-ending supply of energy.

J.R., Helaina, Paul, Cassie, and Tina were excited to see so many of their friends were enjoying time at the beach. Even Emma, Dylan, Kellie, and Mark were enjoying a picnic on the beach. Soon the kids were all occupied fishing off the pier, riding wave runners, building sandcastles or playing volleyball, even snorkeling in the refreshingly cool water: the adults were all but forgotten.

The adults discussed with William and Jennifer the decisions both set of parents had made concerning J.R. and Helaina's future.

"Dad we know that you are retired now, and you and mom wanted to do some traveling and exploring ..."

"Son, I hear a big *but* coming our way."

"It was wonderful of you to let J.R. and Helaina spend the summer, but we really don't want to intrude on your retirement," Katie began.

"You don't have to agree to this, but considering what has been discovered about their DNA and genes, we think this might be best," Joanna continued where Katie left off.

"We believe that we have to think about what's best for them; and about where they could be best be protected," added Charlie.

Jennifer couldn't take seeing the four of them stumbling around the question any longer and wanted to put an end to their discomfort. "Alright, enough! You want to know if J.R. and Helaina can stay with us and go to school here, because of this new information we discovered. It would be less of a security risk for them here on Hope Island. William and I talked last night, and we agreed that if you felt this was best it would be alright with us. We love having the kids here."

"If we want to travel, Sophia and Mason are here; they are very good watchers," inserted William.

"If they do leave the island, even for a trip to visit you, a watcher would be close by at all times. Well, as close as they can get to those two anyway." Jennifer wanted to assure them they were doing the right thing.

"Then it is agreed, we will talk to them tonight after the younger ones finally collapse from exhaustion," David said.

"That should be early, can you believe they were all up by five a.m.?" laughed William.

"Do you think they will understand? I mean, we aren't giving them a choice, not letting them decide for themselves where they should go to school."

"Joanna it's your job as a parent to let them know you aren't abandoning them and because of things beyond our control we need to do what's best for them and their future," Jennifer acknowledged her concern.

"Don't worry, they know we all love them, they are secure with that. But let's not scare them about their security. I think it might be best that they believe that the school here is a better choice for their needs. That here, they can focus on the things they are interested in, along with the traditional subjects. And that they can easily work together to build their machine here, which would be difficult if one is in Maryland and the other in Florida."

"That's a good idea Dad. We can also point out to them that they have so many friends here already that it would be fun going to school here," David agreed.

The adults than relaxed knowing the decision was made, and they watched the kids enjoy the day. Soon William, David, and Charlie were sound asleep in their loungers, cold drinks still in their hands. As the women kept watch on the kids, they took the opportunity to make a few phone calls. They needed to make a few arrangements, like transfer the kids records to the school there on Hope Island, and have their staff back home pack up and ship the kid's things to William's and Jennifer's home. Joanna and Katie made a very detailed list with everything J.R. and Helaina would need or things they would want to have with them. They even made sure the kid's most prize processions were packed and brought to the island. Including Helaina's lizard and other small pets she held dear and J.R. comic book and trading card collections, his stereo, electric guitar, and amplifier. They made sure that enough things were left in their rooms back home, so they could easily travel between places and feel at home anywhere they laid their heads. Of course, Jennifer and William might regret sharing a home with a few lizards, a fuzzy spider, and a very loud guitar.

CHAPTER TWENTY-NINE
THERE ARE NO SURPRISES

With the younger children exhausted from a long day and settled in their beds, J.R. and Helaina entertained themselves in the large recreation room. They were still wide awake and full of energy possibly due to two large cappuccinos that they had confiscated from the refrigerator around three that afternoon. They were playing air hockey. Helaina was trying to win a few games which was hard because J.R. was the raining air hockey champ of the family. While they played, they also had one of their silent conversations.

"Tomorrow, everyone goes home; do you think they will want us to go with them?" J.R. asked.

"Nah, they would have said something so we could have packed our things," Helaina reasoned. "They did say we could stay the whole summer."

"Want to watch a movie?"

"No. Do you know what I really want to do?" J.R. asked.

"Yeah!"

"I hate when you do that."

"Sorry, the little ones are asleep so why don't you go ask Granddad?"

"He just came in; sometimes I think Granddad can hear when we Mind Speak?" J.R. told his cousin.

"Nah, you know adults, they try to outguess us, when they can."

William, trying not to laugh at what he'd just heard, came into the room. The others were upstairs in the den ready to spend quality time with their two teens. William was sent to get them.

"Granddad, can we see some more stories from the Story Chamber? Please, the little ones are asleep," asked Helaina before J.R. had the chance to do so.

"Sure, let's go to the den; your parents are waiting for us there."

They want to spend some time with you before they leave tomorrow."

Using Mind Speak J.R. told Helaina, "I think they know we drank all those cappuccinos and they are going to gang up on us."

"It was your idea! Besides, no one said we couldn't have them."

"That's true. What story do you think that thing will tell us tonight?"

"Don't know, but I do know something you don't know."

"Yeah! What?" demanded J.R.

"Just wait a few minutes; you will find out."

"Another dream story?"

"No, it's more like a daydream," Helaina told him as they arrived at the den. They found their parents waiting for them.

J.R. couldn't help it, he just had to ask, "Are we in trouble?" Everyone laughed at the question.

"No, son, you two aren't in trouble, even though we do know about those cappuccinos you both drank. Next time just have one. Too much caffeine and you will pay for it the next day, believe me," Charlie told his son.

"I told you so." Helaina just had to remind him she was right.

"We have something we would like to tell you. Come and sit down," Joanna told the teens.

"Mom, you don't have to worry; we would love to go to school here. We can be with our friends Kellie, Mark, Emma, and Dylan. It will be so much fun. But can you send me my little furry friends; they will miss me?"

Now, this kind of stunned the adults in the room, because they didn't know how Helaina would know what they wanted to discuss.

David asked, "Of course Helaina my love, but how did you know we wanted you to go to the school here on Hope Island?"

218

"Because, I saw it in my head while we were making breakfast this morning," she answered.

"When did you start seeing things in the future?" asked her mom.

"When my dream stories stopped," she simply answered.

J.R. listened all this time. He suddenly realized that they would be staying on the island to go to school, and his cousin didn't tell him.

"You mean you knew they were going to let us stay on Hope Island and you didn't tell me? Don't you think you should have?"

"I wanted it to be a surprise. I don't have to tell you everything."

"But, I didn't—"

Helaina interrupted him before he could say another world. "Quiet! Don't be stupid and tell them we Mind Speak!" Helaina said, switching to Mind Speak for a few seconds.

"Sorry, how come I didn't know? I usually can feel when something changes in us."

"Don't know," Helaina said, correcting his grammar.

She turned to her parents. "Granddad and Grandma will take good care of us, and we will call every night, we promise."

"You don't have to call every night sweetheart, but an email would be nice." Joanna hugged her daughter.

"I don't know about staying here. I like it here, but, Dad, what about my friends. And what happened to our plans to build a car in the garage? And what about the rock band my friends and I were starting? And—"

Charlie interrupted his son. "J.R. we feel that with all the changes happening to you and Helaina, you could get the best specialized education here. Just think about it like this. Instead of building that car, you can build that machine of yours. It would be easier if you and Helaina were together for that. And you can call and email your friends back home."

"Please, J.R.," Helaina pleaded with her cousin. "Let's give it a try. And we can go home anytime we want if it doesn't work out."

"I guess I can give it a try for a few weeks. It would be mega cool to go down to Station One anytime we wanted."

"And another plus is we get out of babysitting the younger kids."

"Now that's a great reason for staying," J.R. laughed, getting a little more comfortable with the idea of living on Hope Island.

"Can we see some more stories from the Story Chamber now?" J.R. said, wanting to change the subject before the women got all mushy. But it was too late; his mom came over and gave him a hug. He hated that; hugs were for babies and little kids. But it felt kind of nice anyway.

William retrieved the Story Chamber from its hiding place, and everyone now focused on the machine.

"What would you like to see?"

"You mean we have a choice?"

"Sure, you do. You could see stories from the watchers who came before us. Some are pretty scary. One of our watcher's offspring turned out to be Jack the Ripper. Then there was another man who committed even worse crimes, and he was named Adolph Hitler. Those are examples of when our gene turned to evil. There are plenty of examples of those who carry our genes that did wonderful things. Like Henry Ford, Christopher Columbus, a few kings and queens, and even a few presidents, and plenty of scientists, including Thomas Edison and Madame Currie. All possessed a little part of our gene; of course, they didn't know it," explained David Unity to the kids.

"All of that is in the Story Chamber?"

"All of that and much more," said Charlie.

"How does it work? I don't see any dials or switches. I don't even see buttons; it's not plugged into the wall, and it doesn't have a battery," J.R. observed as he walked around the Story Chamber.

Charlie explained, "It works with the power of your mind, and it will only work for those of us that have at least seventy-five percent of our special gene. You think of something you are interested in or would like to see, and you wave your hand above this crystal imbedded in the chamber. Watch. I will show you!"

Charlie concentrated his thoughts on one subject and waved his hand. Immediately the Story Chamber came to life and there before them was Paul hitting a home run for his team the week before.

"That boy sure can hit that ball; maybe we have a home run king in the makings," observed David, the boy's uncle.

"Maybe even another Joe Montana."

"Aunt Joanna, Joe Montana was a football player, not a baseball player."

"I stand corrected. What would you like to see?"

"How about a story about Thomas Edison. He invented cool things."

"Good choice," William acknowledged. "Now come over here and think about Thomas Edison and wave your hand."

J.R. followed Williams instructions and the Story Chamber swirled into action. J.R. and Helaina settled themselves in front of the machine to watch the story, sitting on cushions on the floor. When they settled down, Peanut crawled out of Helaina's pocket so she could also watch the stories. The machine took them to Menlo Park during the late eighteen hundreds. Two men were working in a shop; machines of all sorts surrounded them. Parts littered the floor, and shelves lined up against the walls contained all sorts of things, including the first light bulbs, Edison's phonograph on which he had successfully made the first recording in 1877 of "Mary Had a Little Lamb." Edison's assistant, Fred Ott, was helping a customer at the counter, trying to repair the turning mechanism for an ice-cream maker. After the customer left, Fred heard Edison call him into the work area.

"Fred, I think I did it this time."

"That's what you tell me every day, Tom."

"I know, but this time I found a film that will maintain the picture; I had to find the right chemistry makeup. Now I can play the image back."

"Let's try it. Why don't you record that lamp over there?"

"It doesn't move."

Having breathed in some dust, Fred sneezed.

"Do that again! And I will record it."

"But I don't need to."

"Well then just pretend," said Edison.

"Alright."

221

Then Fred Ott pretended to sneeze as Thomas Edison recorded the event. This marked the first time in history that movement was photographed and played back. It also made Fred Ott the first actor in motion pictures since it was a faked sneeze. Thomas Edison was nicknamed the Wizard of Menlo Park, and he still holds the record for the most patents ever recorded—1093.

"That was cool; maybe I can be the Wizard of Hope Island," J.R. said as the Story Chambers picture disappeared in a puff of smoke.

"I want to try it."

"What would you like to see or learn about? Jennifer asked Helaina.

"Can it be a surprise?"

"Should we trust her?" William teased. "Alright then, come up here and work it just like J.R. did."

After she waved her hand, Helaina sat back down to see the story she had picked. This time when the story came to life, it took the family back to the day before. There, outside Station One, were Helaina and Marlo Turner playing Hokey Pokey with the giant starfish. Soon the story took them back to earlier that morning when Marlo kept her promise to the starfish. Not only did she go and play with her, she brought along her dolphin friend. The dolphin was now well enough to be reunited with his large playmate. The reunion of the two friends brought tears to the women's eyes. The story ended with Marlo placing her hands on the two, saying good-bye, and amazingly, they responded with a, "Thank You," before they swam away. The giant starfish stopped, turned around, and waved goodbye to her new friend.

"Now that was a good story," said Helaina, wiping away a tear.

"Next time can we see something that they don't cry over?" J.R. complained.

"Get used to it my boy. Women always cry with happy endings," his father told him.

"Let's watch more."

"Not tonight, we need for the two of you to go make up a list of things you want us to ship here. We are already having all your clothes packed and the things we thought you might want. We just need you to make a list, to make sure we didn't leave anything off. Give us the list tomorrow before we leave. I'm going to miss you," Katie instructed the kids, trying not to get to emotional again.

J.R. and Helaina got up, hugged their mothers, and said goodnight. But before they left the room, they stopped.

Helaina smiled in understanding. "You don't have to worry; we will be safe here. Night, see you in the morning."

They went to their rooms to make their list, leaving the family staring after them.

It was Joanna, Helaina's mom, who said what they were all thinking. "They understand more than we give them credit for."

"That my beautiful and wise wife is unfortunately true," David pointed out.

CHAPTER THIRTY
THE HOPE ISLAND FAIR

The next morning, after a nice family breakfast, a caravan of cars left the Unity estate and drove to the airfield where William and Jennifer Unity, J.R. Black, and Helaina Unity said goodbye to the ones they loved the most. Of course, Joanna and Katie couldn't leave without a few tears. It is always hard to leave your child, but neither of them regretted the decision that was made. In their hearts, they truly believed they were doing what was best. After a lot of hugs, promises to email and text, and promises of long, detailed calls at the end of each week, the family boarded their private planes. David, Joanna, and Cassie Unity headed to Maryland, and Charlie, Katie, Paul, and Tina Black went to Florida.

Each family had a long list of things that J.R. and Helaina wanted shipped to Hope Island. Each mother had a memory card filled with pictures of the last few days—pictures that would soon be labeled, "The days of discovery," in their scrapbooks. Being mothers, they would have loved pictures from the visit at Station One, but the high-tech security system disabled any camera that was taken down or brought up to the island, completely wiping every memory card. Even cell phones weren't immune. Pictures could be sent down to the station via computers, but none ever made their way out. Ever! When the scientists needed to document and photograph their work, they used special cameras invented by the original occupants of the ten stations, and transferred their work to special computers. Detailed descriptions could be sent to the various CEOs or Guardians via special computers, but no pictures, and immediately after the file was read, the computers automatically erased the information. Nothing of importance was stored in hard drives outside the stations. Security was the Unity Corporations second objective. The first being, "Unite the two Worlds."

The next week William, Jennifer, J.R., and Helaina settled into a routine. In the morning Jennifer and Helaina, along with Kellie and Emma, worked in the kitchen, perfecting their skills for the upcoming fair. William and J.R., and sometimes Mark and Dylan, worked diligently on the motorcycle. Usually after lunch, everyone under the age of eighteen went to the beach to ride wave runners, go snorkeling, and everything else young people do while at the beach on a hot summer's day.

Wednesday afternoon, a moving truck rolled up to the Unity house filled with J.R.'s and Helaina's possessions along with a few passengers riding up front with the driver. The new arrivals included Iggy the iguana, Tulip the tarantula, and Baby and Sugar—two little hamsters that Helaina had bottle fed when their mother died. They received the VIP treatment for their long journey. When the cages of animals arrived, Mason took them straight to Helaina's room where the girls made the animals comfortable in their new environment, giving them fresh water, food, and a little attention.

Helaina, Kellie, and Emma spent the entire afternoon organizing Helaina's bedroom. They tried on some of her extensive collection of clothes, even experimenting and trying different looks with Helaina 's makeup and jewelry. While they were busy, they enjoyed listening to Helaina's enormous CD collection.

They took a break for lunch. When they returned to put the remainder of the clothes away, they discovered something that Helaina's grandmother wasn't going to like. The top of Tulip the tarantula's container was slightly open, and Tulip was missing. For an hour, the three girls searched the bedroom without any luck. Suddenly they heard a scream in the hall and ran to discover Tulip crawling down the hall towards Sophia, cornering her at the linen closet. Jennifer and William came running up the stairs.

Before William could stomp on the spider with his shoe, Helaina yelled, "Granddad, Don't! That's Tulip; she won't hurt you."

"Helaina what is that thing doing in this house? No one told me you had one of those things!" Jennifer yelled.

Helaina went and picked up her fuzzy friend and put it in her pocket. The same pocket that Peanut was sleeping in. Peanut immediately took to chattering at Helaina as she climbed on her shoulder.

"See she won't hurt you. Besides you are bigger than she is," Helaina told the women.

"Girl, you are scaring your grandmother and Sophia. Go put that thing in a cage and lock its door. Maybe we should send, THAT THING, back to your Mom and Dad."

"But Granddad, Mom doesn't like her either; she would be happier here with me."

"That's probably why your mom sent it here. She was probably glad to get rid of it," laughed Jennifer. "Go lock THAT THING in its cage and keep it there. Since Sophia obviously doesn't like her either, I think maybe you should keep it in the garage."

"If I keep her in the garage, can she stay?" Helaina wanted to know.

"Yes, I guess so. But she must stay in the garage, not the house."

"Thanks, Grandma, I promise. I bet Mason will like her."

J.R., Mark, and Dylan, missed all the excitement because when J.R. got his things he just took the boxes upstairs, shoved them into the closet, and went fishing. The boys did bring back some nice trout that they caught at one of the Nature Park's lakes. J.R. had returned to the park several times trying to find the waterfall, thinking that there had to be some sort of mistake. Unfortunately, they couldn't find one single clue that it existed, and this saddened them.

***

Monday came back around, and it was time to prepare for the Hope Island Summer Fair. Everyone on the island, and under it, looked forward to this event. Those on the island who didn't have *must do* jobs at the moment, participated in preparing for the event. This year

William volunteered himself and J.R. to prepare the go carts and the racetrack. When the fair started, William would be overseeing that event, making sure it ran safely, appointing judges, and acting as the race announcer. J.R. would help by keeping the little go carts in running condition.

Jennifer and Helaina helped organized the different contests such as the pie eating contest and the biggest and best vegetables grown in personal gardens. They were also judging for those events. They helped set up the different arts and crafts exhibits. Helaina, Kellie and Emma enjoyed setting up the different displays. Emma entered a few of her paintings and was excited to be participating in such a grand fair. Where she and Dylan were born, they had no fairs or circuses or art galleries, so this was a very big deal in young Emma's life. Emma and Dylan were more excited about the fair than anyone else on the island, and their new family couldn't wait to share this new experience with them. Jennifer would be one of the judges for the arts and crafts division, a job she always looked forward to.

Everyone worked hard setting things up on Monday, Tuesday and Wednesday. Thursday the residents took a break while the rides were delivered by barges and set up on what would be the midway of the fair. When Friday morning arrived, the small circus which was scheduled to perform paraded their animals down Main Street, followed by clowns and acrobats. When they arrived at the arena, they paraded around until everyone was circling the performance area. Ribbons were attached around the necks of four elephants, each one stationed at the four compass points—north, south, east and west. When the elephants pulled the ribbons, ten thousand balloons were released signifying the beginning of the Hope Island Summer Fair. It was a spectacular sight to see, and the newest residents of the island got the privilege of commanding the elephants to release the balloons. It was something Emma and Dylan would never forget.

Friday night everyone enjoyed the circus, the various rides, and games on the midway. Among the fair goers were two new faces to the island. They arrived that morning on one of the island's helicopters. They settled into their apartments that afternoon, and since they were new, they decided the best way to meet the people of Hope Island was to attend the fair.

Spring Rockford and Eli Carpenter, who recently passed the rigorous screening required for new teachers and employees of Unity Corporation, were finally given the opportunity to come to this exclusive community. Spring Rockford was hired to teach ethology and geography, and she wasn't a teacher by training. She was a twenty-one-year-old grad student who ran out of money and needed a job to continue her studies to get her Doctorate in those subjects. Her father, who worked for Unity Corporation, told her about this teaching opportunity. Spring had an IQ of 156, was the youngest of a large family from Denver, Colorado, and both of her parents were botanists. She stood five foot eight inches tall, had dark hair, and was of thin build with a bubbling personality. Some of her favorite activities were writing and gardening. She was an animal lover who devoted her spare time to an animal rights group.

Eli Carpenter was twenty-four. He was a talented mechanical engineer with a restless spirit, and he wanted to explore the world before he settled down. He applied for this job on a whim, not thinking he could possibly get the opportunity to step foot on such an exclusive island. But his inventions caught the eye of someone from the corporation; he also had a talent for teaching and was good with young people. Those things helped him get this chance to explore somewhere new, and he welcomed challenges. Both Spring Rockford and Eli Carpenter came to Hope Island to teach, but each was hiding a few secrets, including a secret that they themselves didn't know.

On Saturday, the arts and crafts, along with all the farm produce, canned jams and jellies, cookies, cakes, and breads were all judged. The awards and ribbons would be awarded at the awards dinner, the last event of the fair. Saturday afternoon in the sports arena, Olympic type activities for adults as well as children took place. There was javelin throwing, long jump, pole jumping, relay races, and other running, jumping and throwing games. Dylan Roberts was the star of the show, out racing, out jumping, out distancing everyone in his age category and every adult who challenged him. When it came to throwing, Mark was the champion. Having powerful upper body strength, he was very accurate at hitting the targets; Mark was an excellent archer and a marksman with firearms.

Everyone had an amazing time, riding the rides, playing the games, trying new foods on sticks, and watching the shows. J.R., Mark, and Dylan loved the go-carts and the rides, spending many hours challenging each other with the different games on the midway. Helaina, Kellie, and Emma loved the arts and crafts, the exhibits, and most certainly, the animals. When the boys weren't playing games, they were on the go-cart track; they took turns racing around it. Everyone knew the three boys had entered the junior races, but only the girls and William knew that there would be a challenge portion of the go-cart competition, and the three girls were going to challenge the three boys to a race.

Saturday afternoon the Junior Go-Cart races were about to begin. First to race were six to eight-year olds; then the eight to ten-year olds got their chance. As the different groups of kids had their turn to race, J.R. went to check out the car he was to drive in the race he planned to participate in. He wasn't too impressed with the engine, so he made a few adjustments that he thought would help the car move faster.

Finally, he heard his grandfather announce the race for fourteen to eighteen-year olds and pushed the car onto the track. There would be ten cars to race this time, J.R., and Mark, and eight others. Everyone was ready to start, the engines running, protective head gear, gloves and safety belts were doubled check. The starting flag was raised; when it was dropped, ten go-carts went racing down the track. J.R. and Mark were in front of the pack until Mark's go-cart started to wobble a bit, and he was hit from behind causing him and the car that hit him to spin off the track. Mark was out of the race. J.R.'s car started to smoke; it started with just a puff and grew into a thick black cloud that encircled the entire go-cart. J.R. couldn't see a thing; the car slowed to a stop, and the rest of the go-carts passed him by, leaving him behind. Kellie's cousin Justin won that race, and J.R. learned a lesson. Cheating, even though he called it *adjusting*, doesn't pay off.

Now came the challenge races. There was just one challenge race. William announced to the crowd, "Folks we have a challenge. Can Mark and Dylan Roberts, and J.R. Black come up to the podium to meet your challengers."

The three boys came up, excited by the challenge. They thought three guys would be their opponents.

"Boys are you ready to meet your challengers for this race?"

"Yes Sir!" they yelled with excitement.

"Meet your challengers."

This was the cue for the three girls to come up to the podium. The boys couldn't see their faces, because they had helmets on to temporarily hide their identity. The girls lined up on the podium before taking off the head gear and revealing to the boys who had challenged them. The guys couldn't believe who was standing there.

"Ladies and gentlemen, these three lovely ladies are Kellie Garfield, Helaina Unity, and Emma Roberts. Boys, do you accept this challenge from these ladies?"

"We sure do."

"Now shake hands and get into your go-carts."

The crowd cheered and clapped for the young racers. J.R. and Mark had different go-carts after the crash. To make the race fair, they lined the cars six across the track and waited for the flag to drop. When it did, all six took off; the race was close, the six of them raced nose to nose. It wasn't until the last twenty yards that J.R. pulled away from the rest, with the accelerator to the floor, a firm grip on the wheel, and with eyes on the finish line, J.R. was the first to cross over it. He was followed closely by Kellie, Mark, Dylan, Helaina, and Emma bringing up the rear. It was an exciting race, and the crowd was on their feet for the whole six minutes.

"Let's give a big round of applause for these young racers who did a fantastic job." The crowd applauded as the kids got out of the go-carts. They smiled, formed a human chain and all took a well-deserved bow.

CHAPTER THIRTY-ONE

NOT LIKING WHAT SHE SEES

Sunday afternoon was the last chance to enjoy the attractions at the fair. Helaina and Kellie finished their volunteer work at the arts and craft tent and decided they would go to the one place they hadn't explored. The House of Mirrors. It was so busy the few times they wanted to go inside that they'd abandoned their attempts. This time they were in luck; the only one at the exhibit was the attendant.

Inside they found mirrors that made them look thin and fat, tall and short. The mirrors that made them look silly were their favorite. It was when they went into the House of Mirrors that the girls got separated. It was fun to play who was the real girl. Getting lost was easy, because sometimes it was hard to find an opening where you could move along the path. With mirrors in front, behind, on the sides, and on the ceiling and the floor, it was extremely challenging. Their images bounced off so many mirrors that the girls couldn't figure out where the other one was which was amazing fun. Helaina stopped; she laughed so hard she needed a moment to catch her breath.

Unexpectedly, Helaina felt all her senses come alive. It was like her body told her something was about to happen. Taking a deep breath, she shut her eyes and slowly exhaled. When she opened her eyes, she saw her images in the mirrors disappear. Taking their place was a picture of the crowd at the racetrack. Instead of twenty or thirty images, it was like she was standing in the middle of the stadium; it was one continual picture alive with activities. Today was the adult's chance to race; there was a large crowd of family and friends to cheer them on. The picture before her focused on a young mother standing behind a stroller with a brown-haired toddler who had attention-getting, deep brown eyes. The mother was focused on the race, watching her husband, and she didn't notice her little girl wiggle out of the safety belt and get out of the stroller. The girl in a red sundress, with a little yellow bow in her ponytail, was headed for the track, right in front of the racing go-carts. Helaina didn't wait to see what happened next; she shook the images away. Seeing a light peeking around the edge of a mirror, she figured that there was a window or door behind that piece of glass. She pushed it aside, finding she was correct in her assumption. She slipped out of the window and into the late afternoon crowd.

Helaina knew she had to get to that little girl before she got hurt. Quickly, after finding her way out of the House of Mirrors, she ran through the thick crowd as fast as her feet could carry her feeling helpless and confused. Pushing people and things out of her way, Helaina jumped over a wagon that carried a family dog and small children. She took short cuts around tents and through the stores on Main Street, going in one door, and out the back door. She was a hundred yards outside the racetrack area when she heard her granddad introduce the drivers. Knowing that in less than a minute those go-carts would be racing, her heart beat faster. Taking another deep breath, letting it out slowly, and getting in control, she continued moving forward.

Realizing it would be easier to find the little girl if she ran along the edge of the track, she ran in front of the crowd. After all, that is where she saw the little girl.

William, while giving a second by second account of the track action, noticed Helaina running along the edge of the crowd, appearing to frantically search for something or someone. Instinctively, he picked up his camera and zoomed in on her to get a closer look, watching her actions, and at the same time keeping close watch on the progress of the go-cart racers.

Helaina finally spotted the little girl just as she climbed out of the stroller. She rushed forward, pushing someone aside and reached the child before she stepped out onto the track. Picking up the child, holding her so close the girl cried out in protest, Helaina's heart beat hard in her chest. The young mother now noticed what her young daughter was up to and saw the young girl pick up the child before she walked on to the track. Tremendously grateful for her assistance, she came to get her little girl from Helaina's arms, thanking her for keeping her wayward daughter from getting too close to the racing go-carts.

William snapped several pictures of the scene. Seeing that all was well, he returned to his job, just in time to declare the winner of the race. After giving a few announcements, William invited everyone to the barbeque where the trophies and ribbons would be awarded to the winners. Then he went in search of his granddaughter.

William found Helaina sitting alone on the beach. Little Peanut cuddled close to her as she stroked her head and tears ran down her soft pink cheeks. She looked so lost and alone. William sat next to his granddaughter and wrapped his arms around her, giving her a chance to gather strength from him.

"Granddad, something happened, and I didn't like it at all," she sobbed into his shoulder.

"I know. I saw you on the track."

"It scared me and Peanut."

"Do you want to tell me what happened?"

Helaina caught her breath and told William what had happened at the House of Mirrors, how scared she was that the little girl would get hurt, and how she came to save her.

William wanted to know. "Did having the daydream scare you?"

"No, the part about thinking that the little girl would get hurt scared me."

"When you had your daydream, did you see how it finished?"

"No. I shook it out of my head and ran."

"Can I show you some pictures?"

"Why?"

"Because they will tell you how the story would have ended."

"Is that a magic camera or something?"

"No! But hasn't anyone ever told you that, 'A picture is worth a thousand words'?"

"I think my dad did once."

233

"I took these when I saw you were running. This is where you pushed someone out of the way to get to the little girl. Do you remember doing that? What do you see?" William asked.

"I see a safety guard."

"This is the picture before that one. What do you see?"

"The safety guard; he's reaching down towards the little girl. I guess I should have seen the rest of the story. Are you mad at me?"

"No, you just worried me that's all." William hugged Helaina close to him again, knowing how all this was affecting her.

"Granddad, I don't want to see anymore daydreams. I don't like seeing the future. It's scary."

"Sweetheart, the future is scary for everyone because of the unknowns, like all the uncertainties surrounding everyone and everything. But I want you to do yourself a favor."

"What's that?"

"When you have more daydreams, as you call them. I want you to push away your fears and see it to the end. Sometimes you might think it will end one way, but it is supposed to happen another. You understand that?"

"Yes, Granddad, but I just wish I could go back to having regular dream stories."

"I know. But isn't it cool that you can see the future? I sure wish I could," William said, trying to make light of this incident. He hoped this was a way to make the girl comfortable with this new skill.

"Yeah! I guess it is, but how come I didn't see who was to win the race yesterday?" she giggled.

"That, Princess, I don't know. Now let's go get some of that barbeque because it sure smells good from here."

When William and Helaina arrived at the picnic area, Kellie came running up to her friend and asked with concern, "Where did you go so fast; you looked like you saw a ghost?"

"Well in a way, I did. It scared me, so I ran. But I'm fine now. Let's go get some of the pig your dad has been cooking for two days now."

"It's five pigs. If there are leftovers like there were last year, then we will have leftover pork for a few months. You know my mom, she doesn't like wasting anything," Kellie joked.

The girls walked off to get some dinner. William went in search of a nice cold beer and his beautiful wife to explain what had happened. Helaina might want a woman to talk about what happened with her vision. Then he realized that he hadn't seen J.R. for a while. "I wonder what that boy is up to. On second thought maybe I don't want to know," he chuckled.

After dinner that evening was the award ceremony. The kids came out winners in the junior divisions of the contests they entered. Helaina won first place with her blueberry jam, and second for her apple turnovers. J.R. won first place in three go-cart races. Mark won four ribbons for his skills as an Olympian, and his brother Dylan won six ribbons, one for the fastest runner, breaking a world record in the one-hundred-yard dash. His run was recorded just in case of a photo finish, and his time recorded; however, these would not be given to those who kept such records outside the Unity Corporation.

Kellie won first prize for her apple and blueberry pies. Emma was the only one of the six kids who won a cash prize of a hundred dollars. She entered the picture she had painted from the sketch of the six friends, the one she drew the afternoon they found the waterfall. She also entered a painting she made of the waterfall and the trees that protected it from outside eyes. Both paintings were stunning. Someone offered to buy them, but her proud mom and dad wanted to hang them at home.

Everyone went home happy. Even Jennifer earned ribbons for her homemade bread and a gorgeous needlepoint of a seascape that took her six months to complete. When everyone was gone, those in charge of clean up took over, and by morning the rides were down and packed on the barges, the temporary buildings down, and the garbage cans picked up and emptied.

Main Street was just Main Street again, everything was good.

CHAPTER THIRTY-TWO

THINGS TO COME

A few days later, J.R. and Helaina were at the Nature Park enjoying the tire swing, jumping into the chilly water, and eating pork sandwiches Kellie's mom made them. While sitting at the picnic table, J.R. and Helaina had a silent conversation as their friends enjoyed lunch.

"I made another drawing last night, and I think you had another daydream, didn't you?"

"Yeah I did. It was about a dome. How did you know?"

"I just figured you did. That's all. Besides, I drew that dome. I think we should call your so called, "daydreams," something else. The name just doesn't work."

"I thought the same thing. What should we call them? They tell me of something that is about to happen in the future, and sometimes I know little things that might happen on a certain day."

"What about *future predictors*?

"Nah! How about *visions*? Just to make things easy."

"*Visions* it is then. Can I see you're drawing?"

"No, I left it at home, but when I drew it, I actually saw the place where it should be built."

"Where the waterfall disappeared?"

"See! You don't have to see my drawing. You already knew. I wonder why I can't draw remarkably stunning pictures of people, places, and animals like Emma. Yet, I can draw detailed pictures of machines. I tried to draw Peanut and couldn't."

"Grandma says we each have talents that are ours alone, and we should appreciate them. Even though sometimes seeing my visions can be very scary."

"Since you know what my drawing is, and we are a team, what did your vision tell you?"

"First I saw the arms being delivered. They were dropped from the sky. Then I saw a big flash of light."

"Do you think the flash of light was an explosion?" J.R. asked.

"I don't know. But I saw your big dome. It's going to be very impressive."

"I drew something on the front, what is it?"

"Are you testing me?"

"Yep! So, what is it?

"You drew a waterfall with the jewels inside the water."

"You're good!"

"Don't I know it!" Helaina laughed with her cousin.

"We know that the dome has to be build right where the secret waterfall was and no place else," J.R. interpreted everything together.

"That's my feeling also. Later when we get home, we will talk to Granddad and Grandma about this."

The others at the table observed J.R. and Helaina sitting there eating their lunch and thinking hard about something. They looked way to serious. Mark and the others decided it was time to take their fish home and head to the beach.

"Hey, you two, let's get out of here; time to check out the beach."

"You just want to check out the girls in bikinis," teased J.R.

"How true that is. Let's go!"

***

That very afternoon, Eli Carpenter and Spring Rockford were given a tour of Hope Island Progressive School by the school's secretary. They were assigned classroom space along with the workspace that they and their students would use for bigger projects. They were introduced to the other faculty, noting that three quarters of the staff held impressive degrees but no teaching degrees. The only certified teachers on the staff taught the basic subjects, English, Math, Literature, Reading, Drama, Foreign languages and Home Economics. When the tour was complete and the introductions made, the two new teachers finally met with the dean of the school. Eli and Spring had been hired by high level managers at Unity Corporation and not the dean of the School.

The dean heard their voices outside his office, and he called out through the closed door. "Eli, Spring, come in. Please. I am anxious to meet the two of you."

They wondered why Dean Meyers didn't open the door for them, but when they entered the room that question was answered. Sitting on a couch, surrounded by bookshelves of books and trophies, sat Dean Alexander Meyers, his leg in a cast and propped up with several pillows. Dean Alexander Meyers was not what they expected a dean of a school to look like. In fact, he was the complete opposite. Alex Meyers stood six foot five inches tall when he wasn't wearing a cast. Alex had broad shoulders, was very muscular, very athletic, very handsome, and very young for a dean at only thirty-one years of age. Looking around the cramped office, Eli and Spring saw two surf boards leaning in a corner, weights, and other sporting equipment which overflowed from boxes on the floor. The only place in the office that wasn't in use was the man's desk where a lone lamp made its home.

"It's so nice to meet the both of you. Grab those folding chairs and have a seat so we can chat."

The school's two newest teachers did as they were told.

"I'm sure you have questions, so let's get at them. By the way, call me Alex."

Spring was the first to speak, "Alex, it's great to be here; this island is like a paradise."

"Isn't it though! Eli, I'm told that you enjoy hiking and water skiing. When I am up and around, we will have to get out on that boat of mine. That is after the repairs are made. I had a little accident as you can see."

Eli, feeling more comfortable, finally found his voice. "I would love that, thank you. This is rather an unusual school. I'm looking forward to meeting the students."

"I looked at my student list; I have only three students for some of my classes, and about twenty for my beginning classes. Is this typical?" Spring asked, wanting to get this sexy man's attention.

"The kids here can be a little different, and we cater to those differences. You will see you have a Miss Helaina Unity in your advance animal behavior class as well as two others. Let's just say she has a way with animals; I will let you discover the rest."

"Could you tell us what our classroom budget is so we can—"

"Eli, at this school there is NO budget."

Spring and Eli were about to question this, but before they could Alex continued. It was his way of messing with the new teacher's minds.

"Let me explain. At this school the main focus is to advance the students gifts. We do that with an unlimited budget. Whatever it takes. Wherever they need to go to reach their full potential will be provided. You prepare your lessons or projects two weeks in advance, submit them to the approval committee, and when approved, whatever you need will be provided. Take your clues from your students; let them lead you and you just provide the support."

"Isn't that a bit unorthodox?" asked Spring.

"I think that is the perfect word to describe our schools here on Hope Island." It was the only answer Alex Meyers gave them.

"Of course, as with any school, you never discuss your students with anyone outside this school other than their families. Is that perfectly clear?"

"They discussed that with us before we came to Hope Island. We had to sign a legal document to that fact," Eli reminded him.

"From the amount of blood they took for our health check, we could have signed all the papers with our blood," joked Spring.

Alex smiled knowingly and nodded. "Good, you were given copies of those documents; every now and then you should review them. Now you need to write your lesson plans and prepare for the first week, starting Monday. Just make a tentative plan. You will know better when you meet your students."

"Thank you for your time, Alex."

"No! Thank you for being a part of our little family. Now I've got to go; time for some physical therapy."

Eli and Spring left the office with some unanswered questions. Spring wanted to know, "What do you think he meant when he said, 'our little family'?"

"I have no idea. This is one weird school, and it sounds like the inmates run the place," joked Eli.

"I think they do," replied Spring seriously.

That same evening while sitting at the kitchen table eating their dessert of apple dumplings with vanilla ice-cream, J.R. showed everyone the plans for the dome building. Helaina told their grandparents about what she saw and how from now on she would call them her visions. The kids made it clear that the only place they could build the dome would be on the site of the waterfall or where it was supposed to be. The dome would also be the place where they would build the machine.

William and Jennifer were impressed by how the two of them worked together, giving clear instructions and reasons why they had to do things this way. Then Jennifer thought about something.

"You know we can't just call it, 'The Machine' and 'The Dome,' we really should give these plans real names."

"That's a great idea. How about Dome City?" J.R. suggested.

"No! It's not going to be a city, dim wit."

"I have two suggestions," Jennifer chimed into the conversation.

"You have always been good at naming things my beautiful wife. What are your suggestions?" William inquired.

"You are just buttering me up so you can have more apple dumplings and ice-cream. Anyway, I suggest the Waterfall Dome. And what do you think about calling it the Jewel Machine?"

"What do you kids think? After all, this is your project."

"Perfect!" they answered in unison.

"The project is official now that you have proper names for them; The Waterfall Dome and the Jewel Machine it is. Tomorrow I will make some phone calls and get this project started for you. Now I think it's time for more of those delicious apple dumplings."

"Granddad, do you really mean this is our project?" Helaina wanted to know.

"Yes, I do. The two of you are basically in charge. Remember that you two are a team. Something is leading you to build these projects; we think that it is important that you follow your instincts."

"You, Dad, and Uncle David will help, won't you?"

"Of course, we will. We have to take care of the things that you can't, like getting the Waterfall Dome built for one, but the rest is up to the two of you."

"Did you hear that Helaina? We are the bosses, ain't that cool?"

"Sure is, and it's, *isn't that cool*? not 'ain't.' That's not even a word."

"She's bossing me around already."

"Get used to it, J.R., usually the women have the last word."

"Now can we have some more ice-cream and some more of those dumplings? Please!" J.R. asked his grandmother, and all three pairs of hopeful eyes looked up at her as she gave in to their request.

CHAPTER THIRTY-THREE
COMPLETED PROJECTS

Three days left before the school year began. Helaina was busy with her friends, choosing which clothes to wear for the first week, and going to the mall to buy school supplies. J.R. didn't worry about that stuff, knowing he had plenty of clothes and school supplies. His mom had sent him boxes of the stuff and even a brand new computer. J.R. wondered if his mom forgot they had plenty of stores on Hope Island, and if they ran out of something, he could get it himself. J.R. wanted to finish up a few projects before school started.

J.R. and the boys had completely rebuilt the motor, carburetor, and rewired every part imaginable on the old motorcycle. They put on new tires, a gas tank, gears, and brakes; the motorcycle purred like a kitten. Today was the day William, Mason, and the boys were taking it out for a test drive. Afterwards, it would be loaded onto the trailer to go for a professional, custom paint job.

Everyone met at the garage. Mason gave J.R. a lesson on how to operate the motorcycle and a few driving tips. The plan was for Mason to drive with J.R. on his own motorcycle. William, Mark, and Dylan would follow with the trailer attached to the new, black Ford F150 that William had recently purchased.

The two motorcycles roared to life with a turn of their keys. Gloves and helmets securely in place, the two riders started down the road. Driving shoulder to shoulder, they made it down to the main road, stopping at the stop sign before turning onto the four-lane road.

Mason turned to J.R. "Let's see what that baby can do. It's a mile to that water tower. See if you can get her up to fifty, then stop there and we will put her on the trailer."

Of course, to a fifteen-year-old boy on a motorcycle, it only meant one thing. And that was a race.

"Great! Race you there!"

J. R. took off before Mason could stop him. Regretting his words, he had no other choice but to follow him and hope William didn't fire him for what J.R. perceived as a challenge. He should have known better than to phrase it like that; after all he used to be a fifteen-year-old boy at one time. J.R. made it to the water tower a full thirty seconds ahead of Mason and did as he was instructed and waited. By the time Mason got there, J.R. had already dismounted the motorcycle and removed his helmet.

"What took you so long?"

"We weren't supposed to race."

"But you said, 'see what that baby can do,' and that's what I did. I swear I didn't go over fifty."

"I guess I am just slower than you then, but don't take off like that; you could get us both into trouble."

"Sorry, here's Granddad now. You think while mine is in the shop, I can practice on yours?"

"That's a definite No! Get a license, and I will think about it," Mason replied.

"That means maybe, right?" J.R. pushed.

"No, my friend, that's a big NO on all levels."

"Hey guys, that was sure cool," commented Mark, who was now approaching the two motorcycles with William and Dylan.

"Sure was, and she didn't sputter once. She is going to be cool after that custom paint job she's going to get."

"Let's get her on the trailer; I need to get this to the shop and get to the office. I have some business to do this afternoon," William instructed them.

After helping get the motorcycle onto the trailer, Mason went back to the house, having some work to do himself on the yacht. Since they were in town anyway, William dropped Mark and Dylan off at their home, and went to the office with J.R. J.R. watched as William made the calls that would begin construction on the Waterfall Dome, and he made arrangements for the Jewel Machine Arms to be stored at a warehouse they owned in Seattle until the building was completed. J.R. and William also had a conference call with his dad and Uncle David. The big discussion was about the plans he and Helaina had made. They were a high priority. This made him feel like an adult, like he was a part of something big and what he and Helaina wanted to build was something very important. It was. This was serious business; J.R. and Helaina knew it. With plans made and assignments given out, J.R. and William returned home for lunch.

With the motorcycle being painted and the Waterfall Dome project in the proper hands, J.R. found himself with some time on his hands. He remembered the box of gadgets he was given when he was down in Station One. He hadn't had any time in which to investigate its contents, so he decided that now was the time to do that.

He found some interesting looking things: an odd-looking scale, a bunch of gears, wires, a machine that was supposed to cut metal with a laser, and something that looked like a water pistol. He also found tools of all sorts, a plasma cutter for cutting metal and glass, screw drivers, wrenches of all sizes, a mallet, a hammer, a brand-new socket set, and a chisel set that looked like it had never been used. There was a soldering iron, an electric screwdriver, and a drill. No wonder the box was so heavy. The big box was almost empty when he discovered something interesting on the bottom. Operating manuals to the gadgets he was given. He also found what looked like two pen lights hiding under the operating manuals.

These caught J.R.'s attention in a big way. Taking a closer look, he discovered that the silver, pen-sized tube had what looked like a light on either end. One end was marked with positive, the other negative. Taking the operating manuals out of the box, he shuffled through them until he found the one that belonged to the odd pen lights; their picture was on the cover.

In large letters across the top it read, ANTIGRAVITY.

For two hours, he studied the diagrams and compared them to the gadgets he held in his hand. Setting down the manual, he picked up some paper and a pencil and began to draw. When finished, he compared the manual with the drawing and started making adjustments, making the same changes to both pens, but something was missing. He looked at his watch to see the time, then an idea came to him. If a drop of his blood made the gene meter in his watch work, maybe it might work for the antigravity pens? With his pocketknife, he stabbed his finger, pinching it until a nice sized droplet of blood appeared. Taking some cotton swabs, he carefully placed some of the blood on the two odd looking batteries in one of the antigravity pens. Waiting until the blood dried, he closed the casing of the pen. He planned to keep one of the pens and give the other to Helaina, but he would use her blood to give it power. Each pen, therefore, could only be used by the one who gave it power. That is, if it worked. He wasn't sure if it worked like that, but he was going to give it a try.

Pushing down on the positive symbol, he felt it move into the instrument and return to its original state. Feeling a warmth come from within the pen, J.R. knew he'd figured out how to make the pens work. When a light beam appeared, he pointed it at a washer lying on the work bench. When the light touched the object, J.R. moved the beam up. With it came the washer, but it fell back to the bench a few seconds later. J.R. was a bit disappointed with the results but not discouraged. Hearing William calling him for dinner, he placed his pen in his shirt pocket along with the one he wanted to give his cousin.

Maybe if I put a drop of both our blood inside it would become stronger, he thought as he went in for dinner. He hoped they were having his favorite, Mexican food, he especially loved quesadillas.

Helaina was already in the kitchen telling William and Jennifer about her shopping trip to the mall that afternoon. Peanut was sticking her head out of her shirt pocket, waiting for a treat. When he saw they were having tacos and quesadillas, J.R. fully forgot about the antigravity pens in his pockets and enjoyed his dinner. That is, until Helaina noticed the one sticking out of his shirt pocket and asked him about it.

"Is that a laser pointer," she asked.

"Much cooler, there're antigravity pens." When William heard this, he dropped his taco on his plate. He listened. That is all he could do considering he had his mouth full of the taco as J.R. and Helaina talked.

"Where did you get those?" Jennifer asked.

"They were in the bottom of the box I brought back from Station One."

"I thought it was just filled with some tools they gave you."

"There were tools, but they put some other stuff in there. It was just a few things that they couldn't get to work. I was taking the pens apart and I made a drawing. Someone made it all wrong, so I fixed them," J.R. explained quickly.

"You got them to work?" Helaina asked.

"Yes! But they aren't very strong, I got one for you too, but I need your blood."

William felt alarmed with this statement.

"Did you use your blood to make it work like the gene meter on your watch?" he asked J.R.

"Sure. I figured, if it worked once, it might work again. I was going to use Helaina's blood in this one to see if that works."

"How powerful is that thing?" William continued questioning him, concerned at what he was hearing.

"Not very. I was thinking that maybe if I mixed my blood with Helaina's, I might be able to make it more powerful."

"I don't think that is a good idea."

"Want to see it work?" J.R. ignored William's last statement.

"Can you pick me up?" his cousin wanted to know.

"No, it has to be something small."

J.R. looked around to find something small to use in his demonstration. He found it when Peanut jumped on the table to get a piece of tomato. Since she only weighed three ounces, Peanut was the perfect test subject.

"Watch this!"

J.R. pointed the antigravity light at little Peanut and moved it up. Up came Peanut. She started fussing as J.R. moved her away from her dinner. Higher and higher she went, hanging there above the kitchen table.

"Put her down!" demanded Helaina as she tried reaching for Peanut. J.R. had her suspended inches from the ceiling, and Peanut was out of her reach.

"Oh alright!"

J.R. returned the frazzled Peanut to her dinner. Peanut snatched up the piece of tomato and took it to Helaina's pocket to eat it in peace.

"You made me one; let's see if my blood will make it work." Helaina was excited about getting a new toy.

"Not now and not unless we are in a controlled environment." William took control of the situation. "I think we will have our scientists do that little experiment next time we visit Station One. Now please hand me both of those gadgets. Please!"

J.R.'s notion of mixing his and Helaina's blood put William on high alert. He didn't know why, but he had to act on it.

"But, Granddad, these are harmless fun. Next time Peanut won't get down from somewhere, I could use it to get her down," J.R. protested.

"I will give them back as soon as I know they are safe. I'm sorry, but what if it gets to strong, and you point it at Peanut or at someone else, and it hurts them?"

"Your granddad is right. Give them to him now, and we can have some dessert. Remember, he always keeps his promises," Jennifer stepped in to give William some support.

"J.R., just one more thing. Whatever you do, don't mix your blood with Helaina's."

"You think something awful might happen?" asked Helaina.

"I feel that it might be dangerous."

"Don't worry; I won't let him take my blood. That's gross anyway."

J.R. handed both the antigravity pens to his granddad and accepted a big piece of chocolate cake from his grandmother. William was grateful for Jennifer's support as he took the pens, thinking that locking them up in his safe might be best for now. Later he would send them to the scientists. Right now, he was relieved that such a potentially powerful device was out of J.R.'s hands. He was glad J.R. showed him the pens before he mixed both his and Helaina's blood together. He believed mixing their blood wasn't a good idea.

CHAPTER THIRTY-FOUR
SCHOOL STARTS

What a beautiful day to start the new school year. The day began with a warm eighty-five degrees; a gentle breeze blew off the ocean, and there wasn't a cloud in the sky. It was too bad that the students had to spend most of their day indoors. Because she was starting a new school, Helaina didn't know what to expect and was so nervous she changed clothes five times that morning. Finally, Jennifer told her she looked beautiful, and if they waited for her to change clothes again, they would be late for their first day. J.R. on the other hand was relaxed, dressed in jeans and a T-shirt that read, "Scuba's Cool." He couldn't wait to get to his beginner mechanical engineering class; too bad it was the last class of the day. Their class schedules arrived a few days in advance, along with the school rules, dress codes, and a book that gave them descriptions of their classes with an introduction to each and every teacher at the school. Of course, a complete list of supplies that they would need was right on top. The package even included the books they would be expected to read, all brand new of course. Students kept their books when they completed the class, in case they needed them for future reference.

Helaina discovered that Jennifer would be teaching Home Economics three times a week. She was happy that she would have beginning ethology—Animal Behavior Science—and she would be able to bring Peanut or an animal companion with her on the days she was in that class. After all, they were going to study the behavior of animals, so it made sense that they needed animals. Geography would be a big class filled with all her friends and J.R. for it was a required subject.

The first day at Hope Island Progressive School was like that of any other school. You found your classes, learned your schedule, met the teachers, got your locker, met your new classmates, and discovered what the food is like in the cafeteria. Helaina and J.R. had the normal everyday classes like English, history, algebra, and gym but it was their extra classes that excited them most. The teachers at HPS preferred a more relaxed and informal atmosphere in their classrooms, so they preferred you call them by their first names.

J.R. bonded with his mechanical engineer teacher, Eli Carpenter, immediately. Eli showed the class some of his cool inventions, and he let his students tell him what they wanted to do in class and the kind of things they wanted to get their hands on. Eli was impressed by the things they were interested in and what they wanted to accomplish. He wrote everything down, of course, adding a few ideas of his own, so he could build an effective lesson plan. One young man brought a sketch pad of machines; Eli believed they weren't feasible, and they were much too unrealistic. However, he was impressed by the boy's skill at drawing, none the less. J.R. thought it cool that the students could tell the teacher what they wanted to do.

Helaina, who was not comfortable with new people or places, spent the first day of classes quietly sitting in her seat following instructions and taking notes. She met Spring Rockford during her last class of the day. In Spring's class, Helaina found a collection of small animals, a box turtle, mice, two rabbits, an aquarium filled with sea horses, four iguanas, and sitting on Spring's shoulders was a sugar glider. Having left Peanut home that day, she was instantly drawn to the animal. She didn't say much, not yet, and Spring didn't push her, but this small thing gave the student and the teacher a connection, and that was a beginning.

***

While J.R. and Helaina were at their first day of school, something more interesting was happening on Hope Island. At the Nature Park, that very day, they began construction on the Waterfall Dome. The measurements were completed, checked for accuracy, and the markers staked out earlier that morning. Now the digging began, all according to J.R.'s precisely detailed drawing. William watched from a distance. He wondered if they would find any evidence of that waterfall. When he became bored, he took his fishing pole and headed to the lake to do some fishing. After all he was retired, and wasn't that what retired folk did?

The week progressed slowly. J.R. and Helaina got used to their new schedule. Jennifer kept busy with her charities and teaching Home Economics. William was busy with a few interests of his own that included fishing and working on his antique cars. Right now, he was rebuilding a 1929 Ford.

Each afternoon when the kids arrived home, they hopped on the ATVs and checked on the progress of the Waterfall Dome. Everyone came together for dinner, Sophia and Jennifer took turns cooking. Helaina became more interested in cooking, getting more confident with her skills. She tried new recipes on the family.

***

One afternoon, during that first week, needing out of his apartment, Eli Carpenter, went to explore the Nature Park. He hiked for about five miles, enjoyed watching the wildlife, and marked out possible places to try his hand at fishing. Eli also wanted to try out the different hiking trails available. Eli was known for exploring and taking the trails not marked by the rangers. That's how he found the construction site.

While hiking through some trees, he came upon the site where they were building the Waterfall Dome. Being a mechanical engineer, he took interest straight away because the way they were constructing it was truly unconventional. Without being seen, he took pictures on his digital camera and shoved it back into his pocket, planning to study them later that evening. Before he could advance towards the strange building, he heard the sound of two ATVs and remained where he was, completely unseen. The ATVs drove right past him, and he got a clear

251

view of the two teenagers driving the vehicle. He recognized J.R. Black and Helaina Unity immediately.

He wondered out loud, "Why is my student at this construction site?"

Eli watched as the construction foreman welcomed the two teens and showed them around the site. They were there for half an hour before they left to return home It was then that Eli decided to take a closer look. But before he could get closer, he was stopped by security guards.

"Sir, can we see your security pass please?"

"I don't think I have one; I was just hiking. What are they building?

"I am afraid you will have to leave. That's a secured Unity project."

"I'm a mechanical engineer teaching at HPS; maybe I can be of some help."

"Sir. leave right now. Or you shall be put in lock up."

"Alright, I'm leaving."

"Sir, before you leave may I see your phone, and that camera in your pocket, along with your identification please?" It was more of an order than a request.

Eli handed over what the two security personnel asked for. They removed the memory cards and returned his phone and camera to him without them. They wrote down his name, address, and driver license number and returned that also. Lucky for him he had a photogenic memory, and the moment he returned to his apartment, he planned to draw what he had seen. Unfortunately, he only saw a little of the project. With all the security, the project piqued his interest, and he was determined to see what they were trying to hide. He would have to sneak over one afternoon or evening to get a closer look without interference, he decided. But for now, two security personnel escorted him away from the area, even going so far as to drive him out of the park to his car. They watched as he left the park and returned to their duties.

This experience left him curious about the two teenagers. Why were they at the odd construction site? Why the security? Eli decided that tomorrow he would definitely take a closer look at the detailed drawings of J.R. Black, maybe even photograph them. He knew of someone who might be interested in such a unique building and the boy's unusual imagination. But first, he needed to get home and do some drawing himself.

The next day was Friday, the last day of the first week of school, and there would be a pep rally. That was the opportunity Eli waited for. He told the students to leave their back packs in the room and dismissed them to the rally, telling them that they could return for their back packs later. Staying behind in the room, he waited until the rally started before finding J.R.'s sketch book neatly stored in his backpack. He quickly took photos of every page and returned it to the backpack. Spring came in while he was taking the photographs.

"Eli what are you doing?"

"Taking interest in the work of one of my students. He has amazing drawing talent. I want to take these photos to the art teacher, maybe she could nurture his talent with a few classes," Eli lied to his friend.

"I have many talented students in my class; and some are so exceptional that I believe they are smarter than me," Spring laughed.

Putting the drawing back into J.R.'s backpack, he put the camera securely in his classroom safe. Then Eli and Spring headed for the first of many school rallies. That evening he emailed the pictures to a friend. Saturday morning, he got a call back from his trusted friend.

"Eli, keep watch on that young man! Understand?"

"Yes, I understand."

Before Eli could say anything else, his friend hung up. Eli thought that had to be the shortest call he ever took, and the strangest.

CHAPTER THIRTY-FIVE

STATION ONE, THINGS BECOME CLEAR

Friday Night William got a call from John Garfield at Station One. Jennifer, J.R., and Helaina were in the recreation room playing video games on the big screen.

"William, I hate to disturb you, but could you bring J.R. and Helaina down tomorrow morning? There are a few things that we need to discuss."

"About the test we did?"

"That and so much more; this is extremely important William."

"We will be there, tomorrow about nine; is that convenient for you?"

"That would be perfect; see you tomorrow."

"Bye, John. See you then."

"Was that Kellie's dad? Did he ask you if we could go water skiing with them tomorrow afternoon?" Helaina inquired while she continued to lose a game to her cousin.

"Yes, that was Kellie's dad. He would like it if we would go down to Station One tomorrow morning. He has some very important things that he wants to talk to us about."

"Will it take all day? We really wanted to go water skiing tomorrow afternoon."

"I don't know, J.R., but if we don't finish at a decent hour, I will have Mason take you kids water skiing on Sunday, alright."

"Alright, but I must take Peanut with us tomorrow; she misses me while I'm at school. I was thinking that I might get a friend for her. Like another sugar glider."

"Remember how Sophia took care of Peanut while we were at the Oceanic One? And she told us she would love to have one of her own?" Jennifer asked the family.

"Yes," the three of them nodded.

"Sunday is Sophia's birthday; I went and bought her a sugar glider and everything she needs to take care of it. Even pouches in different colors to match some her outfits."

"Great! Now Peanut will have a friend."

"She is going to love that. But where are you hiding the little sugar glider?" Helaina wanted to know.

"She's right here." Jennifer unbuttoned her sweater revealing a hidden pouch containing the baby sugar glider."

"Can we see her? Look, Peanut is excited."

The new little face with eyes the size of saucers and the color of a fluffy cloud was introduced to the family and her new friend. As the kids were distracted with the two sugar gliders, Jennifer talked to her husband.

"Dear, do I need to go with you tomorrow? We are having a luncheon for the two new teachers, and I have a lot to do."

"I don't think so, my love. But don't you worry; I will tell you everything that happens like you will tell me every detail of that luncheon."

"Thank you, dear. I will bring you all a piece of that carrot cake you love from the bakery."

"I am guessing that little sugar glider is going to spend the next few nights in our room."

"You guessed right, dear, won't that be fun?" Jennifer asked, teasing her husband. Not expecting an answer, she went back to watch the two sugar gliders get acquainted.

Early the next morning, William, J.R., and Helaina, with Peanut tucked into one of her pouches, went down to Station One. Just like the first time, they were met by John Garfield and Selena Blanchard.

"Selena, I wasn't expecting you here today. I thought you would be at the luncheon for the new teachers."

"Normally I would be, but, William, this is such extraordinary news I felt I should be here. Besides, John sometimes has a hard time explaining things simply, so I am here to translate. Let's get to my office where I have diagrams."

"Great this is going to be just like school!" J.R. fussed.

John not knowing what to tell the teenager simply said, "Sorry about that."

"At least can I go back to the mechanic building later, I might find something else to fix."

"If he can go there, I want to go visit the aquarium," demanded Helaina.

"Now how are you going to do all that and make it in time to go water skiing with your friends?" William wanted to know.

The kids had to think about that one. Besides they needed to be more careful on what gadgets they gave J.R., now that they knew what he was capable of. For now, it was best to keep things out of his reach. They got to the station manager's office; it was obvious that John liked modern furniture and electronics. His furniture was made of steel and glass. He had a complete wall filled with computer monitors, several state-of-the-art computers, and a few things even the two teens didn't recognize. If they looked into John Garfield's pocket, they would find two telephones, one that had everything that the modern world offered, and the other, everything his world offered. With one touch he was able to video conference with, and check into, any lab he wanted for updates on experiments, or to check up on other work that was being accomplished for the Unity Corporation. The group passed through his office and went directly into the conference room where coffee and tea, along with some homemade snacks provided by Johns wife, were available for this all-important meeting.

Everyone settled around the table with something to drink and sat back to listen to John and Selena. Selena being the geneticist began this meeting. She took a deep breath before delivering the news. Since this was about J.R. and Helaina, it was them whom she addressed.

"J.R., Helaina, first of all I want to say we are sorry that we did these tests without your knowledge. But what we found, you need to know about, and your parents should be told immediately. Also, I advise that your brother and sisters be tested. But right now, let's discuss what we discovered about your DNA."

Selena continued, "We have samples of DNA from those who came from Unity. As you know our people carry a special gene, a gene that through the generations has changed, and we believed it became less pure with each new generation. It is possible that the pure form of our gene can be carried yet lay dormant and not able to be used to its full potential. Until now! That is what has happened here. J.R., Helaina, I compared your DNA and genes; I discovered each of your parents carried the dormant gene, then passed it on to both of you. This created a super gene in your DNA. When I compared your samples to that of our ancestors, I discovered that both of you have the gene in its purest form. This makes the two of you quite special."

"So, what you are telling us is that since both of their parents carried the pure gene of our ancestors. they passed a set of the pure gene to J.R. and Helaina, creating a super gene. This is how I understand it." William was trying to clarify this amazing discovery about J.R. and Helaina to himself, as well as, everyone else in the room.

"That's what the research indicates. We ran the test several times just to make sure our findings were correct," John assured them.

"Is that why we are a different?" asked J.R. and Helaina in unison.

"That's the gist of it," Selena told them.

"That's cool; does that mean that our brother and sisters can have the same gene we do?" Helaina wanted to know.

"There is a one in four chance of that happening; remember your biology lessons. But we will test them to see if they do."

"Are there any others like us?" J.R. asked.

"We don't know. Maybe!"

"Are we going to get stronger, or smarter, or be superheroes, like Superman, when we get older?" Everyone laughed at Helaina's question.

"We just don't know. But we need to make sure that the two of you and your secret stay a secret from the rest of the world. Protecting the two of you is a number one priority," said John.

257

"Gee, and Cassie thought she was the special one because she is the baby in the family."

While everyone laughed with Helaina, a thought came to J.R.

"Granddad, what would happen if I mixed a drop of my blood with Helaina's? Would that make the blood even more powerful? Could our blood actually power some of the machines here, like it did with my gene meter and the antigravity pen? Would someone want to kill us for our blood?"

William listened to J.R. and realized the boy was starting to become frightened at the prospect of what a drop of his blood could do. The urgency in his questions told him that much.

"That is why we are going to keep it a secret. Don't worry you are completely safe; I promise. Don't I always keep my promises?" William asked the boy. J.R. and Helaina nodded.

Selena then spoke, "I'm sorry I scared you, but I was extremely careful. I did the test myself. No one outside this room knows about our findings. The only other people who will be told will be your other grandparents and your parents."

"J.R., that idea of yours to mix yours and Helaina's blood, I don't think that's wise, and you must not try it on your own. We must study that to discover what the ramifications would be," John told the boy.

"I promise I won't try it on my own."

William noticed that Helaina was sitting quietly, concentrating very hard on something. He wondered if she was having another vision.

"Helaina are you alright?"

"NO! I don't want to be different anymore. I want to be normal again. Can we do something to make us normal again? I don't like this at all!" Helaina said as tears started streaming down her checks.

William and Selena rushed to her side to comfort her. They felt her shivering from the fear she was feeling. They understood that things were happening much too fast to the two teens and it was beginning to sink in to Helaina's head that they weren't to have a normal life. Selena pulled the girl into her arms, rocking her slightly to comfort her. William kneeled down beside Helaina's chair and took her cold quivering hand. William tried to think of just the right words to comfort his granddaughter, but he couldn't find any. Instead, he took out a handkerchief and handed it to her.

To his amazement, it was J.R. who was the one to help his cousin the most. "Helaina look at me!" J.R. demanded as he took charge of the situation.

Helaina did as she was told, a little angry at J.R. for demanding something from her.

"Everything is going to be different from now on, because we are different. We have to accept that! We have to follow this path we are on. It's going to be hard and sometimes impossible, but together we are strong, and we can do this. Together we can do anything! We are a team, and we are, "The One's," who can do great things for our people. Together, as one, we are stronger and smarter. Apart, we are weak and helpless. I can't do this alone; I need you and you need me. I'm a bit scared also, but think of this as an adventure, as a mystery we have to solve together. We will be just fine, because we have the support of our family and our people. Do you understand?"

Helaina stood up and smiled at J.R. as she pushed the tears aside with the handkerchief.

"I think that was the biggest speech I have ever heard from you. And it was perfect! I understand; I'm not so scared now."

Then she went to her partner and gave him a hug; this time he hugged her back. Their partnership was now unbreakable.

"Damn! I hate it when women get all mushy when you tell them something,"

Everyone else in the room stood and smiled. Even Selina got a little choked up at J.R.'s words.

"Let's have a snack and let this information sink in a little before we move on to your big project," suggested Selina.

"That's a great idea; a ten-minute break is just what we need," agreed John.

After their break of tea, coffee, and sweet cakes the meeting continued. Because John knew more about mechanics than Selena, he took over this part of the meeting. He turned on a screen to demonstrate his findings.

"J.R., Helaina I would like to share my research with you. First there are no other round jewels. We think yours are the only ones brought here by our ancestors. The machine is unique also. Watch the screen. Here is your Jewel Machine and the exact spot where you told us it must sit, right under the Waterfall Dome." John let them examine the pictures before he continued.

"Here is Station One as it lies under the island. And here are the coordinates of the planet of Unity."

Before he could continue, J.R. saw exactly what he was talking about and stepped up to the screen.

"I see where this is going. If you draw a straight line from the center of the Jewel Machine up, it goes directly through the center of Unity, then it goes down through the middle of Station One to the ocean floor."

"That's correct; now let's go on a little field trip."

Everyone piled into a large air car. Using his GPS, John flew over the exact spot that connected the Jewel Machine to Station One, which was right over the middle of the park. John directed everyone to look down. What they saw left them all speechless. Sitting underneath the fountain was the Unity symbol, chiseled in the marbled floor. At the North, South, East and West position on the outer circle, something else had been carefully chiseled into the floor. The arms of the Jewel Machine, and they were each pointing down a walking path. Something no one took notice of before. If it wasn't for J.R. and Helaina connecting all the pieces to the puzzle together, this discovery wouldn't have been made, and it was right under their very noses. The adults looked at the two teens.

J.R. and Helaina looked at each other and said in unison, "Together, two minds can do great things."

GLOSSARY OF TERMS

Guardians-Are leaders of the population of aliens. There are ten sectors around the world, and each has a set of Guardians. The Guardians are also CEO's of corporations. The corporations are collectively a conglomerate called Unity.

Unity-is also the surname the head Guardians adopted and was also the name of the planet for which they came.

Elders-The adults in the group. Can refer to parents, grandparents, Guardians, and Watchers.

Seekers-Those who seek the truth about "Who" and "What" Unity Corporations really are, and especially what their objectives are.

Watchers-Can be any adult who is assigned to "Watch" someone in order to protect them and help them achieve their destiny. They can be family, friends, teachers, or elders.

Mind Speak-This is when two people can connect their minds together and speak to each other with just their minds. Mind Speak can only be done with the person that is your partner, or equal. This connection usually happens to cousins, or twins, who were born on the same day, and year.

The Story Chamber-A six-foot-tall crystal which stores stories of the past.

Nature Park-A Nature preserve were the Dome will be located.

Balls-Four balls, that later are discovered to be precious jewels used to operate a machine. They later just call them "jewels".

Unity One-William and Jennifer Unity's Yacht.

Hope Island-The home for the Unity family, and the conglomerates home base of operations.

Station One-The secret city that is hidden under Hope Island. Nine others exist, there are ten all together.

Logo-This is also referred to as the Unity Family Crest. It is the symbol that the people of Unity recognize one another with.

Acknowledgements

I also dedicate this book to my special friend. You have given me so much, and I could never repay you.

You gave me courage through the tough times.

Your strength when it was needed.

Hope for better things to come.

You were my sounding board, listening when I needed someone to listen to me.

I can depend on you for your honesty, helping me move in the right direction, leading me to find the strength that was hidden deep inside myself.

You showed me respect.

You are my best friend, giving me the friendship no one else would.

You renewed my faith in myself, to do what I always wanted to do but was afraid of what others would think.

You gave me the courage to accept defeat, and not to be afraid to fail.

Because of this, I now have pride in what I have accomplished, and look forward to accomplishing more.

My dear friend, most importantly you gave me your heart, loving me for who I am, loving me unconditionally with all my flaws.

I can never repay you, for all you have given; I can only return the gifts you have given me, for there are no greater gifts to give.

You will always be in my heart.

Forever and a day.

Sandra Golden

About the Author

Sandra Golden was born in San Jose California and is a graduate of Gunderson High School. She joined the US Army where she met her husband David. In December 1989 she graduated from Memphis State University with a B.A in Education, a month later her only son James Robert Golden was born on January 4, 1990. Sandy was a dedicated stay at home mother who was a room mother, school volunteer, and cub scout leader.

When her son J.R. was killed on New Year's Eve of 2008 Sandra turned to writing to help deal with her grief. It has always been a dream of hers to become a published writer. Sandra's hobbies include traveling, cooking, writing, gardening, and scrapbooking. Sandra and her husband share their home with a few cats, and a sugar glider named Peanut. Sandra hopes her readers enjoy the adventures of J.R. Black and his cousin Helaina Marie Unity as they search for Unity, and acceptance, in this unique book series.

Time Will Tell
Unity Objective Series Book2

In the second book of the UNITY OBJECTIVE series, J.R. Black and Helaina Unity accomplish putting the mysterious machine together. With the Jewel Machine completed, they discover that the impossible is possible, and their lives become quite complicated. They are given the gifts of special powers and the wisdom of their elders. J.R. and Helaina must accept the powers given them and prove to the elders that they are capable of conquering the challenge their ancestors have put on their young shoulders. The elders of the present as well as the elders of the past help J.R. and Helaina move forward, guiding them, and at the same time trying to protect them from the evil that wants to take everything away.

www.ingramcontent.com/pod-product-compliance
Lightning Source LLC
Chambersburg PA
CBHW020820260626
47169CB00003B/753